PENGUIN CANADA

CHARLIE WILCOX'S GREAT WAR

Sharon E. McKay is an award-winning author
of many books for parents and children. Her
most recent books include *Charlie Wilcox* and,
from the Our Canadian Girl series, *Terror in the
Harbour*, *The Glass Castle* and *An Irish Penny*.

From a neighbour in Saskatoon
Friday Feb 08, 2012
Canada

Praise for *Charlie Wilcox*

"A riveting story of friendship, loyalty, bravery and honor. There are no glorified heroes here, only ordinary people caught in extraordinary events doing what they believe to be right."

—*School Library Journal*

"McKay's prose is scintillating, and she's at her best when she's describing the fighting—you can almost hear the deafening shelling, smell the mucky odor of the trenches, see the blinding flash of the guns, hear the ping, ping of the snipers' post-battle bullets."

—*The Hamilton Spectator*

"McKay depicts small-town Newfoundland with humor and verve, catching us instantly with her straight-speaking characters and their long-standing knowledge of one another."

—*The Toronto Star*

"An absolutely great book. It is one of the best adventure stories to come out of Newfoundland, and it will become a classic!"

—*The Telegram,* St. John's

CHARLIE WILCOX'S GREAT WAR

SHARON E. McKAY

PENGUIN CANADA

Penguin Group (Canada), a division of Pearson Penguin Canada Inc.,
10 Alcorn Avenue, Toronto, Ontario M4V 3B2

Penguin Group (U.K.), 80 Strand, London WC2R 0RL, England
Penguin Group (U.S.), 375 Hudson Street, New York, New York 10014, U.S.A.
Penguin Group (Australia) Inc., 250 Camberwell Road, Camberwell, Victoria 3124, Australia
Penguin Group (Ireland), 25 St. Stephen's Green, Dublin 2, Ireland
Penguin Books India (P) Ltd, 11, Community Centre, Panchsheel Park,
New Delhi – 110 017, India
Penguin Group (New Zealand), cnr Rosedale and Airborne Roads, Albany, Auckland 1310,
New Zealand
Penguin Books (South Africa) (Pty) Ltd, 24 Sturdee Avenue, Rosebank 2196, South Africa

Penguin Group, Registered Offices: 80 Strand, London WC2R 0RL, England

First published 2003

2 3 4 5 6 7 8 9 10 (WEB)

*Publisher's note: This book is a work of fiction. Names, characters, places and incidents either are
the product of the author's imagination or are used fictitiously, and any resemblance to actual
persons living or dead, events, or locales is entirely coincidental.*

Manufactured in Canada.

NATIONAL LIBRARY OF CANADA CATALOGUING IN PUBLICATION

McKay, Sharon E
Charlie Wilcox's Great War / Sharon E. McKay.

ISBN 0-14-301471-4

I. Title.

PS8575.K2898C473 2003   jC813'.6   C2002-904894-X
PZ7

Visit the Penguin Group (Canada) website at **www.penguin.ca**

CHARLIE WILCOX'S
GREAT WAR

SHARON E. McKAY

PENGUIN CANADA

Penguin Group (Canada), a division of Pearson Penguin Canada Inc.,
10 Alcorn Avenue, Toronto, Ontario M4V 3B2

Penguin Group (U.K.), 80 Strand, London WC2R 0RL, England
Penguin Group (U.S.), 375 Hudson Street, New York, New York 10014, U.S.A.
Penguin Group (Australia) Inc., 250 Camberwell Road, Camberwell, Victoria 3124, Australia
Penguin Group (Ireland), 25 St. Stephen's Green, Dublin 2, Ireland
Penguin Books India (P) Ltd, 11, Community Centre, Panchsheel Park,
New Delhi – 110 017, India
Penguin Group (New Zealand), cnr Rosedale and Airborne Roads, Albany, Auckland 1310,
New Zealand
Penguin Books (South Africa) (Pty) Ltd, 24 Sturdee Avenue, Rosebank 2196, South Africa

Penguin Group, Registered Offices: 80 Strand, London WC2R 0RL, England

First published 2003

2 3 4 5 6 7 8 9 10 (WEB)

NATIONAL LIBRARY OF CANADA CATALOGUING IN PUBLICATION

McKay, Sharon E
Charlie Wilcox's Great War / Sharon E. McKay.

ISBN 0-14-301471-4

I. Title.

PS8575.K2898C473 2003   jC813'.6   C2002-904894-X
PZ7

Visit the Penguin Group (Canada) website at **www.penguin.ca**

My thanks to Dr. David Parsons, M.D., St. John's.

In memory of Major William Henry Parsons M.C., M.D., R.A.M.C. Born in 1880. Served with the Royal Army Medical Corps as a medical doctor. Awarded the Military Cross in 1916. Became Assistant Deputy Medical Services for Newfoundland. Served in France until 1918. Died of complications from an illness suffered overseas and was buried in Harbour Grace, Newfoundland, in 1929.

"We Keep the Vision of his Chivalry"

"And to be boy eternal."

—William Shakespeare,
A Winter's Tale

ACKNOWLEDGMENTS

Ontario Arts Council, my thanks.

Barbara Berson, Senior Editor, Penguin Books.

Catherine Marjoribanks, editor.

Sarah Weber, proofreader.

Catherine Dorton, Production Editor, Penguin Books.

Julia Bell, illustrator extraordinaire!

Tim Love is the illustrator's model for Charlie Wilcox and Michele Spink is the model for Claire. My thanks to you both.

Phillipa Campsie, *merci,* yet again!

Helga Stuermer, Kathy Green, Andrea Langhammer.

Maxine Trottier, who thinks outside of the box.

Wendy Lewis.

Mr. and Mrs. Winsor, I always knew that you were there.

Dr. Daphne Parsons, M.D., brilliant support staff!

George Richards, past resident of Brigus, Newfoundland.

Ian (D.J.) McKay, father and diligent copy editor.

David and Joe and Sam MacLeod, husband and sons.

Plum Johnson and Ylva Van Buuren.

Jon Slan and Pete McCormack.

Wayne Rose, Town Clerk, Brigus.

Elsie Percy, librarian.

And, as always, the residents of Brigus, Newfoundland, who continue to treasure and protect their beautiful village.

WHO'S WHO

(ALPHABETIZED BY FIRST
OR COMMON NAME)

Newfoundland

Charlie Wilcox, born 1900 in Brigus, Newfoundland, the only son of Lucy and Samuel Wilcox. (Charlie has two older, married sisters.)

Claire Guy, born 1901 in Brigus, Newfoundland. Claire is Charlie's childhood friend.

Clint Miller, four years older than Charlie, a bully. Works on his father's fishing boat.

Eliza Norton, Jim's mother and Lucy Wilcox's best friend, lives across the street from the Wilcox house in Brigus.

Emma Fields, nineteen-year-old maid in the Wilcox home in Brigus, engaged to Murphy Milford.

Jenny Jackson, Phil Jackson's mother.

Jim Norton, Charlie's best friend.

Lambe, Mr. & Mrs., butcher and his wife, residents of Brigus. (Mrs. Lambe has a sweet shop.)

Lily MacKenzie (Mac) Daniels, Charlie's nurse in St. John's, married Dr. Robert Daniels in London, England, during World War I. Mother of baby Charlotte (nicknamed Charlie).

Lucy Wilcox, Charlie's mother, considered a wonderful cook and a local beauty.

Murphy Milford, resident of Brigus, joined the Newfoundland Regiment, engaged to Emma.

Philip Jackson, four years older than Charlie, sidekick to Clint Miller.

Pinkstone, Mr. & Mrs., smitty and his wife, and residents of Brigus.

Robert Daniels, Dr., born in St. John's, Newfoundland, respected doctor. Husband of Lily (Mac) MacKenzie.

Samuel (Sam) Wilcox, Charlie's father, often called Skipper Sam, a well-known and respected ship's captain.

France

Chantal, waitress in a bar located in occupied France.

Daw, Mark, captain who allowed Charlie to stay in the trench and work.

Gracie, VAD (Voluntary Aid Detachment) from Vancouver, B.C., ambulance driver. Friend of Helena's.

Hank Boil, Newfoundlander, medic, prankster, and father of three little girls.

Helena McFarland, a VAD. Nursed Charlie back to health after a harrowing bout with influenza. (Her brother Rory McFarland was attached to the Scottish Regiment. Died in battle, age eighteen, at Ypres, France, in 1914.)

Martin, friend of Michael's, also met Charlie on the ship over to England.

Michael, friend Charlie met on the way to England. Died at the Somme during the Battle of Beaumont Hamel, July 1, 1916.

Tom Alcock, stretcher-bearer. Charlie met him at the Battle of Beaumont Hamel in *Charlie Wilcox* and again after the battle in *Charlie Wilcox's Great War.*

Weston, Charles Askwith, nineteen-year-old flier for the Royal Air Force.

PROLOGUE

In the first book, *Charlie Wilcox,* the Great War in Europe (now called World War I) blundered on, with no end in sight. Meanwhile, in Brigus, Newfoundland, fourteen-year-old Charlie Wilcox was making plans to follow the family tradition and "go to the ice." Like his father and forefathers, he planned to become a sea captain. He'd been born with a club foot, but at last an operation had put it right, and now nothing was going to stop Charlie from making his dreams come true. Sam and Lucy, Charlie's parents, had another idea, however. They had their hearts set on their son going to the university.

With his spy glass in hand, Charlie ran from the sheltered coastal village of Brigus to the port city of St. John's. His plan was to stow away on a sealing ship and prove his fitness for the sea.

As bad luck would have it, Clint Miller, a goon from Brigus, was also in St. John's and about to board a ship for the ice. Clint and his sidekick, Phil Jackson, both four years older than Charlie, had bullied and tormented him for years. But when Clint offered to help him stow away on a sealing ship, a desperate Charlie accepted.

There were two types of ships in St. John's harbor in 1916, wooden and steel. During the war, the wooden ships continued to be used as fishing and sealing vessels, while the stronger steel ships were used to transport soldiers and supplies to the battlefronts of Europe. Clint helped smuggle Charlie into a container that was loaded into the hold of a seafaring ship. Charlie nearly died in that container. When he finally emerged from his hiding place, he discovered that he was surrounded not by ice, but by soldiers— hundreds of soldiers! Thanks to Clint, Charlie was on his way to war.

Michael and Martin, two young soldiers, pulled Charlie out of the container and set him straight. It was a sad thing to say goodbye, but once the troop ship docked in England, Michael and Martin were sent up to Scotland for training, leaving Charlie on his own.

Not knowing what else to do, Charlie crossed the English Channel in search of the Newfoundland Regiment and Lily MacKenzie, "Mac," a nurse from St. John's. But Charlie soon found himself in the thick of the war. To keep body and soul together he worked in field hospitals in exchange for food and lodging.

Luck brought Lily and Charlie together, but their reunion was a disappointment for the love-struck boy. Lily was now married to Dr. Robert Daniels and expecting a baby. Worse still, she was ill. When a ticket back to Newfoundland arrived from home, Charlie made a choice that would again spin his life out of control. He gave his ticket to Lily, then headed to the front to tell Dr. Daniels that he was to be a father. What began as a simple mission of mercy ended up catapulting Charlie into battle.

He arrived at the front on July 1, 1916, in time to witness the Battle of Beaumont Hamel, at the Somme. When it was over, the Newfoundland Regiment had been decimated.

Charlie put his own life on the line to save Martin, the very same boy whom he had met on the ship to England and who had saved his life. Michael, who had planned to become a pastor when he had done his bit, was dead. Ingenuity on Charlie's part kept Martin alive, but it was Dr. Daniels's skill that ultimately saved the young soldier's life.

Finally, Charlie and Martin boarded an ambulance that would put them on the road to "Blighty" (England) and home. It was then that Charlie remembered the spy glass—he had left it in the front-line trench, the same trench that was now filled with the dead and dying. He had to bring it home. He had to! Running back to the trenches, Charlie again plunged into an uncertain future.

Three years passed before Charlie Wilcox next laid eyes on Brigus, Newfoundland, in 1919. Charlie had spent his youth watching young men die. He had suffered the death of friends, felt the strength of courage and the power of true love. Like all who returned from the Great War, he had stories to tell but not the will to speak them. And he carried with him a secret that might unite or tear apart this frail little village. Brigus has suffered so much loss—would Charlie be the bearer of more grief?

This is the story of a young man's quest to find his courage and fulfill his destiny on the great battlefields of Europe. But at what cost?

CHAPTER 1
NEWFOUNDLAND, 1919

"WAKE UP, BOY." A sailor gave Charlie's bunk a thump. "We're coming into Brigus. Captain wants you on the bridge." The sailor ducked through the hatch and was gone.

Charlie, gummy-mouthed and blurry-eyed, tried to focus. He gazed up at the wooden slats of the bunk overhead and listened to the groans of the ship. Brigus! He was home. Right! He sprang up, whacked his head on the upper bunk, took a turn, and stuck out his hand to break his fall. A bolt of pain ran up his arm. Jeeze!

In no time he was making his way up to the bridge. The swipe of a fine spring wind met him as he made for the bow on the lower deck. He stopped to take a breath of the sweet, salty air. It went through him like a gulp of cool water.

Below, the ship carved a gash in the deep, black sea, sending up waves of pristine white curls. The water was thick with fish. Above, dark rain clouds threatened off to starboard and potbellied seagulls dove for the scraps Cook tossed over

1

the side. Charlie clambered up more metal stairs, each step resonating with a tinny clang.

"Morning, Captain." He grinned as he landed on the bridge.

"There ya have it, young Charlie Wilcox." Captain John Tripp motioned to the land ahead. "Ye're home."

Charlie looked toward his country as the ship tacked into Conception Bay. He could make out the harbor through a thin mist. It was a sight. Brigus, trim and proper, was the finest fishing port in all of Newfoundland—leastways that was what Charlie thought. The fog began to lift, revealing pale, snug clapboard houses. Some were pink or light green; most were white. They gripped the rocky shore as if expecting a gale to hurl them inland.

"Looks like we've been spotted." Captain Tripp pointed to the shore.

A broken cloud revealed a figure on a far hill. Could it be? Could that be Jim Norton? "Jim!" Charlie whispered. A surge of joy ripped right through him.

The Captain chuckled and looked at Charlie steady-like. A good-looking lad, tall and broad-beamed for all his seventeen years. He had the regal bearing of his father, Captain Samuel Wilcox, but coloring all his own, blond hair with blue, regarding eyes. Away at war three years, give or take. His antics at the front were well known. He should have come home a decorated hero. But then, maybe it was enough just to come home.

Captain Tripp gripped the rail in front of him and turned his face into the wind. Thoughts of his own dear son lying in a foreign grave came over him unbidden. What he wouldn't give to hold the hand of his boy just one more time.

"Get yourself ready, Charlie-boy," he said, willing away the pain. "We'll near be tossing you over the rails for the length of time we're to spend in harbor."

"Yes, sir. I will, Captain. Thank you, sir."

Charlie plunged down the metal steps, back into the bowels of the ship. With a swipe of his good arm he gathered up his kit, stuffing everything in any which-way. The last thing that went into his haversack was his spy glass. It was tarnished and damaged beyond use, but be had brought it home, and that's what counted.

He could hear the ropes being tossed from ship to shore as he raced back to the lower deck and hurled himself down the gangplank. As he was about to put foot to land, something caught his eye—a girl, running. He recognized the run, but not the girl.

He saw his father, Captain Samuel Wilcox, right off. Skipper Sam they called him.

Skipper Sam stood among the crates, barrels, and coils of crusty rope and brine-coated twine on the dock. His beard, once salt and peppered, was now more salt than pepper. His gray-blue eyes still held the mystery of fog rolling in from the bay, but now they were rimmed red, with tears spilling out of them. His arms were around Charlie's mother. Though her face was buried in his father's shirt, Charlie could see her shoulders rise and fall with sobs.

"Father," Charlie whispered. Then he found his voice and called, louder, "Father!"

Charlie caught his father's eyes. They lit up with recognition. Sam whispered something and Charlie's mother spun around. Her black hair, streaked with silver, had come loose and fallen to frame her face. Her skin was smooth. There was a touch of pucker between the eyes perhaps, and a bit of smocking above her mouth, but she was handsome just the same.

Lucy Wilcox looked past her son, her eyes darting every which-way as she scanned the ship. Then she looked back at the young man in front of her.

"Mother, it's me."

"Charlie?"

It was a look of pure astonishment on her face. Just that.

A moan escaped from some place deep within her as she stumbled forward. Lucy reached out and touched him gently, almost tentatively, as if he were made of glass. While her eyes cried, her mouth laughed, and then, in an instant, he was wrapped up so tight, in so many arms, that everything past was forgotten, and nothing yet to come could possibly matter.

"You didn't lose it!" Sam motioned to the spy glass that stuck out of Charlie's haversack then threw his head back and laughed.

"Never."

"Glory be! You're home, my son." Mrs. Eliza Norton, Jim's mother and his own mother's dearest friend, came flying down the road and darted about like a spry little pony. She'd give him a cuff if she could. All that worrying. Dear boy.

The word was out. Charlie Wilcox was home.

Mr. Rabbitt, himself a Brigus resident going back six generations, came at a jog, pulled up short, and rapped Charlie on the back. "Good tar see ya!" He spoke and gasped for air at the same time. Mrs. Rabbitt, hot on his heels, chimed in, herself with a tear in her eye.

It was as if an underground, mystical current charged through the village, spreading the word. The homecoming had begun. Charlie was passed around like a collection plate at church, and by the end of it, his back hurt from the thumps.

"Mother," Charlie shouted over the heads of the gathering crowd.

Laughing, still in shock perhaps, Lucy turned and looked at her son through shining eyes.

"Yes, Charlie?" Oh, she could say those words for the rest of her days.

"There was a girl, running away. Was that . . . ?" He could hardly say her name.

"That was Claire," piped up Mrs. Guy, Claire's own mother, as she elbowed Eliza Norton to one side. "Sure, Charlie, you wouldn't expect her to be greeting you in a plain frock, would you?"

"Charlie!"

"Jim!" Charlie yelled right back.

Jim, tall and strong from three years on the boats, barged through the gathering crowd and grabbed Charlie's hand. There was too much to say, so they said nothing and grinned like two fools while taking the measure of one another.

"Jim," called out Sam. "Run over to the Jubilee Club. Tell young Bill I want a barrel of his finest ale. And tell him to close up shop and come too."

"Yes, sir!" Jim gave Charlie a flash of a smile. "Later!" he hollered as he ran.

"To home," Skipper Sam called out to the increasing throng. "We'll break out Lucy's finest blueberry wine . . ." And to the men that were within earshot he added, ". . . and something more besides."

"Charlie?" A little woman as faded as bleached paper reached a thin, vein-striped hand out to Charlie as he passed. "Have ya news of my Philip?"

Charlie stopped in his tracks and gazed down at the tiny woman. Could this be Mrs. Jenny Jackson, Phil's own mother? She was smaller by half than the woman he remembered.

Lucy turned and gently laid an arm across the little woman's shoulders. "Jenny, join us, won't you?"

"No. No." Mrs. Jackson dithered and looked up through hooded eyes. "I don't want to interfere. I just wanted to know . . ." Her voice, like the rest of her, was reedy and thin. She stepped up close and took hold of Charlie's hand, a grasp so tight he winced. "Would you come by my house tomorrow and tell me about my Philip?"

"Yes." Charlie nodded.

"When?"

"Ten o'clock?" He chose the time out of the air and might well have said midnight, for his brain had stopped working. Mrs. Jackson released his hand. Only then did he feel the blood return to his fingers.

"We'll cook up a scoff," called out Mr. Pinkstone.

Charlie looked up and laughed. When he looked back again, Mrs. Jackson was gone.

CHAPTER 2

CHARLIE LOOKED UP FROM HIS BED at the wallpaper that bloomed with pale-yellow flowers the whole year through. He reached behind him and put his finger on a cluster of greenery and let it trail along the pattern. Brown vines and dusty pink ribbons connected one cluster of flowers to another. He stopped, his finger resting lightly on a rose. The rose exploded.

"Wake up! Your bath is waiting, your worship." Emma gave Charlie's bedstead a nudge.

Charlie bolted upright and let out a blood-curdling scream.

"Mother save us!" Emma clutched her heart and staggered backwards. She stumbled, floundered, batted the air with her outstretched arms, caught a heel in the hem of her skirt, mouthed a series of tiny squeaks, and, in a flurry of swishing petticoats, landed on her backside. The thud shook Charlie's bed—shook the whole house, for that matter.

"I, I, I'm sorry," he sputtered. "I forgot where I was."

"Well, I never . . ." Emma was flustered. Oh, she was downright infuriated!

"Emma, I *am* sorry." Charlie stared down at Emma. Her skirt was up past her white knickers. Her black-stockinged

7

legs, as round and fat as two sausages, lay sprawled out in different directions, and at the end of each leg was a kipper-sized foot, one pointing north, the other south. In a flash the nightmare vanished, and a giggle rose in his throat like a bubble up the neck of a bottle.

"Well, we're all glad to hear it." Emma rolled over and struggled to her feet.

"Bottoms up!" Charlie couldn't help thinking. And it was a mighty big bottom, too. He slapped his hand over his mouth. It didn't help.

"What are you laughing at?" She had no time this day for a spoiled rotten lad. That's what comes, she thought, from being the only boy. "Well, *Mr. High and Mighty Prodigal Son,* you can sleep the blooming day away for all I care." She smoothed her dress with a flat palm, paused a bit, and looked like she wanted to say something more on the subject. The moment passed. "Your mother is doing the shopping and your father is up Carbonear way. As for your two sisters, I hear that they are to make their way down from the Cape tomorrow. Although, with families of their own, can't say how long they'll be staying. If it's in your lordship's plans to eat this day, then get up." With that, she turned and clopped down the hall.

"Emma, really, really I am . . ." he called after her. But it was a waste of breath, and he knew it. Charlie flopped back onto his pillow. Emma had always been a misery, and now she was angry, too. But who could blame her? He sighed and threw his legs over the side of the bed. She had expected to be married by now, have a house of her own, and here she was still, coming on to twenty years old, no more than an old maid in the Wilcox home. Murphy Milford, the man she'd set her cap on to marry, was lying stone cold in France. With so many boys missing in action or dead, a whole generation fed to the war, there'd be slim pickings for the girls at home.

Charlie poured water from the jug into the wash basin, splashed it on his face, then reached for a towel. The smell of lavender leapt out of the cloth. He looked in the mirror and thought of his fine homecoming celebration. The whole village had made their way to the Wilcox home last night. Walter Spracklin came with his fiddle, and Mr. Brown and his old father shared the accordion. Mrs. Cozens came with her unmarried twin daughters, Renee and Dulcie. "Girls" they were called, even though they were coming on to sixty. John and William Weeks standing, as always, in the middle of the room argued about the color of rain. And Mr. Lambe, who, according to Emma, could put the dead to sleep, prattled on to no one in particular. There were Mrs. Cotton and Mrs. Fox, both tinted pink with half a glass of blueberry wine, heads together, giggling in their cups.

Each by turn had done what they could to tell him that he was missed. No hugging and kissing, mind. That was not the way of Newfoundlanders. A cuff to the head or the promise of a fine feed was the way they said "Welcome home, my son." Fine feed indeed. He'd had his fill last night. There'd been squirrel cakes, jay buns, bread pudding and figgy duff, pork cakes, baked beans, and jellied salads of all descriptions. He must have eaten an entire flipper pie by himself. "A feed of flipper pie divides out the Canadians from the Newfoundlanders," Charlie's Grandfather Moses had been known to say. "Only a born Newfoundlander can get the joy out of flipper pie." And the desserts! There'd been no end to them, the best being Lucy's own Pineapple Upside-down Cake. No, Emma could keep her breakfast. He'd not be needing any food for a bit.

Charlie sprinkled tooth powder on a brush and gave his teeth a rub before pulling on his clothes. His hand knocked an atlas on the bedside table. It fell open to the first page and the inscription: *"To my African friend. Carpe diem, quam minimum credula postero."* He did his best to push the memory aside.

Memory! Like a shot in the head! He was supposed to stop by Mrs. Jackson's at ten o'clock. Charlie yanked his suspenders over his shoulders and pulled open a top drawer. He caught his breath as he looked down at the lovely sight, and he let his hand drift across the rolled socks and pressed handkerchiefs.

Mrs. Jackson. Right! He shoved a hankie into his pocket.

"What time is it?" he hollered to Emma while thumping down the stairs two at a time. Charlie caught the look of himself in the hall mirror and tried to flatten his hair. It refused. "Hair like hay" was what his father always said.

Emma, standing in the parlor, pointed her duster at him. "What do you mean, what time is it? Have ya forgotten how to tell time? Don't they have clocks in France or is everyone too busy kissing?" Emma had heard about those Frenchmen and their kissing.

The clock struck ten.

"Got to go." He pulled on his boots.

"Go? Where to? Your father brought in the cod before he left and there's hard tack soaking." Emma put her hands on her hips with such force that the dust from the duster formed a gray cloud around her ample body.

"Sorry. I promised."

"Charlie!"

He bolted out the door.

IN NO TIME Charlie was down North Street and, huffing and puffing, he stood on Mrs. Jackson's gallery. He didn't need to knock because there was Mrs. Jenny Jackson holding the screen door ajar, her doughy face made paler by her dark mourning clothes.

"Charlie dear, you had a lie-in I'll wager. I'll just get the tea. And I've made some brewis. You will have some, won't you Charlie?"

"No, I . . ." Charlie stuttered.

Mrs. Jackson looked crestfallen.

"Yes. I'd love some. Thank you." The screen door squeaked shut behind him and the winter door slapped shut after it. Trapped.

"Into the parlor with you. Go on. I won't be but a minute." Mrs. Jackson trundled down the hall. The water must have been near the boil because, true to her word, within a minute the kettle began to whistle.

Charlie shifted from one foot to the other, uncomfortable-like. Newfoundlanders spent their time in kitchens. The parlor was for laying out the dead and celebrating Christmas.

On the mantel, above the coal fire, stood a picture of Phil in uniform. His red hair, shaved off for the adventure, could hardly be seen under his hat. Trim, trying to hide the grin—

everything about him looked eager. Hard to think that Phil had once been Clint Miller's sidekick. Clint the Bully. Clint the Tormentor. But that was a long time gone. In France, the German Empire was enemy enough.

"Here we are, Charlie." Mrs. Jackson bustled into the room, holding a tray with two china cups, a teapot, milk, sugar, and a plate piled high with brewis. A glob of butter, bigger than his fist, sat smack in the middle of the cod and hard tack mixture. And there was a plate of buttered bread besides. "Sit yourself down now. There's a boy." When he dithered she said, "Sit."

He sat, as did Mrs. Jackson.

"Now, Charlie," Mrs. Jackson leaned forward and gave the coal fire a stir, "tell me what you know." She lifted her heavy eyes to look into his. They were desperate and full of pain.

"Well, Phil, Philip," Charlie swallowed hard, "was a great soldier. Very popular."

"Yes, yes I know." She reached over to a china cabinet and opened a little drawer. Out came a blue-and-yellow telegram. Charlie didn't need to look to know what was written.

Dear Mrs. Jackson,

On behalf of the Battery, I write you this letter out of respect for your gallant son, Philip, who heroically met his death while on duty. He died instantly and felt no pain. His death is felt by all who knew him, for he was looked upon as a good soldier, and admired by all who knew him.

Captain Mark Daw, Royal Newfoundland Regiment

"Would you like to see it, Charlie?" He turned away, and Mrs. Jackson didn't press. "Maybe next time. I sent him many letters. Do you think he received them?"

Charlie nodded. There was one letter that Charlie knew for a fact Phil had received. This little, broken woman in front of him must never know that it was one of her own letters that had contributed mightily to her son's death.

Charlie tackled Mrs. Jackson's brewis. He shoveled spoonful after spoonful into his mouth. Jeeze, it was like forcing down mud.

"I tried to stop him from joining up, dear, dear. Heard *the call to the colors,* he said. *The Old Gray Mother needs me,* he said. And, with all the boys going, well . . ." Mrs. Jackson took a hankie out of her sleeve, dabbed her eyes, then twisted it in her hands.

"It was like holding a young one back from a great scoff, wasn't it? It was supposed to be a lark, wasn't it? A bit of sport. Boys playing soldiers. No harm would come to our lads. None a'tall. They'd have a chance to see the world. They'd be home by Christmas with plenty of stories to tell."

Mrs. Jackson looked up to her boy in the picture frame. Then it just sort of hit Charlie. She blamed herself for her letting him join up! But there was nothing she could have done to stop him. Nothing.

At the start of it, every boy in Newfoundland, in Canada too, had wanted to be part of the adventure, to fight for God, King, and Country. In the beginning, when they called the Newfoundland Regiment the Blue Puttees, on account of the blue woolen material used to wrap around their legs, they'd thought the war would be over in months, weeks even! Boys rushed to join, afraid that if they waited too long they'd miss out on all the fun! How could anyone, let alone a little woman sitting in Brigus, have known what was to come? How could they have known that it would last four long years, take away their very best, and return nothing?

"Charlie?" Mrs. Jackson leaned forward.

"Yes?"

"Philip mentioned a young woman named Helena in his letters. Did you know her?"

Helena. The blood rushed to his face. His stomach tightened and his eyes beat a hole into his plate. Please, please don't ask me about Helena, Charlie prayed to the teapot.

"Why . . ." Charlie stuttered, begging for time, "why do you ask?"

"Philip said she was a nurse, Scottish I think, maybe English. Philip was born in England you know. On the coast, place called Liverpool. Sure, but you do know this. Can't think why I mentioned it. I get muddled sometimes. What was I on about? Helena, that's right. Philip mentioned her several times. He seemed to have taken a shine to her."

Charlie shoved a spoonful of brewis into his mouth to keep it occupied.

"There's more to it, isn't there, Charlie?"

"No, I . . ." Charlie scooped the last spoonful of brewis into his mouth and willed himself to swallow it.

"Charlie, is there something I don't know?"

"No. No." Charlie eased back into the chair. His stomach threatened to explode.

Mrs. Jackson's mouth drooped in disappointment. "No mother should outlive her child. It's awful to grow old, alone," she whispered. "Awful to think of the future."

There she was, more money put by than she could ever use, and for what? What good was money when there was nothing, and no one, to spend it on? Her teacup rattled in her hands, then in an instant she gathered herself together.

"Oh, Charlie dear, I lost myself. I am sorry. Here you are just home and I'm going on. Don't mention this to your mother. She does worry. She would mind mice at the cross-road, as my own dear mother would have said." A sad silence came over the two. "Maybe you could come back another time, when you are more settled."

"Thank you for the brewis. It was the best."

"My Philip always said that I made the best brewis in Brigus."

"He was right." Charlie stood.

Mrs. Jackson gazed into her muddy tea. There would be no more talk about Helena.

"MORNING, CHARLIE." Mrs. Pinkstone stood, round and proud, in her tiny front garden. She lived not five doors down from Mrs. Jackson.

"Morning." Charlie paused at her gate. Pausing was his first mistake.

Mrs. Pinkstone motioned to Charlie with one hand as she tucked wisps of kinky gray hair into her home-knit woolly hat with the other. "Come. Come!" Her chubby cheeks, propped up by a broad smile, blossomed into two cherry-red balls with

the May breeze. "Come in for a cup of tea and a bite to eat."
The smile grew broader.

"I must get home." Charlie spied his own house down the
road and tried to make a break for it.

"Nonsense!" Mrs. Pinkstone grabbed his hand and he was
lost, caught like a fish dangling from a pole.

"Arthur, Arthur," she bellowed in no particular direction. "I
have Charlie Wilcox here."

Arthur Pinkstone, as long and thin as his wife was soft and
round, popped up from behind the woodpile.

"You do that," he grinned, and he adjusted the spectacles
that perched precariously on his nose. "Bring him in for a
feed."

"I will," hollered Mrs. Pinkstone. And to Charlie she said,
"I made Arthur here a feed of brewis just this very morning.
Isn't it a lucky thing I have so much left over?"

"There's the ticket," said Mr. Pinkstone as he came upon the
two. "Nothing like seeing a boy eat, now, is there, Mother?"

"AGGG." A groan erupted from Charlie's mouth. A bellyful of
brewis shifted in his stomach. He looked up at the sun. It was
almost noon. He waited until the wave of sick passed then
carried on down the road. Only once did he actually clutch his
stomach, bend over, and feel the earth shift.

"Charlie," Emma snarled from the gallery of the house.
"Where have you been? Your mother has a king's helping of
brewis waiting for you in the kitchen."

The world turned shades of gray. He teetered. He tottered.
He swayed like a tree in a storm. It was all he could do to pitch

himself toward the side of the house and hang his head over the fence. It all came up. Cod and hard tack, with maybe a potato or two thrown in, and butter, lots of yellow, greasy butter. He couldn't stop until his insides were outside. This day could not get any worse.

"Hello, Charlie." Claire stood by the gate, as pretty as if she'd stepped out of a Paris shop.

The day had just got worse.

CHAPTER 3

CLAIRE SAT CURLED IN A WICKER CHAIR on the gallery. The steam from her mug of tea coiled up and vanished in the cool, spring air. She tucked a curly wisp of light brown hair back into a soft bun that had been wound at the nape of her neck. Her deep brown eyes, her skin tanned pink in the crisp spring breeze, her gentle smile astonished Charlie somehow. He had never thought of her as, as, well—as a real woman! He used to think that she had a face like an egg and eyes like pies, but things had changed. She just didn't look at all like a can of worms anymore. Fact was, she was the most beautiful girl he could imagine. Not a delicate beauty like Lily MacKenzie Daniels, and not dark and mysterious like Helena. Claire was altogether different, but just how he couldn't say.

"Feel better?" she asked, too sweetly.

Charlie nodded dumbly as the gallery door thumped closed behind him. Neither mentioned the contents of Charlie's stomach, which were now buried on the other side of the fence.

"Emma brought me tea. She's sure to bring you a mug too, if you ask her."

Charlie was equally sure she would not. "It's nice that she brought you one."

"It's the day she's to boil the sheets but, with your home-coming, she's got a bit of a holiday. It's put her in a good mood."

Claire looked at him from the corner of her eye. He was more grown up, of course, but there was something else. He was older in his heart somehow. That's what she had thought last night at the party. She had watched as he moved about the room, nodding and laughing, his eyes serious. Once or twice he'd looked her way and tried to push through the crowd to reach her, but she'd ducked out. Thing was, he near took her breath away. His broad shoulders, square jaw, and hay-colored hair falling over his face made him look—oh, what was it? Had he always looked like this? Why hadn't she noticed? And he was so tall. He now stood head and shoulders above her. What was he thinking? There were times, many times, when she could hear his thoughts as if they were her very own. But then, they often did think and feel the same way about things. And his eyes, ocean blue, they were the same, but . . . but what?

This was foolish. He was Charlie! Plain old Charlie. Nothing had changed, and yet everything was different!

Claire sipped her tea. She had loved Charlie forever, but *being* in love was different from *falling* in love, and how do you stop falling once you have stepped off the cliff?

Charlie looked out past the garden fence to the house across the way. No sign of Jim yet. He looked at Claire but not straight on, sort of sideways. Why was she looking into her mug of tea? And what was she thinking? He had to say something. They couldn't just sit there like two frogs on a rock.

"That's a pretty coat." Charlie offered up the compliment like a pig trying to make a bargain with the butcher.

"Thanks." Claire put on her slightly bored face.

Well, it *was* a pretty coat. It had buttons and pockets and a collar and it was made of cloth. Oh, what did he know about girls' clothes? She looked nice, that was all he'd meant to say.

"Maybe we could go for a walk?"

"Sure."

Charlie turned and bellowed down the hall, "Mother, we're off for a walk."

"Yes, I know." Lucy came down the hall with a rug and thermos bottle in hand. "I made you some tea. It's plenty sweet." She tucked it into an old blue haversack. "I put in mugs and biscuits. And take this old rug to sit on. There now, you two can have a nice spring picnic." Lucy looked pleased with her planning. "Be careful," she added.

Charlie grinned. Be careful? With three years spent on the battlefields of the greatest war the world had ever known, it wasn't likely that he'd meet his maker on the roads of Brigus.

"Yes, Mother." Charlie gave his mother a peck on the cheek. Tears instantly filled her eyes.

Claire and Charlie made it as far as the front gate.

"Charlie." Emma stood at the far corner of the house and motioned to him. Now what?

"Back in a minute," said Charlie, as he made his way over to Emma.

"I've been meaning to ask . . . I just wanted to know," she said in a hushed tone, "about my Murphy. You remember him? We was to be married. I wanted to ask you before this but, I just wanted to know, did ya run into him over there?"

Charlie shrank back. "I . . . I . . ." What could he say? "No," he lied.

Emma's lips quivered.

"Mornin', Charlie-boy!" Jim, flushed from standing the last of the winter wood on end at the bottom of his mother's garden, shouted from the front gate.

Charlie waved to Jim then turned back to Emma. "Emma, I . . ." He caught sight of the back of her skirt as she disappeared around the house.

"Come on, Charlie," Claire called out.

"Where are we going?" Jim asked, innocently enough.

"*We* are going for a walk." Claire gave Jim a hard look.

"I'll walk with you . . ."

Jim could hardly miss Claire's glare. What was wrong with her now? Claire was like a pendulum on a clock. One minute she was this way, the next the other way, and heaven help the poor beggar caught in the swing.

"Sure," Charlie said, a mite too eagerly and definitely too loudly, as Claire scowled.

"What did Emma want?" she asked him.

"She just wanted to know when we'd be back." Lies, all lies.

They came to a small bridge that crossed the stream that ran into Bishop's Pond.

"Watch this." Charlie took a run at it, leaping over the loose planks. "I'm brilliant," he announced as he two-stepped about while Jim cheered.

The two peered over the rail. The stream below was shallow, the water running clear, the rocks on the bottom plain to see. Ugly black sculpins, ugliest fish ever to swim upriver, scooted about madly.

"Bubbles." Charlie pointed upstream to gathered foam that lapped against the stream's bank.

"Old man spitballs," bellowed Jim, and again, the two laughed their heads off.

"Oh grow up, both of you."

Charlie laughed, spun about, then stopped suddenly and grimaced. A bolt of pain ran up his arm. He grabbed hold of it and held it to his side.

"How'd ya hurt it?" Jim gestured to Charlie's arm. "Get wounded in battle? Shot maybe?" He looked over Charlie's shoulder. Charlie could see his friend's face suddenly lose its color. You could all but see his heart drop into his shoes.

Charlie turned around. "Bloody hell." All three stared.

"Well, hello there, Hoppy-boy."

Clint, as mean lookin' as ever, planted himself in the middle of the road. The last three years had changed him some. He'd been big to begin with, and now he was bigger, but stooped, his arms dangling ape-like from his shoulders. Tufts of uncombed, dirty brown hair stood out from under his cap in muddy clumps. The muscles on his neck rippled, and one of his ears was curled into the shape of a cauliflower. He hunkered down like a barnyard dog and sneered at the trio.

"Leave us be, Clint." Jim edged forward and put himself between Clint and Charlie.

"Come on, Charlie." Claire gave him a nudge.

"Look at this, the war hero still needs his little pal to protect him." Clint gave Jim a cuff with the back of his hand. Jim raised his fists and made ready to return the favor.

Panicked, Claire grabbed Jim's hand and pulled him away. "Come on, Jim."

"Yeah, Jimmy-boy, do as you're told." The snicker turned into a sneer revealing chipped, yellowed teeth. Spittle collected in the corners of his mouth, and his lips, pulled tight, all but disappeared.

"I'm not a war hero, Clint," Charlie said softly.

"Just the same spineless coward you always were, huh?" Clint moved in close, closer, until he was a smelly breath away. "Heard you and Phil Jackson became pals over there in France. Best buddies, huh? Bosom pals. Ha! Knew he wouldn't make it."

"He was your best friend. How can you say that?" Claire sidled up right alongside of him, jutted out her chin, and glared. Clint was mean, but he'd never hit a girl, and they both knew it. Hitting a girl was the lowest thing a guy could do.

"Well, he's dead now, ain't he? Stupid beggar." He backed away.

"Let's go, Charlie." Claire tugged at Charlie's arm.

"Yeah, you run along, soldier-boy. I'll catch up to you later." Clint hawked, spat a glob at Charlie's feet, then sauntered past the three.

"He has a hate on for you." Jim shook his head. "Ya'd think that after all the trouble he got into he'd just leave you alone."

Charlie spun on his heels. "What trouble?"

"Cripes, Charlie, for locking you in that crate," said Claire. "You know, the one that got you to England in the first place."

"How? How did anyone find out?" Charlie's eyes widened.

"It was Clint himself that told," Jim butted in. "Bragged about it. Laughed himself silly. Said he found you on the wharf in St. John's looking to stow away on a sealer bound for the ice. Then he locked you in a crate that was put on a war-bound ship. Said he planned the whole thing. Well, ya can't go saying you got Charlie Wilcox drove off and not expect it to get around."

"I didn't know," Charlie whispered.

"What didn't ya know?" asked Jim.

"I didn't know that he did it on purpose. I thought, maybe, that it was a sort of an accident. That maybe he really did think that crate was being put on a sealing ship."

"He knew all right. His own father near beat him senseless over it."

An old memory rose up in Charlie's mind. Clint would have been ten or eleven years old at the time, and he would have been seven or thereabouts. Charlie had heard yelling from the road. He had crept around Clint's house, careful not to trip over strewn nets and broken barrels, and peeked around the summer kitchen. That's when he saw Clint's father holding Clint with one hand while he yanked off his belt with the other. The belt flew up into the air and hung there for a second, poised. Then it came down on Clint's back and butt. *Smack, smack, smack.* Clint twisted, spiraling in all directions. He screamed, "I'm sorry, Pa. I'm sorry." Still, the belt went up and came down.

After his da was done, Clint crawled behind the old water barrel, buried his head in his arms, and sobbed, "Pa, I'm sorry. I'm sorry." Charlie tucked himself between the summer kitchen and the woodpile and listened to the bully cry, and then he cried too.

"Clint and Phil were planning on joining the New-foundland Regiment together," Jim carried on. "They went off to St. John's. But Clint's father dragged him back. Said he couldn't join up on account of their fishing boat. There was another fight that night. Whole village heard it. Everyone came running. It was your own father that broke it up. He stood there, between Clint and his da. Your father said loud and clear, 'You'll have to get past me before you hit this boy again.' Clint's da yelled out, the worse for drink, 'Your own boy would be home this night if it weren't for him.' Then your father said, 'Two wrongs don't make a right. No boy will get beat when I can put a stop to it.' That's what he said. Heard it myself."

Claire's head bobbed up and down. She hadn't been there, her mother not being one to let a young girl see such a carrying-on, but she'd heard the story all right. "My mother says that if a rat came to the back door and himself to the front, she'd know right enough who she'd let in, and it wouldn't be Clint Miller."

"See how Clint walks now? A little to one side?"

Charlie turned back and watched Clint lope down the road.

"He's deaf in one ear on account of that beating. He tried to run off and join up again, but not even the Canadians would take him on account of him having that turned-in ear and being half deaf."

"So, he blames me?" Charlie asked, although it wasn't really a question.

"Blames you for the weather, I expect," said Jim. "He's turned real mean, Charlie."

"He was always mean." Claire kicked the dirt and then, remembering that she was wearing her good shoes, brushed the dust off.

"We thought that maybe he'd calm down a bit after his father up and died last spring. But if anything, he's worse now," said Jim, and Claire nodded in agreement. "Just watch your back."

Jim stopped. They'd come to the fork in the road. "I'm to help with scunning the McCormacks' nets. Where are you two going?"

Charlie turned to Claire. She shrugged nonchalantly.

"Up Grave Hill to Norman Lookout," was all Charlie could think to say.

"I'll stop by your house after dinner?"

"Yeah." Charlie thumped Jim on the back. Jim was away. Claire and Charlie trudged on.

CHAPTER 4

"NOT SO FAST. My feet hurt," Claire grumbled.

Charlie glanced down at Claire's feet, which were encased in pointy, laced boots with stout, stubby heels. The heels left square marks on the sandy road, rather like odd animal tracks.

"Why are you wearing them?" It seemed a fair question but for some reason Claire got all huffy.

"Just stop walking so fast."

"Sorry." Charlie slowed to a dead crawl.

"Don't all the ladies in London wear smart shoes?"

Charlie shrugged again. "Some."

The old road up the hill toward the lookout, and past Rockwell Kent's house, wasn't so much steep as it was slippery. (Kent was an American painter who had come to Brigus to roost on the side of a cliff, like a chicken on a nest of thorns. He was gone now.) Claire trailed behind, digging her heels into the hard earth, arms slightly extended, as if hoping an air current might keep her upright. Without thinking they both veered left and took the fairy path that ran behind Kent's place. Neither Charlie nor Claire had ever been afraid of fairies. Jim used to be. Most children were afraid of walking along a fairy path and being snatched away for their impertinence.

"Tell me about the war," she asked, too casually.

"You can't climb in those things." Charlie spun around. "We should go back."

"Leave my shoes out of this. I can climb mountains on stilts if I have the mind. Are you going to answer me?"

Claire stopped to catch her breath and studied him. He might be older, he might even be wiser, and he was certainly better looking, but he was still annoying.

"What do you want to know?" Charlie walked on.

"You haven't said a word about it. It's like you were just away at school." Claire took far too big a step. "Ohhhh . . ." She teetered. "Ohhhh!" Her arms flapped in the breeze.

"Watch out!" Charlie grabbed one of her arms, pressed his other hand to the small of her back, and swung her toward him. Her cheek brushed against his lips. He could feel her breath on his face, a sweet scent. His mouth was almost on hers, almost. He released her so fast she near took another tumble.

"Oh! Careful!" He made a second grab for her and hugged the wind instead.

"Leave me be! I can take care of myself!" Claire flapped about a bit before regaining her balance. She was past embarrassed and right on to mortified.

As for Charlie, his face was on fire. Best not to look at Claire directly. He needed to say something, anything!

"Remember when we flew that kite of yours up here, the one made of paper and crating? You let go of the string, remember?"

"I'm not ancient yet. Of course I remember. And I didn't let go of the string, you did. Stop getting off the topic. I just want to know—what was it like?"

The Great War, where millions died for no reason Charlie could name. "It was fine." Charlie bolted ahead.

"Fine! Fine? It was a fine war? What are you talking about?"

Claire lunged after him and grabbed hold of his arm. Her eyes, usually so steady and sure, blazed black. Her hair flew around her face. She squeezed his arm to steady herself and Charlie winced.

"And what's wrong with your arm? You set off with a bad foot and come back with a bad arm. Maybe you should have had your head knocked off!"

"Tell me instead," Charlie took a deep breath as they came to a leveled-off spot on the hill, "about what you've been doing." He put on his pleasant face.

"Me? I've been knitting a million ugly green socks, that's what. I've been having a swell time. And guess what?" Claire skirted around him and blocked his way. "Once in a while we'd run out of that ugly khaki color, and you know what happened then?"

Charlie was afraid to ask.

"They gave us ugly gray wool to knit with!"

"Ah, well." That's all he could think of, so Charlie repeated it, "Ah, well."

"Ah, well? Ah, well? Is that all you can say? Not a house in Brigus, in Newfoundland, has not had a loss. Look down there." Claire pointed to the homes below. "George Akerman, remember him? Gone. And Rupert Bartlett—dead at a place called Cambrai. What sort of place is that? He's got a Military Cross and Bar to show for it and something called the Order of the Crown of Italy. But he doesn't know about it, does he? He's dead. And what about Fred Wilcox, part of your own family? William Bartlett, Charles Leary, and William King. Thomas Jackson, John French, dead. George Clarke and Bertha Bartlett, too, a VAD. And Frank Jerrett. We knew them all, Charlie. Why? What about their parents? What about the people they were to marry? What about the children they were supposed to have? What will New-foundland do without more children? They were fighting for the King—the King! Do you think the King knows that Phil's mother is all alone now? Does he care? What about Emma? What's to happen to her? Why did it go on, and on, and on?"

"Because," Charlie said softly, "because . . . no one knew how to stop."

"Stop!" Claire was fit to be tied. "You stop killing by not killing." Claire's body was rigid with fury. There she stood, in an outfit that had taken her a month to make, that had cost her every blessed cent saved from hauling eggs around town, in shoes that pinched so badly she could hardly feel her toes, and shook. She shook and shook until the tears were rattled right out of her. "Why didn't they just stop?"

"I . . . I don't know."

Take up our quarrel with the foe: / To you from failing hands we throw / The torch . . . Charlie hung his head . . . *If ye break faith with us who die / We shall not sleep . . .*

"Charlie, answer me! Why?"

"Too many had already died. We couldn't let them down." His voice was barely above a whisper. How could she understand? Charlie reached out to put his arms around her.

"Don't touch me." Claire stepped backwards, covered her eyes with her hands, and stumbled.

"Claire!" Charlie lunged after her again. Too late. Maybe it was a fairy squall after all, but a sudden wind came up. "Claire!" There she went, hurtling down the hill.

Charlie, himself nearly taking flight, ran after her. He leapt, dove, and now the two, clutching onto each other, rolled like one down the hill. For a brief second, almost too short even to register, he felt her in his arms, and it felt good.

Thunk. Charlie heard the sound before he felt the pain. "Oh," he moaned. His arm had smacked against a protruding rock. They had come to rest against a small mound of earth.

"Charlie, speak to me! Are you all right?" Claire, her hair and clothes a wreck, struggled up on an elbow. "Charlie?"

Dazed and thoroughly bewildered, he gazed up at the blue sky.

"Oh Charlie, are you hurt? Say something."

What was there to say? Had he survived the war only to get killed on a peaceful hill in Brigus? What would his mother think?

"Is it your back? Is your arm all right?" Claire was blubbering. Her nose was running and the hankie she had shoved up her sleeve was missing.

"I'm fine. How are you?" Charlie struggled to sit up. He looked around, then up the hill at the blanket and haversack.

"Yes, I'm fine too."

"Here." Charlie passed Claire his handkerchief.

"Thank you." She blew her nose. The honk was impressive.

Charlie struggled to stand and, taking it slow, trudged back up the hill to retrieve their things. When he returned, he noticed that Claire must have run a hand over her face, leaving a black streak across her face. She looked like the little girl he'd once played with.

He laid the rug out on the near-frozen ground. It was a pleasant spot, all things considered. The bay was spread out in front of them, the village down below, and the hill behind gave them shelter. He sat down beside Claire and, for a moment, they were alone in the world.

CHAPTER 5

SHE HAD GONE TOO FAR. She had made a mess of it all. Claire rubbed her eyes with the backs of her hands and then unscrewed the top of the thermos bottle. What was he thinking? She used to know. Not words exactly, but it was as if she could *feel* his thoughts. Now, it felt as though there were a wall between them. As if the war were right here, on this hill.

It was Claire who finally broke the silence. "I know it must have been awful for you, but it was awful here, too. They would post the names of the dead and missing on the window of the post office. Names, just names. Like they were not real people at all. It was as if one side of the world was bleeding to death and the other side was drowning in tears."

Yes, yes, that's how it must have been, Charlie thought. *Keep the home fires burning while your hearts are yearning.* Waiting for the telegram that said he's dead, but he died heroically, quickly, without pain. Charlie watched Claire pour out the tea. Tears gathered in her eyes but didn't fall.

"Thing is, those who have made it home want to forget, and those who stayed at home want to remember." Charlie spoke more to the wind than to Claire. "But they want to remember the war that was supposed to have happened. A glamorous war with lots of flags and courageous men charging into battle. A war of honor. That's not the war I remember."

"Charlie, you said that they didn't stop killing because no one wanted to let down the ones who had died. But if no one talks about them, then they *are* let down. They are forgotten. Don't you see?"

What could he say to her? There was a pact between soldiers—not spoken to be sure—to not tell those at home the truth. To not mention lice as big as grains of rice. To not tell them about feet so bloodied and raw they looked like skinned animals, about obese rats and how they came to be so fat. But most important, to not tell how their loved ones died, really died, with bits missing off them, crying out for their mothers, for their homes. Best they thought it all a lark, lads off for an adventure. But what Claire had said, there was truth in it.

He looked down over his village. There had been so many times when he'd been sure he'd never set eyes on this place, or this girl, again. No, she wasn't a girl anymore than he was a boy. She was a woman, almost seventeen. He turned. He looked into her eyes. Brown eyes, with streaks of crimson shot through like bolts of lightning. He could drown in those eyes. She wanted to know. She had the right to know. Everyone did.

"I don't know where to begin."

"At the beginning, where stories start."

"But you know the start of it. It all happened by accident, me being there and all. I was in France. After I gave Mac— Lily I guess ya call her now—my ticket home, I went to the front to tell Dr. Daniels that he was going to be a father. I never intended on doing more. I never intended on staying. I knew my parents were worried about me.

"I arrived at the front on June 31, 1916. The next day, over eight hundred men from the First Newfoundland Regiment went over the top. It wasn't a battle, it was a slaughter. Sixty-eight soldiers answered roll call the next day. Some came straggling, limping, and crawling back after that, but only after having spent one, two, maybe three days lying out there in no-man's-land." Charlie ran his hands through his hair. "The Brits, *the Imperials* is what our lads called them, lost twenty thousand men at the Somme. Three times that were wounded, some dying after. And ya know what they say now? That hardly any Germans lost their lives that day."

"Charlie, if it's too hard . . ." Claire laid her hand on his arm. He shook his head, then sipped his tea.

"If you want to know, I'll do my best to tell you."

Charlie paused and looked about. The sun, high in the sky, shone down on a few skiffs that bobbed about on anchor in the bay. Other small boats lay belly up on the far beach. Some were painted dark blue for a season of mourning. Why was it so hard to feel like he was home for good? The thing was, the war was more real to him than this very place. He took a deep breath.

"After the battle I just wanted to get home. It was July 2, 1916. My friend Michael had been killed the day before, and Martin, another friend, had got himself wounded. It took the better part of a night and day to get Martin help, but I found Dr. Daniels and he set him straight. Martin was put into an ambulance. At first I thought I'd go with him, back to the hospital and then onto England, Blighty they call it . . ."

CHAPTER 6

1916, FRANCE

CHARLIE JUMPED OUT OF THE BACK of the ambulance and ran. Martin was yelling after him, screaming, "Charlie, no." And then, "Come back!" Charlie didn't even look back, he couldn't. Instead he barreled down the road as if the enemy were behind him, not in front of him.

He needed to find his spy glass. It had been passed down from Wilcox to Wilcox for generations, and he'd promised his father he wouldn't lose it. After he found it, he'd catch up to Martin and get home—somehow.

He kept an eye out for Dr. Daniels. It was best to avoid him. He'd have something to say if he found Charlie heading back into the trenches.

The roads were jammed. Charlie dodged lorries, horse-drawn wagons, water and munitions trucks, automobiles, and men on the march. He passed the farmhouse that served as a field dressing station, FDS they called it. That's when he spotted the tracks. Flatbed railcars were used to haul the wounded from the front lines. They were powered by mules or men and unloaded near the FDS. All he had to do was follow the tracks back to the front. Charlie hurled himself onto the last railcar. At first glance it looked like the floor was painted red. He sniffed. Blood. There was blood everywhere. Charlie sat, pulled his knees up to his chest, and waited.

Ten, maybe fifteen minutes later he arrived at the front. Paths, cut sharp and clean through the hill, led to the trenches. You could smell the stink of them from a distance—blood, piss, petrol, and enough shell fire to scorch the nose and back of the throat. He plunged onward, then downward.

The reserve trenches were at the back. Next was the support trench, and just before no-man's-land was the fire trench. Connecting them, and running perpendicular, were communication trenches. The spy glass was in his old haversack in the fire trench.

"Look out there!" A soldier, carrying a wounded man on his back, stumbled toward him. Charlie pressed his back against the mud wall to let him pass. A stream of misery was bearing down on him, dazed men, all exhausted and desperate. How could he reach the fire trench?

"Where have you been?" snarled a grim-faced stretcher-bearer. He was tucked into the side of the trench and puffing on a cigarette, a gasper they called it. On a stretcher beside him lay a soldier. Charlie peered into face of the stretcher-bearer. He knew him! It was the same fellow he had worked with two days ago, before the battle. Charlie opened his mouth to tell him that he'd been at the FDS, that he'd put his friend Martin on an ambulance, that he was just here to find his spy glass and then go home, but it was plain to see that the soldier wasn't interested.

"You still wearing that?" The stretcher-bearer pointed to the filthy Red Cross band that circled the upper part of Charlie's left arm.

"Yeah," said Charlie, although, truth be told, he'd forgotten about it.

"Good. Here!" The stretcher-bearer flicked his gasper into the pool of muck at his feet, whipped the helmet off the man on the stretcher, and flung it at Charlie. "Take that end."

Charlie put the helmet on his head and looked down at the soldier lying on the stretcher. He peered closer. "He's dead."

"Dead or alive, we've got to clear out these trenches."

"No, I . . ."

"LIFT!"

Charlie picked up the two poles of the stretcher. It was obvious that the only way to find his haversack was to help clear the trenches. He spent the rest of the day removing bodies, or bits of bodies. Occasionally they found someone alive.

Around mid-afternoon they scrambled up and out of the back trench, tumbled two more wounded men onto the push-train, and slumped to the ground. The guns were surprisingly quiet.

"Here." The stretcher-bearer tossed Charlie a canteen. Charlie slugged back the warm, stale water. He was sweating. A feeling of sick was on him. "Eat." A can of sardines was winged in his direction. Charlie caught the tin, then curled back the lid with a small key. His hands were shaking as he tipped the oily sardines into his mouth. They were disgusting. Damn things near slithered down his throat.

"My name's Charlie Wilcox, from Brigus. What's yours?" Jeeze, he sounded like he was trying to make friends in a schoolyard. Thing was, he hadn't thought to ask the stretcher-bearer his name before this, a battle not usually being the place for introductions.

"Tom."

"Tom what?"

"Just Tom. No sense getting to know anyone around here." Tom looked at Charlie from the corner of his eye. Too young for this war, he thought, but what the kid was doing here was none of his concern.

"Do you know where the Newfoundlanders are?" Charlie spoke above a series of rumbles. The two sides were making halfhearted attempts at shelling one another.

"Heard they've regrouped in the St. John's trench, what's left of 'em, plus the 10 percent they held back in reserve."

"The what?" A blast had obliterated Tom's last few words.

"The 10 percent," Tom yelled.

"What 10 percent?"

"They hold back 10 percent of the Regiment in any battle. They'll move up soon enough. Heard that they're thinking that the Huns might counterattack. I would if I was them. Finish us off. But maybe the Huns feel sorry for us, eh? Come on."

Tom made a sound that might have passed for a laugh, then stood up and dusted his backside. Charlie, despite the queasiness in his stomach, scrambled up after him.

CHAPTER 7

THE NEXT FORTY-EIGHT HOURS PASSED IN A BLUR. They ate and slept when they could. Day became night and then day again. There was no accounting for time.

Charlie slid down onto a box labeled "Munitions" and fell into a dreamless sleep. When he awoke everything was spinning. "Tom," Charlie called out. And then, "Father. Father." He shook his head. Greasy sweat coated him, and heat pressed down on him like a flat palm. He was burning up.

Somewhere, somehow, in the midst of all this, he had a thought. He wouldn't be catching up to Martin, and he wouldn't be seeing England anytime soon. He had to find the Newfoundlanders. Where were they?

Charlie grabbed a bedroll that had been left in a funk hole and tucked it under his arm. What had Tom said about the Newfoundlanders? Something about regrouping in the St. John's trench then making ready for a counterattack. All the trenches were named after places from home. Now, how to get there?

"WHAT IS IT?"

"It's a kid. Must be French."

"Hey, wake up. *Levez-vous.*"

Charlie felt a poke in the ribs. He squirmed away from the offending hand. He was dead cold but sweating just the same.

"Is that a Red Cross band on his arm?"

"Hey, who are you?"

Charlie looked up expecting to see Tom. Four eyes, black and pointy, gaped back at him.

"By God, it's Charlie Wilcox from Brigus. Least I think it is. That you there, Charlie?"

The black eyes moved in close. Charlie struggled to sit, rubbed his eyes, then rolled out of the funk hole. He tried to stand but his legs gave way.

"Hold on there, boy, sit yourself down now."

A wooden box was kicked toward Charlie and he thumped down on it, hard. He pulled the sleeping bag behind him. It was lined with balled up newsprint, now soaked through, making it heavy and smelly. The ends fell through the duck-boards at the bottom of the trench and dipped into a pool of brown water.

"Where am I?"

"It *is* you, Charlie-boy!"

Charlie peered up at the face and placed it. Oh Jeeze! Phil Jackson, not a face he particularly wanted to run into.

"Good to see you, boy."

"Where am I?" he repeated.

"St. John's Road. Charlie-boy, you look like death warmed up."

Phil took a hard look at Charlie. The boy was yellow. What little weight he had on him had melted away. As for his clothes, they seemed to be a collection of castoffs—a torn tunic, khaki pants, boots not fit for the bin, gray puttees, and all caked in mud and guts. Phil thumped down on a wooden crate across from Charlie, poured out tea from a thermos bottle, and passed the cup over to Charlie. Phil held his feet up out of the slimy water but Charlie couldn't muster the strength.

"Keep a lookout there, Garth," Phil said to his pal, who nodded and took up a spot a way down a bit. Garth motioned an *all clear* to Phil by nodding his head. The Captain was nowhere in sight.

"Feel better?" Phil passed Charlie a biscuit and a can of bully beef.

"Yeah." Truth be told, he didn't feel any better, and he didn't even know how he'd got there. But what did it matter? He gnawed on the biscuit in between mouthfuls of the beef.

Phil screwed the cap back onto the thermos bottle and shoved it into his haversack. "Never in all my born days did I expect to see you. But we see things here we never expected to, and that's God's truth."

Just then a water-resistant rat paddled happily through the foul black sludge that covered the trench floor. Phil gave it a swift kick, then looked into the funk hole. Surely the kid couldn't have been hiding in there for long!

"What's the date?" Charlie looked up to the sky.

"July 5th maybe."

Four days had passed since the battle.

Charlie gulped down the sweet, warm tea. It wasn't sitting in his stomach right. The beef, the biscuit, and the tea were now churning together.

He peered at Phil over the lip of his mug. He was older than Charlie by almost four years and near twice as big. Since he was seven he'd been fishing on his father's skiff. His back and shoulders had been broadened by two seasons on the ice. Thing was, Phil looked as fresh as a daisy.

"Where've you come from?" Charlie asked.

"We arrived just before the battle. We're part of the reserves, the 10 percent held back, me and Garth both." Phil motioned to the other soldier who stood a ways off.

"Been up in Scotland training afore this. Thought we'd be in the thick of it by now, mind. Didn't see myself clearing out and shoring up trenches. What are you here for?" He passed Charlie another biscuit.

What *was* he here for? The shelling was picking up. It took Charlie a moment to think. He was muddled. The spy glass, now he remembered.

"I'm looking for something. Soon as I find it, I'm going home."

"Find what? What are you on about?" Phil hollered over two shells that near landed on top of them.

"Stand to!" Garth yelled out. The Captain was coming down the line.

"You'll get us put on report. Hide!" Phil hissed.

The biscuit fell into the water between the slats of the duckboards as Charlie dove into the funk hole and pulled the sleeping bag over him. Phil rammed the haversack on top of Charlie and then turned his back.

"Steady on, boys," the Captain bellowed over the advancing thunder. "I'm looking for volunteers to go on a raiding party tonight. Capture a few Boche. There's a week's pass in England for any who come back alive."

"What does he mean, come back alive? I hardly think we'll want a pass to England if we come back dead!" Garth muttered under his breath.

"What's that, soldier? Speak up." The Captain gazed at Garth—a big fellow, ruddy faced, a woodsman.

"Nothing, sir."

"Good of you to volunteer. Report at twenty-three hundred hours."

"Yes, sir." Garth's face lost its color entirely.

The Captain passed Phil and went on his way without further comment. Phil's sigh of relief was loud enough to bring Charlie out of hiding.

"Raiding party, ha!" Garth muttered. "Just a jaunt across no-man's-land and back again, and with a little Hun in tow, no less. There's a way to get killed for nothing good. Besides, what do I want a pass to go to England for? We've been here no more than a week."

Garth crashed down onto a crate, propped his Lee Enfield rifle between his legs, and scratched his chest. Phil scratched his chest too. Fact was both of them were alive with lice. Charlie knew the signs. A blind man would know the sight of lice making a meal of a body. They could do a man in, drive him crazy. The scratching would go on and on until the skin was scraped raw. Then infection would set in.

"Got a candle?" Charlie asked.

Phil shook his head then hollered down the line, "Anyone got a candle?"

It took a few minutes but a candle was dug up.

"Give me your tunic." Charlie lit the candle.

There was no reason for Phil to obey Charlie, but he did anyway.

Scrunched down on his haunches, Charlie set to work. Slowly, he moved the flame up and down the seams of Phil's jacket and listened to the satisfying little pops as the lice copped it. There was a trick to delousing a jacket. Go too close with the flame and the threads would shrivel and break, too far and the lice would not burn.

"Hey, look here," Phil called, and Garth, plus four others, gathered round to watch Charlie fry lice.

A new lot, Charlie thought. Green.

"Could you do mine after that one?"

"Mine too?"

"Looks like you have yourself a job, Charlie-boy."

CHAPTER 8

WITH DAYLIGHT came the *Moaning Minnies,* as the lads called them. Minenwerfers. Shells. Red-tailed comets that fell like stars and shattered the air like glass. The Huns were saying "Good morning."

Charlie rolled over in the funk hole. He wanted to find Tom, he needed to find his haversack, and he hoped to go home. He was feeling no better.

"Boots!" Phil tossed a pair of leather, ankle-high boots, only two sizes too big, into the funk hole. One landed on Charlie's head.

Charlie gathered them together and considered. He did need new boots. He looked down at his father's old Parker & Monroe sealer's boots. They had done their bit. But if Phil thought Charlie was going to be grateful, he could bloody well think again.

"Come on, Charlie-boy. No hard feelings, huh? Let's let bygones be bygones."

Charlie sat up and peeled off his old boots. It might have been a hard thing, giving up his father's boots that way, had not the sudden movement made the sick rise in his throat.

Whatever illness had come over Charlie showed no signs of wearing off. If anything, it was worse. The sweat now poured down him, making a stink that he could hardly bear. A bath would be some good.

The trench was waking up. There was yelling, snap-to orders, soldiers checking their gear, saying their prayers. More bombs.

A carrier came down the line with rations. Charlie, his chin tucked into his tunic and as muddy and worn as the rest of them, was counted in. There was black bread, hard cheese, a can of stew, and a can of plum and apple jam to share. Charlie ate, threw it up, tried to eat again, and vomited that up, too.

"Want to hear a joke?" asked Phil as he wolfed down the stew with positive relish. "New recruit is told to bring Maconochies up to the front line. Recruit says, 'Let Maconochie bring his own up.'" Phil chuckled. "Get it?"

Charlie shook his head. It throbbed.

Phil held up the tin of stew and pointed to the label. "See, Maconochies makes this stuff. Makes the plum and apple jam, too."

"What do they use in the jam?" Charlie peered into the jar. There weren't any plums and apples in that guck, that was for certain.

"Here, drink this." Phil pushed a mug of black tea under Charlie's nose. Charlie drank it, but it took all of his will to keep it down.

Thing was, Charlie didn't entirely trust Phil Jackson. Why should he? He was a bully, or at least a bully's sidekick, and people didn't change overnight. Maybe people never changed at all. In any case, Phil wasn't his problem now. His biggest enemies were sickness, mud, rats, and lice. Even the Huns came in a poor fifth.

"Garth didn't come back from the raid last night." Phil hadn't really known Garth long, and he relayed this news with detachment. He stood, stretched, and took off his helmet. His red hair was cut short and stood out from his head like miniature, red-hot iron spikes.

They heard the sound, *thunk*—like a fist coming down on a table.

"Down! Sniper!" The soldiers all threw themselves onto the soggy duckboards and lay there, as still as dead men.

"You all right there, Charlie-boy?" Phil lifted his head slowly. His face was covered with muck and his lips were pulled so tight they were a thin line.

Charlie picked himself up and shook like a dog and then checked, just by instinct, his arms, his hands, his legs. He was all there.

"Where is it?" Phil hissed.

"There!" Charlie pointed. The sniper's bullet was lodged in the trench wall a mere inch above Phil's head, or where his head had been a moment ago. "Bloody bugger missed," Phil muttered. "Ya hear that, ya great bloody bugger, ya missed me!" Phil shouted over the top of the parapet, all the while hunching over and ramming the helmet back on his head. He'd have done the strap of his helmet up too if his hands hadn't been shaking.

Charlie put on his own helmet then rolled up his filthy sleeping bag. Three shells fell, one after the other. They waited, steadied themselves, then carried on.

"Remember Murphy Milford?" Phil asked.

Charlie nodded. He was Big Emma's intended, poor sod. Imagine a life with Emma!

"He's down the line a bit."

"You sure?"

"Sure, I'm sure. He's been in the thick of it since the start." Phil slung his rifle over his shoulder. "See here, Charlie," he hollered.

Charlie bent forward to hear him better. "What?"

"I said . . . I been meaning to tells ya . . ." But Phil's words were lost. "Never mind. I'll find ya, when it's over . . ."

Phil joined the line of soldiers slogging by on their way to the fire trench. Maybe a counterattack was being planned. Nobody bothered to tell the soldiers in the trenches a whole heck of a lot. With bowed heads and at least sixty pounds of equipment bogging them down, they moved forward as if they were battling a storm. Mess kits bounced against their butts. If it hadn't been for the overhead din they would have sounded like cows clanking about in the field. No chance of surprising the Huns, not with all that racket.

Charlie tucked himself back into the funk hole and waited until the line of soldiers passed by. His teeth chattered. The sweat had dried on him and now he was clammy and cold. After the last soldier was gone, Charlie stood and steadied himself. No sense even trying to get up to the fire trench to search for the haversack. Home seemed as far off as ever. If he could just see this through . . . but it was hard to think straight.

He started down the reserve trench. He'd make his way to the communication trench, then down toward the aid post. No one cared who held up one end of a stretcher. No one asked your name, or age, if you were trying to save a life or take a life. But Phil was right, he couldn't stay there much longer. He'd be in some trouble if he was caught wearing the uniform, such as it was.

Charlie was halfway down the reserve trench when he stumbled over a foot. "Sorry." His eyes trailed up the legs. He half expected to find this was a corpse.

"Murphy? Murphy Milford? Is that you? Murphy, it's me! Charlie Wilcox. Charlie, from Brigus." He bent down and rested a hand on the soldier's shoulder.

Murphy's head emerged from his uniform like a turtle coming out of its shell. "Charlie-boy, heard you was here somewheres. Surprised I didn't run into you before now."

The look of him near took Charlie's breath away. It was Murphy all right, or the shadow of him. He was as thin as a rope, with rheumy eyes and flat cheeks as long and gray as slabs of sheer rock. Charlie peered closely.

The bursts of artillery fire increased. Murphy didn't flinch at the barrage, didn't even seem to notice. And he did nothing to hide his tears, just let 'em roll down his face, like pearls dropping off a string.

"It's going to be all right Murphy, you'll see," Charlie yelled. A shell landed. Hunks of dirt fell off the trench wall and splashed into the water. Charlie leaned against the wall and tried to keep his balance.

"I'll come to me end afore this war comes to its. We're forgotten, ya know. The world has forgotten us." Murphy's eyes, red as fresh meat, seemed to turn in his head. He inched closer to the wall, as if trying to crawl right into it.

"We have to go on, Murphy. We have to beat them. We're their betters. Think of home, Murphy."

Murphy didn't need to be reminded of home. In his mind he was already in Newfoundland. He was with his brothers and father. Maybe setting off for a day's fishing. He could see the sun come up over the water. It was a mystery to Murphy why man mined the earth in search of diamonds when all he had to do was look out on the water at dawn to see more brilliance than the eye could take in. It was a cruel thing to take a man born to the ocean and have him die in this godforsaken, landlocked spot. For sure, if Newfoundland was a bit of heaven fallen from above, this land was a piece of hell chucked up from below.

"Think of Emma," Charlie yelled. Two explosions, one coming on the tail of the other, landed nearby. Again the earth revolted and coughed up chunks of dirt.

"Ah?"

"I said, think of Emma."

"Grand girl, Charlie. I loves her. I do." Another shell landed. They were coming fast and furious now. Charlie jerked forward. Murphy didn't wince. Instead he gave Charlie a hard, bold look. "You'll not say . . . Emma . . . found me. Promise . . . word . . . Newfoundlander."

"What?" Charlie cupped a hand to his ear and shook his head.

"You're not to tell her . . . how you found me. Your word." He yelled as loud as a man could yell.

"My word, Murphy."

"A grand girl."

"You're not dead yet, Murphy." Tears rushed up the back of Charlie's throat.

"Yeah, I am, Charlie-boy."

"What?" Charlie shouted.

Murphy, his great height bent forward, staggered into battle, defeated.

CHAPTER 9

Tom leaned against the entrance of the aid post like a boy waiting for his date. The post was carved into the trench wall, bolstered with timber and coils of tin. A piece of canvas slung across the entrance made do as a door and a Red Cross banner hung over the top.

"Where ya been?" Tom didn't wait for an answer. "Here." He chucked Charlie a bulging Red Cross bag. Charlie lurched forward to catch it. He opened it and checked the supplies. All there.

"Anyone in there?" Charlie motioned toward the aid post.

"You're safe enough. Medical unit hasn't arrived."

The shelling was constant now. The breaks in the barrage came like short, labored breaths. Charlie pulled the straps of the bag taut across his chest and checked his mask and water bottles.

"You're looking bloody awful. Didn't know people came in that particular color. It would look fetching if you were a plant."

"What?"

Tom waved him away.

Charlie thumped down onto a stool in front of the aid post and hung his head. His temperature would be up around 102, if he was counting, which he wasn't. Finding his haversack seemed less and less likely as time went on.

What was that? Charlie cocked his head. Between lulls in the shelling he heard loud voices coming up from behind.

"Oh Jeeze!" Charlie dove behind Tom. "Cover me!"

"What?" Bewildered, Tom looked around him.

"Shut up," Charlie hissed and stood, back to back, directly behind Tom.

Two medics and a doctor, all carrying hospital supplies, passed close enough to brush Tom's shoulder. Tom's face, as blank as a plank, looked directly ahead.

"You all right, soldier?" Dr. Robert Daniels stopped and stared into Tom's wide eyes.

"Yes, sir. Fine, sir."

Dr. Daniels nodded and ducked into the aid post.

"Let's get out of here," Charlie whispered into Tom's ear. Like boys caught playing with matches, they picked up the stretcher and made a run for it into the trenches.

"Stop," Tom hollered. "Why are we running? Do you know that sawbones?"

Charlie, his back against the wall, leaned over and hugged his stomach. "Yeah. Dr. Robert Daniels. He runs the FDS."

"He's one of the good vets. Why are you ducking him? What'd you do, kill someone?"

"I saved his wife and baby."

"Well, that explains it."

"He doesn't know that I'm here. If he finds out, he'll send me packing. And it's too late to catch up to Martin."

"What are you babbling on about, boy? Who's Martin?"

"Met him on the ship coming over. He's . . ." Oh Jeeze, up it came again. Charlie lurched down the trench, heaved himself over the trench wall, and vomited. Nothing would stay put in his stomach. His gut was having its own war. Everything was spinning. If he could just lie down for a bit. Jeeze. He looked about. This was a good way to get shot. He rolled back into the trench, cleaned himself up as best he could and stumbled back to Tom. "Thing is, I want to see this bit to the end. I need to think about what to do next."

"Think? You picked just the spot. A nice quiet war to help you *think*. You're off your head, you know that?" Tom propped the stretcher against the trench wall.

A distant whistle blew. Something was up. An attack, most likely. The first bunch would be going over the top. *Snap . . . snap . . . snap.* With practiced grace, bayonets were being fixed onto rifles. *Snap . . . snap . . . snap. "Dear Lord, You know what I must do this day. If I forget Thee, do not forget me."* You didn't need to hear the prayers to know that the soldiers were whispering them.

There was a howling and wailing from somewhere off in the distance.

"Where's that coming from?" Tom searched his pockets for his tobacco pouch.

"The shelling?"

"No, the bloody bagpipes."

"Maybe it's the Huns playing. They're trying to confuse us." Charlie rubbed the sweat away from his face with the back of his hand, then slid down to crouch on his haunches.

"Huns got Beethoven, and what about that Bach fellow, ain't he German? They got lots of musicians. They got better taste than to play the bagpipes." Tom took out a pouch of Prince Albert Tobacco and rolled himself a gasper. "Do you suppose those Scots play the pipes to drown out the screams, or do you suppose the men scream to drown out those bloody pipes?"

"My father loves the sound of the pipes." As far as he knew, every Newfoundlander loved the sound of the pipes. Father, Mother—what would it be to sit at the kitchen table this very moment, hear the kettle whistle, and laugh at a good crack?

"Maybe so, but count me out," snarled Tom. "My old father used to say that a real gentleman was one who could play the pipes, but don't." Tom finished rolling his cigarette, jammed it into the corner of his mouth, and fished around in his pockets for a light. "Gotta wonder at the Scots, going over the top the way they do, in their skirts, all hairy legs and bare arses. What do you call that thing that hangs down in front?"

"What?"

"The hairy thing that dangles in front. What's it called?"

"Oh, a sporran," said Charlie.

Tom lit his gasper and took a long drag. "What's it for?"

"What's what for?"

"A sporran."

"It's a sort of purse."

"Who would have thought that we'd be fighting alongside men in skirts who be wearing purses!"

Another shrill whistle blew. Whistles had been going off the past half hour.

Tom looked over at Charlie. "You look like something the cat coughed up."

"Jeeze, and I was just thinking how nice you looked."

"I'm just saying that ya looks bloody awful, and there's more that can kill ya here than a bloody bomb." Tom took another puff then flicked his gasper into a pool of stagnant, murky water. "Come on, Florence Nightingale, time to join the party."

Charlie eased himself up and took hold of his end of the stretcher just as a riptide of noise washed over them. They careened head-first into the forward wall.

"Gawd damn, Jeez'murphy," Tom grumbled as Charlie spat out mud and checked his hands for cuts. "Them Huns have something to answer for." Tom shouted as he made a fist and shook it heavenward. "Come on."

Once again they staggered forward, down the communication trench and finally into the front fire trench. "This will do." Tom pulled a boxy periscope out of his pack and peered out into no-man's-land. It was a rare thing for a stretcher-bearer to have a periscope, but Tom was always coming up with rare things—hunks of cheese, biscuits from some posh shop in England, cans of sardines, clean underwear, new socks.

"Look here." He passed Charlie the periscope.

Charlie pushed his eye against the box and looked out into that scrap of land that divided the enemies. It was a haunting, ravaged place, a moonscape. The once green, rolling French hills were now black and pockmarked with craters—some as big as a house, others small enough to camouflage a single German machine gun and gunner. The sounds of the German artillery had been replaced by the *ping, ping* of snipers' bullets as they hit the curly barbed wire that lay in fierce loops along the battlefield. The bullets gave off startling flashes of light.

Through the haze Charlie could see soldiers lumbering and lurching forward in clumsy attempts at a charge. They might have been men, or they might have been hulking, prehistoric beasts at the dawn of mankind. And beyond no-man's-land lay the Germans' own barbed wire. Miles of it, as sharp as sharks' teeth.

Charlie slid down the wall of the trench and hung his head between his knees.

CHAPTER 10

IT WAS MORNING AGAIN. Maybe it was morning, hard to tell. There was no sun to speak of. Charlie hadn't seen Phil all day. Not that he'd expected to, but knowing that there were others close by from his part of Newfoundland made him feel better. And what of Murphy? Had he gone out on the attack?

Slumped on a crate, Charlie looked up at a passing soldier. He had the insignia of the Newfoundland Regiment, a caribou, on his collar.

"What's going on?" asked Charlie.

"Some of our lads were sent out on attack last night." The soldier never looked at him, just answered and carried on.

"Stretcher-bearer, over here!"

Charlie gave Tom a shove. "Get up."

"Yeah," Tom mumbled.

Ping, ping. A sniper was at his post. Tom and Charlie did up the straps of their helmets as they scurried forward, hunched over. The sleep, what little there had been of it, hadn't done Charlie a bit of good.

"Over here." A soldier, crouched on the trench floor, held up his buddy in his arms.

59

Tom made it to him first, bent down, and picked the soldier up by the shoulders. "Okay. Up." Tom and Charlie lifted the stretcher, Tom in the lead.

The strain of hauling near-dead weights was tearing Charlie apart. His sides, his legs, his arms, his entire body pulsed with exhaustion. Run. Run again. "Bad times don't last," that's what his mother used to say. Charlie repeated it to himself as his feet plunged into the muck.

He heard a roar, like the sound of a wounded beast. Charlie looked up. A soldier, smeared in mud and clutching his chest, hovered, then wavered above the parapet. Charlie let go of his end of the stretcher as the soldier toppled into the trench, while Tom dragged the stretcher onward. The soldier landed at Charlie's feet. Blood poured out of him like paint running out of a pot. He was shot right through.

"I got ya." Charlie bent down over the soldier, turned him face up, then fumbled with his medic bag. He dammed up the hole with a length of bandage but there was no stopping the stream of blood. Shells hit. The trench quivered. Putty-colored hunks of mud fell into the soldier's open wound. Keeping the blood in was one thing, keeping the mud out was another.

"Mother!" The soldier's body went into a spasm, vibrating and quaking. He clutched Charlie's arm. Another shell hit outside the trench and another after that.

"Let go! It's all right. You're going to be fine, just let go." Charlie tried to peel the fingers off his arm. The trench wall began caving in around them. Charlie held up his arm to fend off the downpour of flowing earth but the wall continued its inward slide. "Let go!"

"Get out of there. Leave him," Tom, a few yards ahead, yelled. Charlie looked over. What was he screaming? Tom's arms waved like pinwheels.

"Get away!" Tom screamed.

"I'm trying," Charlie yelled back. He pried the soldier's fingers off and leapt back just as the trench wall gave way entirely. "No!" Charlie grabbed hold of the soldier's feet, pulling and tugging before throwing himself on the pile and digging. More earth fell in, a small, contained avalanche of mud. Charlie scrambled backwards, crying, shrieking. The soldier was buried alive.

"Over here." Tom was bent over a soldier who was cradling the better part of his leg in his arms.

Charlie stumbled, then slumped against a trench wall. His teeth chattered. Worse, his vision blurred. He couldn't think straight.

THE GUNS WERE QUIET NOW. Occasionally Charlie and Tom could hear a German voice from across no-man's-land. People said that at the beginning of the war the two sides had sung Christmas carols to each other. There was another story, too, of how men on both sides had crawled out of the trenches on Christmas Day, claimed their dead, and then had a soccer game. The idea disgusted Charlie. Consorting with the enemy. The Huns had to be driven back. God was with us. We were their betters and had to teach them so. Charlie was sure of it. If he didn't believe that, what was the point?

"Hear that?" Charlie raised his head. It was a voice all right, but not German.

"Dieu, je vous donne ma vie librement pour ma patrie."
The voice had an echo to it that made his skin creep.

"What?" Tom muttered.

"There's a Frenchman out there." A sniper would get him
if he wasn't quiet.

"A Frenchman in France, imagine that! Get some sleep,"
which was Tom's way of saying, "Shut up."

"You speak French?"

"Enough. *Mon cheri, comment ça va?*"

"Tell me what he's saying."

Tom cocked his head and listened to the Frenchman's rant.
"He's saying, 'God, I give you my life freely for my country.'
What God wants with his life is something else entirely. Seems
to me God has enough company of late. Get some sleep."

Charlie was too tired to sleep.

"Tom, why are you here?"

"Jeeze, boy, are you daft? What kind of a question is that?"
Tom crossed his arms, tucked his hands into his armpits, and
rolled over.

"I was just thinking, lots say it's for the adventure. Is that
why you are here?"

Tom, whose hair was brown with bolts of blond woven
through, who had a round, cherub-like face and horsy teeth,
looked up at the strip of sky. "My father said that he'd be
ashamed of me if I didn't sign up, so I signed up. When I was
getting on the boat in St. John's, he said that if I brought
embarrassment to his name, he'd shoot me himself."

CHAPTER 11

IT WAS MID-AFTERNOON. Charlie had fallen into a half sleep. His head lolled about on his shoulders.

"Stretcher-bearer." It was a Newfoundland voice, and it was coming from no-man's-land. Charlie didn't have the strength to respond.

Tom gestured with his thumb toward the voice. "That lad's going to attract unwanted attention if he doesn't shut up." Then he squirmed around as if trying to accomplish the impossible and find a comfortable position for a nap.

"Help me."

Charlie struggled to stand. He peeked over the parapet. Where was the voice coming from?

Ping, ping.

"Get down!" Tom leapt up and made a grab for Charlie. "Are you off your head? What's wrong with you?"

"Sorry." Charlie wiped the sweat from his brow. Thing was, for a moment he had forgotten where he was.

"Help!"

"Never mind," Tom muttered. "There's nothing to be done. There is more than one sniper out there. Wait until the sun sets."

"That'll be hours yet."

"Get some sleep."

"Stretcher-bearer." The voice out in no-man's-land was weak and thin.

Charlie pulled his knees up to his chest and rested his head on them. He covered his ears with his hands. Why didn't he shut up? What was the point? No one would help him. Battlefields can speak, but they can't hear.

"Help."

"Give me the periscope," said Charlie. Tom, annoyed, unfurled himself and flung it over. Charlie struggled to stand and pressed his eye against it.

"Oh no. Please no . . ." The soldier's face, as big as a moon, looked directly at him. It was Murphy. He was caught in their own barbed wire not twenty feet away.

"Murphy," Charlie hissed. "Murphy!"

"Who's that?" Murphy's eyes were wide and bright, like a trapped animal's. His face glistened with sweat and tears.

"Not so loud, and don't move. It's me, Murphy, Charlie Wilcox."

"Charlie-boy," Murphy gasped. "Can you see my mates? Did they make it back?"

Charlie swiveled the periscope. He could see rotting horse carcasses. He could see swarms of rats. He could see dead men but had no way of telling one body from another. They all looked like gray husks with the occasional splash of color, like smashed fruit. But over there, in a shell hole, he spotted the caribou on a collar. There were maybe four of them, all curled up like kittens, dead.

"Yeah. I see them. They're all alive."

"Good." Murphy took a deep breath. Even from a distance Charlie could hear a gurgle in his throat. "Didn't I tell ya, Charlie? Didn't I tell ya I was done for? Remember your promise to me, Charlie. Remember, you're not to say a word to Emma about how you found me. Not a word." He was gasping now.

Charlie could see the top of Murphy's head clear enough and bits of his legs and feet. They were angled out. It looked as though both feet were tangled in the barbed wire. One hand was hung up on the wire, poised in the air as if he were waving hello. But where was he hit?

"No worry, Charlie-boy." Murphy's voice was just above a raspy whisper. You could only hear it if you were meant to. "No worry."

Thing was, Murphy didn't look too bad. If he could reach him, if only . . .

Ping, ping, ping.

Charlie slithered down the trench wall. There was nothing to do but wait for dark and hope Murphy lasted.

THERE WAS NO TELLING what the time was. Dust and ash choked out the sun's rays.

"Tom, lend me your watch."

Tom, with both eyes shut, passed Charlie a pocket watch. It was near five. His mother would be starting the dinner right about now.

"You there, Murphy?" Charlie fumbled with the periscope.

"I'm not going any place special at the moment."

"Not long now. Hang on."

"Charlie-boy, do you mind the sun coming up and the nets lying out in the water? Was there ever a prettier sight, do you think?"

"No, Murphy. But don't talk so loud."

"And do you mind the smile on my Emma's face? Was there ever such beauty born?"

"She's a grand girl, Murphy."

Flies, there were always flies in the afternoon.

IT WAS COMING ON to six o'clock when Charlie next called out.

"Murphy, you still there?" No answer. "Murphy!"

Ping. Ping.

Murphy responded with a cough.

"It won't be long now, Murphy. Hang on."

"I was thinking about being a donkey, Charlie-boy. Donkeys don't think of their own deaths. Best to be a donkey."

HE CHECKED TOM'S WATCH. Seven o'clock. Time couldn't have gone any slower if it had been going backwards.

"Murphy?" Charlie hissed. No response. "Murphy?"

Charlie raised the periscope to his eye. There were two shots. The first one made Murphy cry out. The second one took off the top of the periscope.

"Gawd damn." Tom jolted forward. The periscope, now in two parts, lay in the mud at his feet. "You know how hard it is to get one of those things?"

Charlie's whole self vibrated. Anger, as sharp and hot as lightning, set fire to him. Bloody Huns. Why? Why were they doing this? What did they want? He lunged toward a lone Lee Enfield propped up against the trench wall. Rifles always went with their owners. If a rifle was hanging about, more then likely its owner had gone west, meaning he be dead.

"Don't be daft. Put that down." Tom leapt up and stood in front of Charlie. "You're not a soldier. You'll get yourself killed."

"Get out of my way."

"Why? You want to join in the killing? As if there's not enough going on?"

"Leave off." Charlie ducked around him, grabbed the gun, hoisted the rifle up to his shoulder, and pressed his eye to the sight. He could see him right enough. Murphy was lying dead still.

Sweat streamed down Charlie's face, near blinding him. Something moved in the corner of his eye. A wounded German was wiggling toward his own front line. He was dragging his leg like it was a dead weight. Kill the wounded so that they won't get patched up to fight another day. Kill him. Charlie breathed heavy. Ya know you're alive when you can take a life—wasn't that what war was about? He focused. He squeezed the trigger. The gun went off. The shot went wild.

Tom grabbed the rifle. "Feel better now?" He stopped himself short and looked at Charlie real close. "You're off your head. You're sick, boy. Oh, Jeeze, what's that!"

Something under Tom's foot cracked. He reached down and pulled up a bag of sorts. It was filthy, soaked through.

"That's mine." Charlie reached for the haversack. He could feel the spy glass inside. Great tears rolled, like melted candle wax, down the sides of Charlie's face as he held the filthy haversack to him. "Close your eyes, Murphy," whispered Charlie. "Close your eyes and float home."

"HE LOOKS LIKE HE'S IN A COMA. He's burning up, that's sure. The influenza most like." Was that Tom's voice? It sounded like Tom.

"He keeps muttering something. A name maybe, Daniels."

"Robert Daniels runs the FDS. Charlie knows him. We'll take him there."

"You're on duty."

"Come on. We'll just drop him off. Wait a minute, he's got me watch. Now, give me a bit of paper, will you? And a pencil. I want to write the boy a note."

Charlie could feel something being slipped inside his tunic. Dead people couldn't feel, could they? "Charlie, can you hear me?" Tom was yelling at him. Why couldn't he answer? "Listen to me, I'm taking you to the FDS. Got it? You're sick, boy."

"He can't hear you," said the other voice.

"Give me more paper. I want to tag him, too."

"WHO IS THIS?" It was a booming voice, hurried and annoyed, the voice of someone in command.

"A boy, sir. French maybe. Look, there's a tag pinned on him. It says, 'Attention, Dr. Robert Daniels.'"

"Daniels, is it? He's busy with our own men. Where'd he get that uniform?"

"Don't know, sir."

"Bloody thieves these kids. This is no time for children playing dress-up. Get rid of that sign. He's a G.O.K."

G.O.K., God Only Knows.

CHAPTER 12

THE GROUND BENEATH HIM was wet. The damp invaded his dreams. The voices. The voices. They were calling. He was at the bottom of a well. The bricks were slimy. He couldn't get his footing. He crawled up a few feet, his fingers and toes searching for gaps in the bricks, then he slipped back down. Down and down into the black water.

"Boy, who are you with? What's your name?"

The voices rolled in like waves. The waves breaking on the shore, rolling in. There was Claire, dancing, light as a fairy. Her legs kicking up a foam, her laughter on the wind, her hair flying and whirling about her.

"Claire!" Charlie called to her. "Claire!"

She turned. She laughed. "Charlie, I can hear you. I'm here."

"Claire!" Charlie called out. Words felt like sandpaper coming up his throat.

"What's he saying?"

"*Air* or something. Is that his pack?"

"Yes, sir. Only a dented old telescope in it. Broken, I'd say. No use to anyone. Some clothes. Nothing else."

"Daniels," Charlie whispered.

"What'd he say?"

"I think he says that his name is Daniels, sir. Blair Daniels or something."

HE HEARD A VOICE, then felt a water flask being pressed to his lips. "You're burning up, boy. Rest easy. I'll have you moved closer to the hospital."

Later, Charlie felt himself being lifted. Later still, he opened his eyes and saw the sun set.

THE SUN WAS HALFWAY UP the sky when Charlie pulled himself into an upright position. He laid his hand out by his side and felt for his haversack. He couldn't think why it was important, just that it was.

He recognized the back of a farmhouse in the distance. It was a dim recollection, but the trapdoor to the cellar seemed very familiar. He had to get to that farmhouse. He didn't know why. Clutching the haversack, he stood, wobbled for a bit, then staggered forward, swaying and weaving, reaching out for invisible walls, as if on a ship during a mighty storm.

He felt the rough wooden exterior of the farmhouse with his hand. He moved his feet to the lip of the worn stone steps, then carefully, cautiously, he stumbled down the stairs and waited for his eyes to adjust to the dim light. The field hospital was in the cellar, two tiny connecting rooms, brick lined, with a rounded roof blackened by the smoke of torches and candles. A tall man could stand up straight only in the middle. The hay on the floor was sticky and clung to his boots. A bald light dangling over the operating table and stubby candles rammed in the cracks of the brick cast a murky, yellow glow. He rubbed the sweat off his forehead and again tried to focus. Acid burned the back of his throat. He'd have vomited if he could have, if there had been anything in him to get rid of.

The place reeked of blood, iodine, urine, and antiseptic. The walls had been washed with chlorine bleach, and lime disinfectant sweated a green bile. Charlie slumped against the wall and looked over at the man in the blood-smeared white coat.

Dr. Robert Daniels wasn't much older than the boy on the table, maybe twenty-four or twenty-five, but by the look of him, you'd have thought he was coming on to fifty. He stood, hollow-eyed and haggard, his feet rooted in bloodied straw, over a wide-eyed patient.

"That will do, soldier."

The young patient grimaced as he eased himself up and gingerly swung his legs over the side. A startling white gauze bandage covered most of his upper body.

"Thanks, Doc." With his filthy jacket in hand, the soldier brushed past Charlie. He picked up his rifle and staggered back up the same steps that Charlie had stumbled down. This soldier was one of the walking wounded. It was back to the trenches for him.

Dr. Daniels looked up. A wave of recognition registered, followed by shock.

"What the hell are you doing back here? I thought you were out of here long ago!" After seventeen hours bent over an operating table, Robert Daniels hadn't the strength to yell.

The most he could offer was a muffled roar. "Why, Charlie? Why on God's earth did you come back here? And where have you been?"

Charlie shrank back against the wall. "I had to . . ." he stumbled. He couldn't think, couldn't collect his thoughts. It was all he could do to reach into his haversack and hold the tarnished, dented spy glass out in front of him. "I thought I . . . lost. Had to . . . to find . . ." He felt the earth sway beneath him. "I promised my father . . . never to lose it."

After that, there was nothing.

CHAPTER 13

CHARLIE ROLLED HIS HEAD BACK and forth on the pillow and pushed his tongue up against the roof of his mouth. It stuck there. A bushel of hay must have been parked in it. There was a rock in his throat, too. And there was something sitting on his chest, an elephant maybe? Wait, was that a pillow under his head?

He stretched and wiggled his toes. The sheets felt clean and cool to the touch. Sheets? His hands drifted across the bedclothes. Sheets and blankets? Was he dead? His eyes, gummy with sick, pulled apart. He turned his head, half afraid of what he might see.

He was in a bedroom, a nice one too, top floor by the look of the sloped ceiling. A faint breeze billowed thin, white muslin curtains in and out. He could see a stand of poplar trees outside. Beside the window stood an enamel washbowl, with a wooden towel rack to one side and a spotty-looking glass above it. A rocking chair sat by the open window and a mug of something grew cold on a three-legged table beside the chair. There was a wardrobe against the far wall. But it was the water stain running the length of the wallpaper that tipped him off. He couldn't be dead. This place was too good for hell, and surely God would have had mucky old wallpaper replaced.

"Charlie, you are awake at last!"

He jumped. There, on the other side of the bed, stood a young woman with chocolate eyes and chocolate hair, rosy lips, and skin as pale as milk. She was a nurse by the look of the uniform, although she wasn't wearing a veil. Maybe he *was* dead, after all.

"Oh dear, I startled you. I'm sorry. Here, let's give your face a wash."

He smelled Pears Soap and felt a soft cloth on his face. "There now, I'll just fix your pillow. My name is Helena. Helena McFarland if ye must know all."

Charlie caught a whiff of the soap as she bent over him and rearranged his pillow and bedclothes. It was the smells that were calling him back to someplace far away, a place he couldn't name, a safe place. He closed his eyes.

"CHARLIE? CHARLIE, CAN YOU HEAR ME?" Helena's voice drifted toward him. He could hear her voice wafting over the waves. There he was, in the middle of an ocean, his feet extending down and down into the water until they were stuck, dead tight, in the sand beneath the sea.

"Charlie, wake up." There was that scent again. It was soapy, clean, fresh.

"Mother?"

"Charlie, darlin'."

Whose voice was that? It was Claire's! He tried to call back to her but his voice made no sound.

"Come on, darlin', you've been sleeping for a whole day."

The voice became the road back. All he had to do was follow it. He tried to regain control of his mouth. He knew he should say something but his brain was woolly. The sheets again. He moved his legs, slowly at first. He was so stiff. Every limb seemed to weigh a ton.

"Welcome back." Helena, that was her name. How did he know her name?

"Hello." The word came out in a whisper.

Helena all but cheered. "It's good to hear your voice! You gave us a scare!"

How did he get here? Where was he? France. Right, he was in France.

"Dr. Daniels brought you here weeks ago. We thought we'd lost you a few times. Do you remember anything at all? You were delirious most of the time."

"Why? How?" Words came out in squeaks.

"Here, drink this." In three short steps Helena was at his side and holding a cup of water to his chapped lips. Some liquid went down, the rest sputtered up and dribbled onto the blanket.

"Sorry," he croaked. Was there no end to this humiliation?

"No need for that. You've been ill." She mopped up his damp blanket. "Many would have given you up for dead. Robert nursed you himself for a great long time. He took your illness very hard. There now, sit up and let's get you into some nice, clean pajamas. I can't tell you how many pairs you went through. Let me help."

Helena put her hand on his back. Slowly, groaning, he sat up. The strain made him woozy.

"Where are you from?" Charlie sputtered between two coughs.

"Now, isn't that grand. You're talking. I'm from Scotland. My auntie owns a farm there. Cows mostly, but some pigs."

No, that's not what he'd meant. He'd meant, what *unit* was she from? Where had she come from just now? But Helena spoke like many nurses he had met, in a sort of rambling babble that was meant to take the patient's mind off what they were doing.

Gently, she slipped a blue-and-white-striped top on him, then buttoned it up. Then, a thought came to him. Not one of those sudden thoughts that arrive in a flash of understanding, but a slow, gradual realization that rises like a wave lapping onto a sandy beach. He could *feel* the sheets. He could feel them *all over*. Helena turned and flung back the window curtains. Charlie lifted the blankets a smidgen and peered down. He was bare-assed naked!

With his top half now clothed, Charlie fell back onto the pillow and clutched the blanket up to his chest. "I can do the rest," he said, motioning to the pajama bottoms in her hand.

"You are a funny one. But no different from our Rory, I expect. You just hang on while I ask our landlady for a bit of soup." Helena vanished from his line of vision.

Again, Charlie scanned the room and searched his mind at the same time. It was coming back to him, but in bits and snaps. Tom. What happened to Tom? And Murphy? He drifted again. It was so hard to think straight.

"Back again." Helena floated into the room. "This landlady is none too pleased about having her house invaded by foreigners. I don't think she sees a bit of difference between us and the Germans." She giggled and placed the tray beside his bed.

"Where am I?" Words were coming a little more easily now.

"Can't say I know the geography of the place, but I believe we're near the village of Elverdinghe." Helena arranged the tray. "You are sharing Dr. Daniels's billet. We're not far from Ypres. This must have been a lovely house once." She sighed as she lifted a spoonful of soup to his lips. Charlie tried to swallow. "That's it. You're doing fine." She dabbed his chin with a cloth and dipped the spoon back into the bowl. "We are well behind the lines. Nothing to worry about. I'm a VAD. That stands for Voluntary Aid Detachment. We are seldom allowed this close to the front. We're not real nurses, you know. We don't have the training that the sisters do. We're just given basic courses, one in first aid, another in home nursing, and here we are!" She seemed very jolly about finding herself in the thick of things.

"Why are you here?" Charlie whispered. "I mean, why are you taking care of me?"

"I had some leave coming to me. And, since Dr. Daniels and *Mrs.* Dr. Daniels are friends of mine . . ."

Charlie looked up, startled.

"Yes, I know that Lily and Robert are married. Dr. Daniels tells me that Lily is an old friend of yours, from Newfoundland. Mac, you call her. Is that right?"

Charlie nodded.

"And, I know that you gave Lily your ticket so that she could go home." Helena continued to spoon soup into his mouth. He felt like a baby bird. "Lily had to tell Matron-in-Chief about the wee one coming . . ."

"The what?"

"The wee one, the bairn, the baby! I'm afraid she left in disgrace, but I don't suppose it matters. She's home by now I expect. When Robert called and asked me to come up and tend to you, how could I not?" Helena smiled broadly. "All gone." She put the spoon down in the empty bowl.

Charlie swallowed the last spoonful and took a deep breath before settling comfortably into the bed. Lily was home, at least he'd got that right. Wait! Where was it?

"My spy glass. Have you seen it?" he asked in a great gasp.

"That poor old thing. It's badly damaged I'm afraid." She glided over to the wardrobe and flung open its doors. There it was. He'd found it.

CHAPTER 14

"HE'S AWAKE!" Dr. Daniels burst into the room and grinned. Black hair fell over his forehead and his face looked as tired and worn as the clothes he had on. "He is, and clear-headed, too," answered Helena, pleased as punch.

"Charlie-boy, do you know how sick you were?" Robert Daniels dropped some packages onto a table and, in doctorly fashion, felt Charlie's forehead.

"Nice and cool," he announced. "I found you some clothes. We had to burn everything you were wearing." Dr. Daniels motioned to the packages. "Your boots weren't too far gone, and these ought to fit you." Dr. Daniels held up a pair of home-knit Newfoundland socks. "Bit worn. Hole in a toe. Oh, and there was that bit of paper we pulled out of your tunic. Where is it, Helena?"

"Right here." Helena reached into a side table drawer and pulled out a bit of smudged paper. Charlie, his hands still trembling, held the note up and tried to focus. It said, *"My name is Tom Alcock."*

"Does that mean anything to you?" asked Dr. Daniels as he pulled the rocking chair up beside Charlie's bed.

"He was the stretcher-bearer I worked with. I didn't know his last name before this. I don't think he wanted anyone to know who he was or to get to know anyone else. He's lost a lot of friends, I guess."

Dr. Daniels nodded. He understood. "It means a lot, then?" he asked.

"Yeah, a lot." Charlie tried to smile but his chapped lips allowed only an odd-looking grimace. "I have something to say to you, Charlie-boy."

"I'll leave you to it then, shall I?" Helena took her long, blue cloak down from a hook behind the door, and, with a practiced swirl, threw it over her shoulders.

"Thank you, Helena. Oh, and Charlie's expecting a guest. Someone from Brigus." Dr. Daniels turned again to Charlie. "He says he's an old friend of yours. His name is Phil Jackson. Lanky fellow, in the Regiment, of course. He came by the FDS looking for you. I told him that you were bunking in with me. He's on rest, stationed over on the next farm I believe. Helena, keep an eye out for him, will you?"

Helena nodded. "Won't that be nice, Charlie? Seeing a mate from home?" She smiled as she sailed out the door.

Dr. Daniels sat down on the edge of the bed and spoke in a low voice. "I don't have much time. There's talk about the Regiment moving on. Charlie, Phil told me about you living in the trenches. I could hardly believe it. I thought that you were in England."

"I couldn't . . ." Charlie didn't know what to say.

"Let me talk. Had you not given your ticket to Lily, you'd be home now. What you did . . ." He ran his hands through his hair. "She's my life, Charlie. And now I'm to be a father. Lily would have lost the baby if she'd stayed in France, we both know that. What you did, you saved all our lives, but almost at the expense of your own. You nearly died, Charlie. You came as close as I've ever seen, and I've seen plenty." The strain on Dr. Daniels's face was so evident that Charlie had to look away.

"Until I can get you a safe passage home, you're to stay with me. You'll be my unofficial assistant. I want you where I can keep an eye on you. The work is hard, terrible, but you'll be out of direct fire. And you're not to go in the trenches, for any reason. Do you understand, Charlie? Do you?"

Sick though he was, Charlie's head snapped up. He had learned a lot about caring for himself these past few months and he was coming on to fifteen years of age. But it was the guilt on Dr. Daniels's face that made him come up short.

"It was my choice," whispered Charlie. "I am not your responsibility." He tried to prop himself up. Then he remembered. He was naked from the waist down.

"I disagree. As soon as it can be arranged, you'll go to England and then home. That's final, and there will be no discussion."

Charlie could hear voices outside the window. They were faint, but one of them definitely belonged to Phil Jackson.

"That would be your man." Dr. Daniels went to the window and peered out. "He's talking to Helena. I'll leave you to have a visit. Now, remember Charlie, just do what Helena says, and you'll be on your feet in a week."

Charlie felt his head nod but didn't take his eyes off the window. The very last thing he wanted was to see Phil. Maybe they had been pals of sorts in the trenches, but that didn't erase all the years of bullying.

"I said, I'll be back tonight." Dr. Daniels gave Charlie a quizzical look.

"Pardon? Oh, yes." What could Phil be saying to Helena?

"Stay in bed." With those words, Dr. Daniels left.

It would be just like Phil to say something embarrassing about him. Maybe, if he just got over to the window, he could hear what they were talking about. Charlie gingerly lowered his feet. It would have been a lot easier if the floor had agreed to stay on the ground. He put his weight on his feet. They turned into liquid. Both legs buckled. The floor come up and hit him in the head.

Phil opened the door and looked down at Charlie's bare butt, shining like a round, pearly moon.

"Hey, Charlie-boy, nice ta see you."

CHAPTER 15

"It was lucky that you were here. He's a growing lad. It would have been a struggle getting him back to bed on my own." Helena spoke to Phil over Charlie's corpse. At least Charlie *wished* it were his corpse. There he lay, like a fish on a plate, a dead fish on a plate, a dead, gutted, gummy-eyed fish on a plate, and said nothing.

"He's a good kid," said Phil to Helena.

Ha! Like he needed Phil's compliments.

Phil couldn't take his eyes off Helena. Charlie could see that right enough, even with his eyes mostly shut. He was going to be sick. Well, he was already sick, but watching Phil make eyes at Helena was enough to put him into a coma.

"Still, it's lovely having a man to help with the shifting," Helena added.

Shifting? What was he, cut timber? Did these two have to go on? He'd be dead in a minute, killed entirely. Death by embarrassment. The least they could do was wait.

"There now, Charlie." Helena spoke loudly and directly into his ear. "Don't you be trying to get up again, do you hear?"

Did she think he was deaf? The whole world would be a lot easier to manage if it would just stop spinning.

"Did you and Charlie know each other well?" Helena asked Phil.

"In a place the size of Brigus, it's hard not to know everyone. It's a grand place. Mind you, I didn't rightly know that until I left. It would suit you. I'm sure of that." Phil looked down at him. "Why don't we step outside and let the poor little fellow sleep."

Poor little fellow? Poor little fellow? If he could have raised his fist, he'd have done some damage. As it was, he couldn't even raise an eyebrow. Just wait, Charlie thought. Just wait. I'll whip your butt. No, he didn't want to think of butts. Especially bare butts.

"Sleep now, Charlie," whispered Helena. Which, despite his best efforts to stay awake, is exactly what he did.

CHARLIE AWOKE TO A CLEAR FALL DAY. The elephant had shifted off his chest, the rock had dislodged from his throat, and the bale of hay in his mouth was gone. He opened his eyes and looked directly into Phil's.

"Welcome back, Charlie-boy."

Oh, Jeeze.

"You're awake!" Helena declared triumphantly from the far corner of the room. "I'll just run down to the kitchen and get you some soup." She made for the door. "Give him time now, Philip. He's that groggy."

"I've been waiting on you," Phil said, tentatively. "Not since yesterday, mind. I've been away and back again. We're out on rest, they call it, billeted down the road. No rest that I can see, though, what with guard duty, marching, and cleaning everything. They have us building a road, for Pete's sake. Imagine, coming all this way to build a road!"

Phil droned on and Charlie, still caught between this world and the next, remembered.

He'd been six years old, or thereabouts. It had been a dirty day in Brigus, rain and fog enough to blind a fellow. You couldn't see a barge in front of your face. He went down to the wharf. What made him coppy down in the square end of a punt? Six-year-olds do things just because. He must have fallen asleep the way small children do, in odd places, trusting in the world. They launched it, Clint and Phil both. Picked up the punt and heaved it out into the bay in weather that could have drowned a fish. And they laughed. Menacing laughter all around, caught in the fog, coming from all directions.

Charlie awoke to their howls. The rain was blowing, and him in nothing but a sweater. There he was, in the fog, out on the water, just a child, not strong enough to work the oars or old enough to swim. He wanted to cry for his mother, for his father, but sounds seemed to echo back in the fog, like he was calling out to himself, like he was all alone in the world. The punt cut steadily out to sea. He was near frozen when they pulled him in. They say it was a miracle he was saved.

"Why? How did it happen?" His mother, shaken to the core, had looked at him with terror. He was a thoughtful child, not given to such foolishness. Why? How?

Charlie never told on Clint and Phil, never said a word, because even then he knew better than to tell. And so it went on.

Bullies feed off good kids, nice kids, kids who don't tell. Maybe Phil hadn't been guilty of the worst of it, but he'd been Clint's pal, and that was enough. You never forget the shame of being bullied. Never.

"I met the landlady on the landing." Helena burst into the room holding a tray.

Phil stopped talking mid-sentence, bounced up, and dragged the three-legged table close to the bed.

"Thank you, Phil," Helena said sweetly.

"Well, I'll be off then." Phil made for the door.

"So soon?" Helena looked genuinely shocked.

"Got to get back to my unit. My mother would have something to say about me going AWOL."

"Maybe you can visit tomorrow." Helena spoke to Phil but looked at Charlie. "What do you say, Charlie?" She had one of those girl-longing looks on her face.

"Sure." What else could he say?

"Grand. Tomorrow then."

"Wait!" It hurt to talk but he had to know. "Any word on Murphy?"

"I hear tell he never made it back." Phil shrugged and sauntered off.

"He seems like a nice sort," said Helena. "Murphy—was he a friend?"

"Just someone from home."

Charlie turned his head toward the peeling wallpaper. He knew better than to cry.

HE LAY IN THE DARK, listening to the night. Thoughts come slowly, but decisions often arrive with a fierce suddenness. Murphy had never harmed a soul in his life. The world had lost a good man, but what use is a good man in a war?

"I'm staying," Charlie whispered into the dark. "Ya hear that, Murphy? I'm staying." And then he made a promise—to Murphy, to God, to anyone who cared to listen. "Long as there is a Newfoundlander fighting, I'll stay."

No matter what the cost, Charlie would see this war to the end. These were his people dying—proud Newfoundland boys, every one. You could hardly credit it, that such a small country in a tucked-up corner of the world could produce so many brave men. Maybe he wasn't old enough yet to join the Regiment, but he could help, and no one was going to tell him otherwise.

CHAPTER 16

CHARLIE SHUFFLED THROUGH THE FARMHOUSE KITCHEN. He still wasn't too steady on his feet, but he'd managed to walk across the bedroom just the day before and now he wanted to poke his nose out of doors.

"Bonjour." He spoke to the landlady, who was hunched over a length of heavy, dark material. Two kitchen windows were already covered in their new black curtains. The stout older woman, dressed in black to mourn any number of people and things, fretted, mumbled, moaned, and seemed to carry on a secret conversation with no one in particular.

"Bonjour," Charlie tried again.

"Boom! Boom!" She waved her hands and pointed to the ceiling. Charlie looked up.

"Boom! Boom!" She made a fist, held it in the air, and dropped it with a thud on the table.

"Ah, zeppelins, yes. *Oui.*" Giant, cucumber-shaped zeppelins often cruised silently across the night sky, dropping little bomb bundles at anything that twinkled. They seldom hit much, but they were a nuisance.

Charlie went out the back door and saw Helena knitting in

a canvas chair on the lawn. He picked his way across the stubby, sharp grass.

"You're up and about, then?" Helena looked up from her work, then patted another chair beside her. "Sit yourself down. You're not to do too much."

Charlie groaned as he lowered himself gingerly into the chair. The cold weather was coming, poplar branches clattered in a soft breeze, leafy trees lined the roadside, and blackbirds bickered from a tumbledown garden fence. In the beyond, farmhouses peeked out of crannies in the surrounding hills. A thumb-sized farmer, strapped behind a plow, worked his land. And yet only a few miles away, strangers were killing each other.

Charlie pulled a needle, a bit of yarn, and the Newfoundland socks out of his pocket. They were grand things. The Brits would trade a pack of cigarettes for home-knit Newfoundland socks, even one with a hole in the toe. He took hold of the holy sock, a long length of yarn, ran it through the eye of the needle, and jabbed himself in the hand. Jeeze!

"Oh, give it over." Helena laughed as she put down her knitting and reached for Charlie's sad sock and needle. "You're no better than our Rory. The closest he would ever come to a needle was if he found it in a haystack."

"Who is Rory?" Charlie had heard Helena mention that name before.

"My brother. He's the reason I came here, to France I mean." Helena jabbed at the sock.

"Where is he now?"

"Gone. Dead six days after he arrived." Helena spoke in a flat, expressionless voice.

"I'm sorry," Charlie whispered. "Where did he die?"

"Ypres, November 5th, 1914. Died instantly they say, but they always say that. Still, dead is dead. And dead in France is even more dead." Helena's needle stabbed the sock over and over.

"What do you mean?"

"No body. No funeral. Just gone! Like smoke. He was all I had, you see. Our mother died just after Rory was born, and our father worked the collieries, the mines. It was the lungs that did him in. Coal dust. There!" Helena bit off the end of the yarn with her teeth and passed him back a perfectly mended sock.

"What did you do? I mean, after your parents died." Charlie rolled the sock over his foot.

"Our auntie took us in, she being our father's sister, a spinster. We were born by the sea, Liverpool."

"That's where Phil was born." Charlie could have clapped his hand over his mouth. What a boneheaded thing to say. The last person he wanted to talk about was Phil Jackson.

"We were talking about just that, he and I. Could you mind the two of us meeting as wee ones? His father was a sailor, he tells me, and met his mother in Newfoundland."

"They didn't live in Liverpool long. But you were telling me about your aunt . . . ?"

"Auntie lived up in Scotland, a wee village. Landlocked place, lovely in its own way. Still, I missed the sea. I was about four and Rory would have been near two years old.

We were never apart." Helena paused. "Auntie was kind, in her own way."

Something in the way she spoke suggested that Auntie was anything but kind.

"It was understood, we was to be a credit to Auntie, who had brought us up by hand. Rory did his best taking care of the farm, not at first, mind, but as he grew. He would have made a good farmer, our Rory. But he and Auntie never did see eye to eye. Oh, he was a bonny wee lad, but you know how boys are. Always up to something. He dressed flash I suppose, and that was not to Auntie's liking! She was set in her ways, still is. Along comes this war and our Rory joins up the first day!"

Helena grew silent and looked out into the distance to see the life she'd left behind. She saw Auntie, her face hard, hooking a rug by a mean fire, the place smelling of boiled beef. Her life had been made stony with the burden of two orphans she neither wanted nor loved. And when the war came along, Auntie welcomed it for the peace it would bring her.

And then there was Rory. Handsome, brave, dressed-to-the-nines Rory. Dear God in heaven, how she loved him. To think of him made her want to double over with pain.

"Hello, there!"

Helena and Charlie looked up as Phil, shiny buttons and boots and all, made great strides across the grass. He swung his rifle casually over one shoulder and presented himself in front of the two like a cocky beagle. Charlie scowled. What did he want, a blue ribbon?

"Ya caught us off in fairyland. You're looking fit." Helena smiled, and Charlie tried to make his face pleasant. Did this guy ever have to fight a war?

"Fit as a fiddle. You're looking fine there too, Charlie-boy." Phil turned his high beams on Charlie.

"Let me make some lemonade." Helena bounced out of her chair and made for the house.

"That would be grand," he hollered after her. "She's a terrific one, eh Charlie?" Phil plunked himself down in Helena's vacant chair. His long legs sprawled out in front of him; his red hair, once shorn to the quick, had filled back in a little.

Charlie eyed Phil suspiciously. He searched around for something to say.

"Why'd ya sign up, Phil?"

"God and King, Charlie-boy. You know that! That's why we all signed up. 'Come forth young man and defend your country.'" Phil beckoned the birds with his arms. "Do you suppose anyone would have signed up if they had said, 'Come second or third young man and defend your country'?" Phil threw his head back and laughed. "Shame you can't sign up. You're doing the work of a soldier, pity you can't get the pay! But there's time enough, don't see an end to this war anytime soon."

Phil seemed pleased at the prospect of a never-ending war. Charlie looked up at the birds chattering away. Maybe the war *would* last forever.

"I was wondering, about Helena, like." Phil leaned in close to Charlie. "She seems right fond of you. Maybe you could put in a good word about me. What do you say?" Phil cast hopeful eyes over Charlie's way.

Charlie shrugged. So, Phil was smitten with Helena. It wasn't that he had any, well, hopes for Helena, not in that way. After all, he was still barely fifteen and Helena, she had to be more like Phil's age, nineteen or handy to it. But now, Phil wanted a favor. Ha! After all those years of being kicked around by Clint and Phil, Charlie finally had the upper hand.

"Has she asked about me?"

"No." Charlie looked thoughtful. "She's never said a word about you." He paused a good long while and then said, "I think she's got a boyfriend somewhere."

Phil's face fell to his knees. Got him!

CHAPTER 17

"Be careful? Take care?" Helena hugged Charlie for the third time. "You have my address in Scotland, and the VAD headquarters in London?"

Charlie nodded.

"What about your traveling papers?"

Charlie tapped his chest pocket. It was the first time he'd had any of these and he wasn't about to lose them between the parlor and the front door.

"Right then." Helena paused and then, throwing her hands in the air, hugged him again.

"I just want to say thank you for—"

"None of that, Charlie."

"But you gave up your leave. You might have gone home to Scotland."

"Truth be told, I don't have much to go home to. Auntie, I expect, is just as glad to see the back of me. And you know what they say, a change is as good as a rest. You're a fine boy, Charlie." Helena's voice drifted a bit as she looked out across the battered yard of the billet. "I guess Philip was sent back earlier than expected. I had hoped that he might stop by. He does put me in mind of our Rory. And to think when he was a wee one, just a baby, he might have lived nearby. Funny, the ways of the world." Helena spoke sadly and looked wistful again. Charlie turned away.

A battered ambulance pulled up. The driver stuck her head out the window and waved to Helena.

"That's my lift. See here, Charlie, I wrote a wee note to Phil. If you see him, pass it on, will you?"

Helena handed Charlie an envelope. She was embarrassed, that was plain to see. Charlie tucked it into his tunic. He had no plans to seek out Phil Jackson.

"Come say hello to Gracie." Helena grabbed Charlie by the elbow and maneuvered him toward the ambulance with the giant Red Cross flag tied to its sides.

"Hello there!" Gracie called out.

"Grace, this is Charlie Wilcox from Newfoundland. Gracie is from Vancouver."

"Newfoundland, is it?" Gracie smiled. Her teeth were uneven and her nose was on the big side, but all together she was sort of pretty.

Charlie nodded. "Yes, Brigus."

"My roommate's from Newfoundland. Her name is Armine Gosling. Know her?"

Charlie shook his head.

"Never hurts to ask. Hop in, Helena. Can't keep the war waiting."

"Goodbye, Charlie," Helena shouted over the engine's complaints. "Dr. Daniels is expecting you. Don't dally. Looks like rain. Goodbye. Cheerio."

Gracie floored the engine. After a lurch and sputter, the ambulance chugged down the road. Charlie waved—waved until they were out of sight—then turned in the opposite direction and began the mile-long hike that would take him to the field hospital and his new job as Dr. Daniels's assistant.

A LORRY PICKED HIM UP not far down the road. Good thing too. Helena had been right, it was raining.

"Thanks," he hollered as he leapt out of the lorry. Cold drops dribbled down his neck as he looked about. The hospital in front of him was under canvas. Everything—wards, operating rooms, billets, and offices—was housed under different-sized tents. In the middle of the canvas compound stood a wooden hut, hammered together in haste. Two orderlies with clipboards stood in the pouring rain among five ambulances as the wounded were unloaded. Filthy, broken, wet soldiers were pulled out of the ambulances like loaves of sodden bread from ovens. It was the orderlies' job to sort them.

Most of the wounded would be patched up and tossed back like puny fish into the stream. The next biggest group was made up of "Blighty wounds" bound for England. Lucky was the soldier with a Blighty wound. Then there was the third group, the ones too far gone. They received shelter from the rain, were covered in brown blankets, often given a shot of morphine and left in peace to die.

Charlie walked into the largest tent. A battered, wooden schoolroom desk and chair were posted at the entrance. Two rows of cots were lined up at the sides. Despite the place being full, it was oddly quiet.

"Is your name Wilcox?" A corporal, barely looking up, knelt beside a squat stove in the middle of the tent and bellowed at him. He shoveled in a load of coal and slammed the iron door shut.

Charlie nodded.

"You're late. Daniels says that you've worked in a hospital before this," he hollered.

"Yes, sir." Charlie stood straight and tall.

"What's that?" Corporal Philpot cupped his hand over his ear and rammed it forward. "Speak up."

"I said, YES, SIR."

"Don't call me SIR! Call me CORPORAL!" He stood and brushed his hands up and down his white coat, leaving a trail of black smudges. "Look here, I don't know what's what with you and I don't want to know. Just keep out of the way when the brass visits. It's not often."

Charlie nodded.

Corporal Philpot was small, dark, and blurry-eyed, like a fish left too long on the dock. And he was deaf as a post, thanks to a shell that had gone off next to him as he slept. "The brass only pop by to dole out the occasional medal. Seeing the results of their handiwork seems to depress them. No sisters here. No old battleaxes about the place telling us what to do. You'll find mops and pails in every tent. Keep the stoves going and the kettles on the boil. Unload the supply trucks as they come in. Empty the bedpans and help with the lifting. And remember, Wilcox," Philpot stepped in close, "you're here because Daniels wants you here."

"Yes, sir. Sir, about the mail."

"What?"

"THE MAIL."

"What about it?"

"I can do the sorting and the delivery too, if you'd like."

Corporal Philpot's fishy eyes narrowed. "What for? You thinking of pilfering packages from home?"

Charlie's own mouth gaped open. The idea had never occurred to him.

"Yes, sir. I mean, NO, SIR."

"Private Hank Boil is in charge of the mail. He's a lazy bugger. You're bunking in with him. Decide between yourselves. Remember, Wilcox, step out of line and I'll turn you in myself, by God I will." Corporal Philpot turned to leave, then hollered over his shoulder, "Swab the operating floor this afternoon. It's the last tent before the arms and legs graveyard."

Charlie made his way to the operating tent, opened the flap, and slipped inside.

"Dr. Daniels?"

Robert Daniels didn't look up from the patient on the operating table. No matter. Charlie wrapped a towel around his waist, rolled up his shirt sleeves past his elbows, and picked up a pail of bloody water.

CHAPTER 18

CHARLIE AND DR. ROBERT DANIELS were posted to several locations over the next few months, Corporal Philpot and a small crew along with them. Philpot was in charge of the medics. It didn't take long for them to become a team.

At every posting Dr. Daniels fired off letters to Headquarters asking for help. All he wanted was some assurance that if Charlie Wilcox, a boy who had more than proven himself as an able assistant, arrived in England he would be assured of a berth back to Newfoundland. Money was no object. But he hadn't heard a word or received a single response from anyone. Again and again Dr. Daniels asked about the mail. "Sorted it myself," said Charlie. "Nothing but letters from home."

Liar. Liar. Liar.

They were usually posted to Field Dressing Stations, but come October 1916 they were assigned to a hospital in Bandighem, Belgium. The good doctor arrived a day ahead of Charlie and the medic team. And, as usual, Charlie stayed behind to see that the surgical equipment was packed properly.

By the time Charlie arrived the weather had turned terrible—cold, rainy, a breeding ground for influenza. A pale moon hung over the lot of them as Charlie entered the surgical tent around midnight. He stoked the stove and filled up the kettle. There was the usual stink about the place—blood, antiseptic, and piss. But this was the best shift. There was no chance of a surprise visit from the brass, and occasionally there was time to sit and jar with a patient or take down a letter or two.

"Dear Mother, I am doing fine," says the soldier with tears streaming down his face.

"Might you not want to tell her . . . ?" Charlie would always ask, but it was a hard thing to tell your mother that you were blind or crippled, legless or armless, or had a fragment in your head that robbed you of all reason.

"Wouldn't want to worry my mother," one would say, and the rest would chime in. Night after night, day after day, month after month, it was the same.

"CHARLIE-BOY, THAT YOU?"

Charlie pushed a cart of bed linen down the ward and passed a sorry excuse for a Christmas tree before he stopped short. The voice was low and raspy but there was no mistaking it. Charlie spun around. Where was he? Which one? The wounded all looked alike—gray, bloodied, bandaged.

"Charlie-boy, over here."

"Jeeze boy, is that you?" Charlie stood at the foot of Phil's cot and looked him up and down. Phil's leg was strung up and his left arm was in a cast. It wasn't a life-threatening injury, you could tell that right off.

"I broke my arm and my leg." Phil was triumphant. "Hurts like the dickens, but it's Blighty for me! Take a load off."

Sharon E. McKay

Thing was, he was actually happy to see Phil. Maybe not happy, maybe more like relieved. Helena's letter was tucked in his haversack along with his spy glass. Many's a time he'd thought about pitching the letter.

"How'd it happen?" Charlie held a cup of water up to Phil's cracked lips.

"Fell into one of those big craters. Just fell in!" He was positively jolly. Charlie mopped up a trickle of water that dribbled down Phil's chin.

"You in pain?"

"Comes and goes. I was laid out flat, I tell you, out there in no-man's-land. I was thinking, if I could just roll over like, and see the sky. Sweet Lord, didn't I just, and then, didn't I see a bird fly by! A nightingale on a battlefield." Phil laughed, but not long and not heartily. "Then I heard it. *Whoosh.* Just that sound. *Whoosh.* A bullet clipped me helmet. Twice now that happened. Twice! You was there for the first time. Remember? Mind that sniper way back? Do ya know what this means, Charlie? Do ya?" Phil reached up with his good hand and grabbed hold of Charlie's arm. "Those bullets were meant for me. Don't ya see?" Phil's eyes were wild. He threw his head back and laughed again. "The Huns can't kill me now. They had their chance. They've had *two* chances!"

"Wilcox." Philpot stood at the end of the cot and bellowed, "Shift that cart, then get this man ready, he's moving out."

"What? At this time of night?"

"Wounded are coming in anytime." Philpot, who didn't like explaining himself at the best of times, carried on down the line barking out commands in every direction.

Electric lights snapped on and the tent was filled with a luminous glare that stung. The wounded moaned, coughed, and shaded their eyes. "What the hell is this?" yelled a few. "Turn those damned things off."

"It's Blighty for the lot of you," hollered Philpot. The announcement was greeted with cheers and more coughs.

Private Hank Boil, Charlie's roommate, appeared at the foot of Phil's cot. "Let's go."

"Hear that, Phil? England for Christmas!"

Charlie, with expertise, lowered Phil's leg and propped it up for travel.

"Didn't I tell ya, boy? Didn't I just! Wait, Charlie." Phil turned his head as best he could. "I've been meaning to say something to you, right from the start. Remember that day when you were sick and Helena was taking care of you?"

Charlie nodded.

"Come on now, we've got a schedule to keep," grumbled Hank. "Pisspot's got his watch out."

Hank stood on one side of the bed, Charlie on the other, and together they shifted Phil onto a gurney.

"Give us a minute," said Phil.

"One minute!" Hank grumbled.

"I came that day to tell you that I was sorry," said Phil softly. "Sorry about all them things Clint did to you and me not lifting a hand to stop him. You remember you asked me why I joined up? I said it was because I wanted to do my bit for God and King and all. Thing is, I don't give a fart about the King. I joined up to get away from Clint. I was afraid of him, afraid of standing up to him. I thought maybe I was a coward. I've learned a thing or two, Charlie, and I'm sorry for it all. I truly am."

"Last bus is loading, mate. You're on it or you can stay and fight another day." Hank took hold of the gurney and began wheeling him out toward the ambulance. There was a great traffic jam at the door. Dozens of wounded were being slid onto trucks, laid on racks. Everyone seemed to be yelling. Doors slammed.

Charlie stopped and stood in the middle of the chaos. He wasn't that boy who was bullied any longer. And if he wasn't that boy, then maybe Phil wasn't that bully, either.

"Don't just stand there, Wilcox, hurry up," Philpot roared.

Charlie walked smartly to the back of the ward, swept back a curtain, reached below a cot, and pulled out his old haversack. Moments later he darted back down the ward and out into the night. One truck, then another, faded away down the dark road. Their headlamps were hooded and cast no real light ahead, just down to the ruts in the road. Hank was sliding the last stretcher onto the back of last truck.

"Wait!" Charlie leapt on the truck. "Phil, where are you?"

"Here. I'm here."

Charlie reached in through the wooden slats that hemmed in the wounded and tossed Phil the letter.

"It's from Helena. She's in London."

Phil's face lit up. "What about this fella of hers?"

"He's dead. Merry Christmas, Phil."

Charlie jumped off the truck. The fact that Helena's fellow had never been alive seemed to be a trivial point at that moment.

CHAPTER 19

FEBRUARY 1917

Dr. DANIELS ARRIVED AT A HOSPITAL near Sailly-Sailsel (dubbed *Silly-Sally*) in France. It was another compound, this one with several hastily built wooden structures. As usual, Dr. Daniels had gone on ahead of the medical unit while Charlie and Hank, along with the drivers and medics, followed with the supplies.

Charlie jumped out of the front of the lorry. Jeeze it was cold. His feet were numb. He blew puffs of frosty smoke into the air.

"Hank!" Charlie pounded the back of the lorry with his fist. "Wake up." He flipped back the canvas tarp that hung across the back of the lorry and peered into the gloom. Hank's great hulk was wedged between boxes of supplies. He had wrapped himself in a sheepskin. His head bobbed but he showed no sign of waking. The truth of it was, Corporal Philpot was right, Hank was lazy. But as long as Philpot wasn't around making trouble for the lot of them, Hank could sleep the war away for all Charlie cared.

Charlie tucked his chin deeper into his coat. Over the past few months he had managed to hoard 10 plugs of Mayo-Lind tobacco, 125 Gem cigarettes, and 2 bottles of whisky. There'd been chocolate, too, but he'd eaten that. He'd then traded his entire booty for this winter coat, and what a grand coat it was! Then, wouldn't ya know, home-knit mitts and socks had arrived from home. There'd been a note pinned on the socks: "From Claire." They were the warmest socks he'd ever had on, but he hadn't needed to be told that Claire had made them. The tops were knitted all wrong.

If memory served, the only thing worse than Claire's knitting was her cooking. Jeeze, he'd like some of her cooking now, anything would do.

He stamped his feet. His boots were holding up, as long as he lined them with newspaper each morning. What he wouldn't give for them old pair of his father's Parker & Monroe sealer's boots.

Charlie grabbed the mailbag and headed for the building with a sign nailed over the door saying "Headquarters." He dumped the bag on a counter and danced about in a futile attempt to thaw his feet. It wasn't a whole lot warmer in there than it was outside. He found what he was looking for. Three letters were addressed to Dr. Robert Daniels, and one was from the War Office in Newfoundland. Charlie slipped it into his own pocket. The mail sorted, Charlie made for the door.

"Wilcox, where's that lump of lard Boil?" Philpot hollered.

"Unloading equipment, sir."

Charlie headed out toward the lorry. Again he flung back the tarp and peered into the back.

"Wake up, Hank. Philpot's looking for you."

"Ol' Pisspot? Such a sweetheart. He does worry about me." Hank pulled himself up and wiped the sleep out of his eyes. He was twenty-three and married, with three little ones at home. If he got out of this alive, he thought, he would never again complain about bawling babies and soiled nappies. Funny thing, to run away to war to get away from the noise at home. The only thing that made Hank's life worth living was making Pisspot's life a misery. Of course, he'd have some reckoning to do if Pisspot could prove that it was him who nailed his locker shut.

"Find us some sleeping quarters, will you?" said Charlie as he tied up the lorry's tarp. Finding a place to bed down was one job Charlie knew Hank would finish.

Charlie was still laughing when he came up to the operating hut. The ice in the water barrel outside was frozen solid. Icicles, as fierce looking as knives, hung from the eaves. He ducked around them, opened the door, and slid inside.

"Charlie, get scrubbed."

He could see the tips of Dr. Daniels's smile at the top of his mask. Charlie nodded and exchanged his greatcoat for a white smock. When time allowed, Dr. Daniels guided Charlie through different medical procedures.

Charlie poured near-boiling water from the kettle into a bowl, plunged his hands in, and scrubbed them until they were pink. The brazier had been stoked and it was surprisingly warm in the operating room. The smell of antiseptic, chloroform, and blood was now as familiar to Charlie as salt air.

There were three operating tables in the room, but only one was occupied. On the other side of a partition was the X-ray room, and opposite it, also sectioned off, was the sterilization area, with a boiler that gurgled and bubbled like a witch's brew.

A new medic, young and goofy looking, stood at the top of the operating table holding a webbed, gold-colored metal disk over the patient's mouth. In his other hand he held a bottle of chloroform.

"Take over, Charlie." Dr. Daniels motioned toward the medic.

"Thanks, sir," said the medic, stepping back from the table. Charlie caught the look of the patient. His lips were blue, his skin chalky, and his head lolled almost unnaturally to one side. His clothes had been cut off and the thin sheet covering him revealed a fit body. He was maybe twenty. The wound was in his hip. Black, crusty blood had been cut away to reveal gleaming white bone. Charlie sniffed. No smell of gangrene. He put the disk and chloroform bottle on the tray and inspected the instruments. They had all been properly sterilized and set out. He had spent weeks training the last lot how to do things as simple as sterilize. The concept of cleanliness was beyond most of them. Hank seldom got the point either.

The operation was routine and it was a quiet day. The last attack a few days ago had fizzled out. Maybe both sides were just too cold to fire a gun.

"Check his breathing, Charlie."

Again, Charlie eyed the pallor of the patient. His breaths were shallow and over forty a minute. Not good, but acceptable.

"Now, look here." Dr. Daniels held back the flesh to reveal a slug buried deep in the tissue. Charlie peered down into the wound. Extracting a bullet from a hip was a simple enough procedure. Dr. Daniels carefully plucked out the shell and tossed it into a ceramic bowl. "Souvenir," he grinned.

"Shell landed on an ambulance," Hank shouted as he flung open the operating room door. A blast of wind set the sheets fluttering in protest. Instantly the place was flooded with flakes of snow, biting cold air, and men frothing at the mouth.

Dr. Daniels turned away from the table. "Close him up, Charlie."

Soldiers who could hobble crumpled into corners. The unconscious ones were tossed right onto the operating tables. Within moments the room was filled with moaning, writhing men. Dr. Daniels moved from table to table giving orders.

Charlie checked his patient. His blood pressure was failing. A soldier underfoot called out to him.

"Water," he whimpered. "Please, water?"

Focus on the patient, that's what Dr. Daniels had taught him. Charlie opened his patient's eyes. They were dilated and his nostrils were pinched. The faster he was stitched up, the better. Beads of sweat formed on Charlie's forehead. His own breathing was short and labored, but his patient's breathing seemed to stop altogether.

"I'm losing him," Charlie yelled. The soldier trembled. His head rolled back and forth. The anesthetic was wearing off.

"Mein Schatz, bitte komm zurück. Komm zurück," the patient cried.

Charlie gripped the edge of the table. He was German!

"Give him more chloroform. Stay with him." Dr. Daniels bent over yet another wounded soldier.

A German? Charlie looked at the wounded around him and then back at the German soldier on the table. Why save his life? It didn't make sense! The soldier who had asked him for water lay at his feet, unconscious.

"Charlie, see to your patient." Dr. Daniels's orders were clear and direct. "Charlie!"

Charlie nodded.

"CHARLIE." Dr. Daniels sat at a desk at the back of the surgical ward. A letter from home was propped up beside a lamp, and his hand was poised over a sheet of paper. His hair, once as black as coal, was now more white than black. It was hard to think of him as a man who had yet to turn thirty. "How is your patient?"

"He'll live." The German would live while three of their own had died, one right under the gurney that the German had been laid out on.

"Sit, Charlie."

Charlie just wanted to go to bed, to sleep. He slumped down on a shaky chair beside the desk.

"If your treatment of a person depends on which side he's on, then you have no business here."

Startled, Charlie looked at Dr. Daniels. He meant what he'd said, that was plain.

"But it's all so pointless. Why save a man who hates us?"

"Does he? Do you know that? Was he born hating us or was he taught to? You hate him, I could see that. Why?"

"He is the enemy."

"Ah, Charlie." Robert Daniels ran his hands through his hair. "Thing is, we have been told that Germans are evil so that it will be easier for us to kill them."

Charlie slumped back down in the chair. "My Aunt Maude once said that."

"What did she say?"

"That in time we'll come to believe that all Germans are monsters. If we knew that they were loved by their parents, and loved their children and wives, then it would be harder to shoot them."

"Your aunt is a wise woman. Wars can't be won, Charlie. They can be fought, but the day the first soldier dies, the war is lost."

"Excuse me, sir." Hank thumped on the doorframe. "The medic told me to come and get you." As usual, the buttons of his tunic were done up wrong. Hank Boil always looked like an unmade bed.

"I'm coming." As quickly as that, Robert Daniels was gone.

"Hey, I glued Pisspot's shoes to the floor. He's asleep now but he's on duty soon. Want to come and watch?" It didn't take much to amuse Hank.

Charlie shook his head. Hank shrugged and loped away.

March 1917

Dr. Daniels and his ragtag crew were posted at a CCS, a Casualty Clearing Station. The work was less frantic. Operations were performed, bones set, amputations done, casts put on, burns treated.

Rules were the order of the day, and, as a rule, Charlie kept out of the way. He was tolerated well enough, so long as he kept to his duties. He was still in charge of sorting the mail, but now he had a new specialty—washing patients who had fleas. Fleas were easier to get rid of than lice. Just scrub the skin with stout, hard nailbrushes, then wash with green liquid soap, then listen to the howls as patients complain of their skin burning.

No one bothered to question Charlie directly anymore. There were sisters at the CCS, but most of the staff took him for granted, and the rest didn't care.

August 1917

They moved to a hospital near Brandhoek, between Ypres and Elverdinghe. Three years had passed, millions had been killed, and here they were again, not far from where Helena's brother Frank had died back in 1914.

It was pouring rain. The mucky heat bent the air and made the stench of the hospital ward rise like a mist. Charlie soaked the sweat off his brow with his sleeve then changed a bandage. The soldier grimaced and mumbled a thank you.

"Nurse, morphine," Charlie called to the sister as she passed by. Then, "Sleep if you can," he told the soldier as he tossed the putrid bandages in the bin.

Corporal Philpot bustled into the tent and, not being one to give a damn about the next man, took off his coat and gave it a shake, sending raindrops off in every direction. Charlie scowled. He'd already mopped that patch of floor three times in the past hour. Nothing stayed dry, and mold seemed to grow at the speed of light.

"What a place! Mud everywhere. We're in hell now, boy. Just heard that a man disappeared in the mud. Sank like a stone." Philpot picked up a towel and rubbed it over his damp hair.

There was no news there. Charlie lifted the bin of soiled bandages. "Lots dying like that," he said wearily.

"He was sitting on his horse at the time," snarled Philpot. "Jeeze."

Philpot hustled down the line of beds. Muffled laughter rose up as he walked by. Charlie looked after him. Oh Jeeze. Philpot's arse was hanging out like the better part of a hot-cross bun. Someone had cut the seat out of his trousers. Hank was going too far!

CHAPTER 20

BRIGUS, 1919

"YOU'RE LAUGHING." Claire touched Charlie's arm.

Charlie looked around. All he could think of was war, and all he could see from this hill overlooking Brigus and Conception Bay was peace!

"Have you heard enough?" he asked, without looking at her.

"What do you mean, *enough? Enough* as in I can't take it? I'm a girl and war is not ladylike?"

Claire took a deep breath. She hadn't meant to sound so . . . so angry. She wasn't angry. Not at Charlie, anyway.

"No, I just mean it's late." For the life of him Charlie could not figure out what she was thinking.

Claire shaded her eyes with her hand and gazed down at the tide, then up at the sky. She'd been raised by the sea. To her eyes, and to Charlie's, the sit of the sun and the tilt of the moon could tell the time of day and night as accurately as any watch. "It's mid-afternoon. Coming up to three, I expect. That's not late." She sighed. The things he was saying, and the things she was feeling—it was a lot to take in, a lot to understand.

"What's wrong?" asked Charlie.

"I just don't understand why you stayed. You said it was because of Murphy, but . . ."

"I stayed because the war was in my way, because it was the right thing to do, because staying was easier than running, because it was easier to be brave than to be a coward."

"But Charlie—three years!"

"I didn't spend all of my time in the trenches." Charlie looked up at the sky. Great puffy clouds, the kind that might be drawn by a child, floated above them. "See those clouds? I hid in those clouds."

"What are you talking about?"

"I haven't told you about Weston—a British twit." Charlie's face brightened.

"A what?"

"Twit. A toffee-nose."

"What have the clouds got to do with a British twit?"

"One day a giant hand came down and scooped me up." Charlie couldn't take his eyes off the clouds. He could almost see himself up there, darting in and out of the wild blue yonder.

"What are you on about?" Claire almost laughed.

"It was in September 1917 that I learned that fliers, aeroplane pilots, had their own problems that were not a bit like ours. It seemed like those in the trenches and those in the sky were in different wars. Not that pilots didn't die, they did. A flier lasted three to eleven weeks if he was lucky. Many got killed the first time out. They didn't have much training and, of course, there were no parachutes."

"Tea is still hot. Want some?" Claire whispered.

The numbers bounced around in her head, *three to eleven weeks*. What must it have been like, to climb into an aeroplane knowing that you were likely to die?

Charlie held out his cup. "Where was I?"

"The fall of 1917 and somebody called Weston."

"Right. It was a horribly wet fall. The dikes had all been blown up and there was tremendous flooding. Dr. Daniels and I were lodged at the top of a chateau. It might have been quite grand once, but by the time we arrived it was a gigantic pile of gray rubble. I hadn't slept in three days. I remember putting my head down on some sorry excuse for a pillow and thinking that the place could be blown to bits for all I cared, I wasn't going to budge.

"It could have been minutes or hours later, I couldn't tell, Dr. Daniels comes bursting into my room hollering, 'Get up. You're leaving.'"

France, 1917

Charlie, more asleep than awake, rolled over in his tin bed. His back ached. The detestable horsehair mattress wasn't so much lumpy as wavy. Maybe the horse was still in it somewhere. He looked at the doctor through bleary eyes.

"It's my day off."

One day. One crummy day. Charlie closed his eyes, rolled over, and pulled the blanket over his head. With only the occasional nap, he had been on duty for three days and nights straight. Sleep, he wanted to sleep.

"Get up." Dr. Daniels pulled the blanket off him, leaving Charlie shivering in his nightshirt.

"What? Why?" He fished around for his blanket. He hadn't even finished unpacking. "Where are we going?" He pulled the skimpy blanket back over his head.

"Not *we*, you. There's a staff car waiting." Dr. Daniels tore Charlie's blanket off and flung it into the corner. Oh, that was really mean.

"Staff car?" Charlie opened his eyes.

"A friend in the Flying Corps turned up. Good man, patched him up a couple of times. Major Piggot-Smith. "Pug" they call him. Ah, here's your haversack. He's British, runs the aerodrome at Bertangles, about fifteen miles from Amiens. Aeroplanes go back and forth to England all the time. He says that his fliers make frequent supply stops in and out of England." Daniels was racing around the room opening wardrobe doors and banging drawers. "Most of the aeroplanes go empty and come back loaded. He'll get you to England. Move! I'll post Helena a letter. She'll set you straight." He stopped long enough to take a breath. "And I've sent a wire directly to the Harbormaster in London. Report to him as soon as you arrive." He turned to Charlie. "This is important. You must report as soon as you can. Understand? Your passage home is paid up. Lily has seen to it. Don't ask me how, I don't know myself."

Robert Daniels looked young, happy almost. He was think- ing that it was possible, just possible mind, that in a few weeks' time Charlie would be on a ship bound for Newfoundland.

Charlie, stunned, threw his legs over the edge of the bed and watched Dr. Daniels collect his bits and pieces. How had this all got by him? He'd intercepted all of the letters, hadn't he?

"Get dressed." Daniels tossed Charlie a pair of pants. "Where is that spy glass of yours?" He reached to the top of the wardrobe and retrieved the battered instrument. The insides slid around like frozen peas in a tin. "Can't leave this behind, now can we?"

"I'm not leaving." Charlie spoke firmly, in a low, even voice. He pulled on his pants, tucked in his nightshirt, and flipped his suspenders over his shoulders. He was sixteen years old now and as tall as Dr. Daniels himself.

"Yes, you are." The doctor was absolute. This was an opportunity that would not come around again, and by God, the boy was going to take it. "Here are your travel papers and a letter of introduction to Pug." Daniels held them out. "Take them." It was a command. Suddenly, all the humor and gaiety had gone out of his voice.

Dr. Daniels, trimmed to the bone, an old man before his time, looked at the young man in front of him. Charlie stood tall, rigid—defiant. There were no words between Newfoundland men that said what Daniels wanted to say, but had Charlie been his own son, he couldn't have been more proud of the boy. He loved him like a son, that he did. And at that moment there was nothing more important to him than to see the boy safe.

"Sir." A fresh recruit stood at the door. "You're needed in surgery."

Charlie scowled. If Dr. Daniels thought he could turn this kid into an able assistant, he had better think again. The kid wouldn't know his right foot from his left hand.

"Be right there." Daniels turned back to Charlie. "The Major has gone into Paris, but his driver is taking his staff car back to the aerodrome. The driver will take you back with him."

Charlie said nothing.

"Look here, Charlie, you're the best medical assistant I could ever hope to have. The lads trust you and you work hard. But it's time you went home." He stretched out his hand.

Charlie looked away. This was all too sudden. It couldn't end like this, not with a handshake.

"Charlie?" Daniels's hand was still extended. "Don't make this any harder than it has to be. You may not be in the army, but this is an order. You are leaving. Think of your parents. Think of what you being here must be doing to them, Charlie."

That was a low blow. Charlie's arm seemed to extend without his say-so. He took the doctor's hand and felt the warm grip of a man he had come to love like a father. How was he supposed to walk away? But what of his parents? Still, he had made a promise that he would stay to the end. What if there was no end?

"Charlie-boy, can we ever explain this war?" Daniels's voice was sad. "It's a nightmare, and when nightmares become real, things spin out of control and the unthinkable happens. Any good we can find, any at all, is a small victory. And seeing you out of this is *my* small victory. Go home, Charlie. Please."

"Sir!" The medic standing at the door grew more impatient.

"Lily has a letter." Daniels waved to the soldier but didn't take his eyes off Charlie. "I sent it weeks ago. It's a letter telling anyone who's interested just what you did here. Maybe you'll consider taking up medicine, maybe you won't, but I'll always be proud to say that I worked alongside Charlie Wilcox. Write me, when you get home. Kiss Lily for me, and baby Charlie too."

"Charlie . . . is that what they call Charlotte?" He couldn't help himself—Charlie grinned.

"I think any daughter of mine would be proud to be named after my friend Charlie Wilcox." Robert Daniels smiled back at him and in a swift moment his arms wrapped around Charlie. Then, just as swiftly, he turned and left.

"Must feel some good, going home." The new recruit stood grinning at the door.

"Just keep the water at a full boil, and lay out the instruments like I showed you. And Jeeze, wash your hands."

"Yes, sir." The smile vanished. The young recruit saluted, not knowing what else to do, and backed out of the room.

He was an idiot. Charlie fell back on the bed. What should he do? What could he do?

CHAPTER 21

The driver, a sergeant, was a miserable little man, small in body and spirit, a footman by trade, birth, and disposition. British, of course. He didn't introduce himself, which suited Charlie fine. Charlie sat beside him in the front seat of the General's Daimler for the better part of the day. Bloody hell, he could have walked faster, and he was hot.

They joined a stream of goods being dragged down the road by sloe-eyed donkeys, broken-down lorries, and limping horses. The beasts pulled guns and cannons, odd portable kitchens, and flatbed pallets. They strained at their harnesses and frothed at the mouth. Every type of lorry seemed to be on the move. There were timbered wagons, transport wagons, ration and water carts, not to mention troops from all over the Empire—Britain, Ireland, Australia, Canada, and now the United States, too.

Then there were the refugees. Worn and thin, they struggled down the road, many pushing wheelbarrows or baby carriages piled high with unidentifiable bundles. The children were the hardest to look at. They were all skinny with round, vacant eyes. Was this who they were fighting for? They didn't seem in the least bit happy about it.

"Pull over. For God's sake, look at her. Give her a lift." Charlie pointed to a woman heavy with child, dragging a suitcase and balancing a toddler on her hip. She staggered under the weight.

"No, no, no." The thought of these disgusting Frenchies dirtying up the General's automobile horrified the little man. All these foreigners running around! "Get away. *Viens ici, viens ici!*" he cried. "What's a matter with these Frenchies? Are they all stupid? *Viens ici!*" He waved his arm frantically out of the window. From a distance he looked as if he were trying to make the car fly.

People charged the automobile, all smiles at first, but then their looks changed to confusion as they were shooed away.

"That's the trouble with this war, people rising above their station in life. No good comes of it. None a'tall. *Viens ici!*"

"If you don't want them to get in the car, maybe you should stop telling them to *come.*" Jeeze, he didn't know much French but he knew that. "'*Viens ici*' means 'Come here.'" Charlie slumped down in his seat. After that, the miserable little man barely said two words to him, and for that Charlie was grateful.

The driver pulled over often. Being the nervous sort, he needed to pee every hour. The sun had come out and the road was drying up quickly. Charlie rolled up his sleeves. There was a muggy stench in the air. The shiver of heat bent the air ahead, and from a distance it looked as if everyone were walking on water.

Charlie leaned against the car and held out a chocolate bar to a small boy. His mother, in a fit of energy, leapt forward and snatched it out of Charlie's hand.

"Merci, monsieur." She bowed her head to him as if he were a general or something.

"Hey, away from the car. Away!" The driver came rushing out from behind a hedgerow. One hand was busy buttoning up his trousers while the other was batting the air. "Away. Away!" Then he turned on Charlie. "What do you mean giving them food? They'll only want more. We'll have half of France down on us in a minute."

Charlie took some satisfaction in noting that the miserable little man had done his pants up wrong.

"Non, Nicole, pour moi!" cried the boy.

"Non, Jean." The boy had called her Nicole. It dawned on him then—this woman wasn't the boy's mother. She wasn't a woman at all, she was just a girl, and not much older than himself. It was just that she looked so worn down, so old. Nicole carefully broke the bar into even pieces and shared them.

It was at that precise moment that he heard it. He knew the sound. It was a drawn-out hiss, like the sound of water just coming to a boil in a whistling kettle. Charlie scanned the sky. Where? Where? *There!*

A black dot came hurtling across the sky toward them. People scattered, horses reared, bundles were tossed aside and goods abandoned. Soldiers and nursing sisters tumbled out of the lorries and ambulances and tried to find cover. Many dragged or carried the wounded. Those too sick or hurt to move lay strapped onto the stretchers inside the ambulances and waited.

Charlie threw himself into the field just as the road erupted. Bits of shrapnel hit a gas tank and it exploded. Red flames shot up into the summer sky. The wave of heat was immediate and suffocating. It happened in slow motion and in a flash.

"Jean! Jean!" The girl was screaming. She had been flung yards away and lay sprawled out in the field. The boy was close to Charlie, running in circles, shrieking.

"Get down!" Charlie lunged toward Jean and fell over him just as the aeroplane made a second pass. *Tack-tack-tack.* Black bullets made nasty, deep holes in the yellow road. *Tack-tack-tack.* Another explosion, but farther away. And then, it was over. Someone in the distance had been taking potshots at the aeroplane.

"C'est finis."

Charlie, breathing heavily, fell back. The boy, round-eyed and tearless, slowly sat up.

"Jean!" The girl ran over and fell on her knees in front of her brother. She hugged and kissed him in quick, frantic movements. She stood and walked toward Charlie, then stood on her toes and kissed him, a quick, feathery kiss that was over before he had a chance to realize how pretty she was. *"Merci, monsieur."*

Her brother ran up and stood by her side. She took his hand and the two walked through the carnage down the road.

Charlie watched as they picked their way through the debris. Where were they going? What would happen to them? He looked around. There was a quiet about the place. Wounded people, bodies, dead animals, burnt-out vehicles littered the road. Charlie bent down to help the wounded man nearest him. When Charlie looked back down the road, the girl and boy were gone.

THE GENERAL'S CAR WAS DEAD. Charlie left the driver sitting on the auto's running board holding his head, moaning and groaning. He'd walk to the aerodrome.

The road underfoot should have been soft, but, like everything else in this part of France, it had been hammered down by lorries and the feet of marching men. He passed fresh troops on the march, British by the look of them, and some Australians after that. They followed their leaders like ducklings after their mother. Ambulance drivers, both men and women, called out to each other as they passed. The new recruits gazed at the ambulances and wondered at their cargo, then someone led off with a song, "It's a Long Way to Tipperary," and so it was.

Once in a while he tried to wave down a truck. One driver gave him a toothless grin, waved back, and carried on. The rest just ignored him. Ah well.

The land around him sloped gently in all directions. Poppies, as delicate as butterflies, grew wild and swayed in the fields beyond. Daffodils, primroses, and cowslips were in the last stages of bloom. Despite the dull roar of the guns off in the distance, skylarks gave noisy performances. What was it his mother used to say about songbirds? Auditioning for God's orchestra, that was it. That sick feeling cropped up, the one he always had whenever he thought of his parents and how they must be worrying about him. Well, it wouldn't be long now. He shifted his haversack and walked on, whistling.

The next day was fine. Charlie was pulled over by the military police and had his papers checked three times. It wasn't spies they were looking for, it was deserters. Charlie took an apple out of his pack, bit into it, and gazed up into a flat, blue sky. It hadn't rained all day.

It took three full days of walking to reach the aerodrome. He slept in barns mostly and bartered for food along the way. On the third morning he woke with the rooster. His dreams were about food now. Cod, what he wouldn't give for a feed of fried cod. He walked down a path to a rundown farm and traded a chocolate bar for a drink of fresh milk and a hunk of black bread. The old woman took the chocolate, grinned, and pointed to a small boy who cowered behind the barn. Her grandson. Charlie smiled at him, then rummaged through his pack and gave away his last chocolate bar.

Finally, Bertangles. The aerodrome was at the edge of a large woods. Wildflowers were scattered about, most dying off now. A collection of drab tents, hastily built huts, and a large tin hangar—a bit like a giant oil drum sawed lengthwise and tipped over—made up the facilities. Even from where he stood he could read the word "Office" painted on a length of wood and hammered above the entrance of the largest hut. Low-slung canvas chairs, better suited to a beach, stood in front of it. Two fliers sat in the chairs sipping tea from china cups. In the distance a bunch of perky little aeroplanes were lined up in front of the hangar. They looked like toys.

Two small aeroplanes buzzed overhead like demented flies. One, coming in for a landing, looked steady and sure, while the second grunted and bucked. It began to cough, its wings seesawed back and forth, and then it stalled. For a brief moment, there was nothing. Then, just as suddenly, the aeroplane banked up, screeched, and in a hairpin turn tumbled to the earth. It crashed less than a third of a mile away.

"Jeeze," Charlie muttered.

Men, fliers no doubt, spilled out of the huts in the distance. They were yelling, or maybe they were singing. They piled onto various transports—a lorry, an ambulance, one climbed on a motorbike, and another jumped on a horse! Driving and galloping they passed Charlie and made their way toward the downed plane. Thing was, they looked rather gay, as if they were off to a party. One fellow, hanging off the lorry, held a champagne glass aloft and toasted Charlie as he went by. Very peculiar.

CHAPTER 22

Charlie stood at the entrance to the office at the Bertangles aerodrome. He rammed his hand into his pocket and fingered the letter of introduction to Pug.

"Hello?" he called out. Nothing, just an echo. He walked in. The place was empty except for a desk, a few chairs, and piles of maps scattered around or pinned up on the walls. "Hello?"

"You there, what are you after?"

Charlie spun around and looked up the nose of a flier, English by the sound of him.

"I'm here to see . . ." He couldn't say Pug, surely? Charlie pulled the letter out of his pocket and scanned the name on the envelope. "Major Piggot-Smith."

"What do you want with Pug?" The flier, who wasn't a day over nineteen, looked at Charlie with contempt.

"I have a letter for Major Pug, I mean, Major Piggot-Smith."

"A letter! Really. Can you read?"

"Yes." Charlie was indignant.

"Show-off," he sneered.

Charlie gazed at the flier. A shock of black hair dribbled down his forehead. His nose was long, or maybe it just appeared that way because of the way he looked down it.

"Where is the Major?" Charlie asked.

"Spot of bother with a new boy. Copped it, from the looks of it. Serves him right, too. He'll not make a bally-hash of another flight plan."

Charlie followed the flier's gaze to the window and the two looked off into the distance. A cone of smoke from the downed plane coiled up into the air, then twisted and broke off into wisps.

"I'll wait." Charlie backed away.

"You'll do what I tell you to do. I'm the Officer of the Day. My name is Charles Askwith Weston. You may call me Weston. And where did you get that dreadful accent?"

"I'm from Newfoundland." He meant to speak proudly, but all he could manage was loudly.

"New Found *Land*, part of Africa, is it? Swazi*land*? Or maybe it's that bit off Australia, New Zea*land*. Now it's not dear old Eng*land*. That goes without saying. There's Ire*land*, Thai*land*, and Green*land*, of course. Or Po*land*! Dear fellow, might you be Polish? I say . . ."

Charlie's mouth gaped open. "No. Newfoundland is an independent—"

"All the same to me." Weston waved him off. "You're here now, it seems. This might be your opportunity to learn to speak English."

Bloody twit! This might also be a good opportunity for the imperial prig to learn a little geography. Then again, the toffee-nose could be having him on. It was hard to tell. Charlie clamped his mouth shut.

"Give me that." In one swift movement Weston pinched the letter out of Charlie's hand and ripped it open.

"Hey!" Charlie lunged at him.

"Watch yourself." He scanned the letter, holding it out first at arm's length and then, turning his back on Charlie, holding it up to his nose. Very peculiar. "Don't forget," he said, "I could have you court-martialed."

"You could, if I were in any part of the service." Charlie glared at his back.

"Don't get your knickers in a twist, my little African friend. Come with me." The Officer of the Day tossed the letter onto what was probably Major Piggot-Smith's desk and bolted out the door.

Charlie scrambled after him. "I think I should wait for—"

"Pug. Everyone calls him Pug. He has a pug nose, you see. Irish extraction I should think. Poor sod. Of course, he could be called Piglet. Looks piggish. Rather hard to eat a pork chop in front of him, say what? Might be eating one of his relatives." He came to an abrupt stop in front of a smaller hut. "Just making a pit stop. Have a pee-pee if you like. No charge." He pointed to a shed off in the distance then ducked into the hut.

Charlie peered in after him. Two well-made bunks lined one wall. A large, partly opened box of pressed shirts lay across one of the beds. The name on the package read "St. James Express Laundry, London." A table that looked as though it was accustomed to better surroundings sported a Fortnum &

Mason's food basket. Tins of foreign stuff, pâtés, cheeses, and cakes spilled out of it. Two very comfy chairs sat under two very large reading lamps, which were beside two matching side tables. There were bottles of brandy and glasses on each table. The shelf behind was lined with leather-bound books and copies of the *Illustrated London News.*

"Where is everybody?"

"Taking care of that nasty business, I should expect. Bloody flamer." Weston motioned toward the smoke that continued to spiral up to the sky.

Charlie followed Weston into the hut.

"Shake a leg there, grunt. Speaking of which, you limp. Are you defective?" Weston looked hard at Charlie's feet.

"No, I . . ." What could he say? "I had a problem with my . . . foot. Now it's fine." Charlie hadn't given a thought to his foot in years. The club foot he'd been born with was fixed, or almost fixed. His gait was a little halting, but only when he was tired. And he had, after all, just walked for three days!

"Here." The British prig reached into the wicker basket, split off a chunk of fruit cake, and tossed it Charlie's way. "Belongs to a fellow from London. He's entirely too fat. We're doing him a favor by eating his food. Eat, but don't drink too much. I did tell you to pee-pee, did I not?"

"I don't have to be told to pee." Charlie, cake in hand, glared at the Englishman. Fact was he was famished. He could have eaten the entire basket, wicker and all, given the chance.

"Really? Are you sure? A defective, illiterate New Zeel Lander who can't speak the King's English. How is one to know?"

"I am not—"

"Help me kit up." The flier turned on his heels and sauntered off.

"Help you what?"

"Come along." He gave an imperial wave.

Charlie couldn't stop himself. He tucked a round of soft, white cheese into his tunic and shoved a packet of crackers into his pocket.

The next building had the words "Pilots' Hut" painted on a bit of wood nailed, not neatly, to the doorframe. Weston charged in while Charlie, stumbling behind, wolfed down the rest of the cake. The hut was empty except for three fleece-lined leather jackets hanging on hooks, boots in various stages of repose, a few scarves, gloves, leather helmets, and a tangled heap of goggles.

Weston helped himself to his jacket then plunked down on a chair.

"Boots, boy." He motioned to a pair of highly polished boots in the corner.

Charlie looked around.

"Oh, do get on with it." Weston stuck out a poised, outstretched foot.

"I'm not your batman." Bloody English gents were used to having their own personal servants about the place. Well, he was no one's servant! Charlie flung the boots over in Weston's direction and stood in the corner with his arms crossed.

Weston cheerfully kitted himself out in scarf, gauntlets, leather helmet, and goggles.

"Don't stand there, grunt. Get yourself kitted out. Never mind the boots. Terribly possessive bunch, these fliers. Just because they bought them, think they own them."

"Why?"

"Why what?"

"Why get myself kitted out?"

"I'm to take you across the Channel. Drop you off like the post, I'm told. Isn't that right, or is there another grunt coming who needs a lift?"

So that was it. This Charles Askwith Weston fellow had been expecting him.

CHAPTER 23

"I DIDN'T THINK . . . I thought I had a few days," Charlie dithered.

"Now or never, boy. Must warn you though, ol' chap, I plan to make a little detour, nothing much." Weston slapped his gloves together, charged out the door, and strode across the great expanse of grass toward the hangar.

Detour? Charlie grabbed a jacket, gauntlets, leather helmet, and goggles and stumbled behind. By the time they'd reached the hangar he was half dressed.

"Afternoon, squire." An older man standing outside the hangar next to an aeroplane nodded to Weston. He had a face like a road map, with creases sharply defined by embedded dirt. There seemed to be no part of him that hadn't been dipped in oil and grease.

"Meet the best rigger in the business," Weston said. "How's it going, John?" Weston moved around the plane, examining the tail and wings as if it were a horse.

"Not quite up to snuff, this one, sir," replied John.

To Charlie's eyes the plane was a beauty—not that he knew one plane from another. Fact was, this was the first plane he'd even seen close up.

"What's it called?" Charlie gingerly touched the canvas wing. It was a biplane, its wings staggered and tilted back, like a hawk in flight. Two-seater. The front seat was filled with sandbags.

"A BE2c, grunt." Weston grinned. "They call it a Quirk. Pretty little thing, wouldn't you say, John?" He gave the wings a rap. "Made with Irish linen. Now who would have thought the Irish would come up with anything useful. Our fine friend here is from Ire-Land, John. A Catholic, no doubt." Weston was pointing at Charlie.

"I'm from New Found Land." He hadn't meant to raise his voice. Was this guy putting him on?

"It can go eighty miles an hour, full out. Looks in good shape." Weston ran his hand down the plane's tail, then gave it a dog's pat.

"Controls a bit spongy, sir." John rubbed his dirty hands on a dirty cloth then mopped his forehead with it.

"Like Nanny's pudding, I suppose." Weston chuckled. "It's a topping piece of junk. Even a grunt could fly it."

"Maybe so, sir." John's voice was as smooth as spilled milk. He'd seen these pompous flyboys come and go with great haste over the last two years. Flying bloody fools. Mind, more might have lived to fight another day had they been issued parachutes. Of course they were bulky things—in a cockpit the size of a small man's arse where would they fit? And it had to be said that a pilot would try harder to land his plane safely if he knew he couldn't bail out. Planes were more valuable than pilots, that's what the brass thought. Now the German pilots, they were protected by armored plates and wore para-chutes. John thought on that a great deal.

"I do believe I'll take her up." Weston grinned. Old John looked uncomfortable. "Well, sir, this might not be the day for it. I can have the Camel ready for you in a jiffy."

"Nonsense. Someone has to test this ol' dear. Up and across the Channel, dispose of my baggage here," he motioned to Charlie, "back in a jiffy."

"Sir, I haven't checked the mount. That gun is a bit sticky."

"Johann, Du machst Dir zu viele Sorgen. Wir haben keine deutschen Flugzeuge in den letzten Tagen gesehen."

John looked every which-way at once. He glanced at Charlie, then hissed to Weston, "Wish you wouldn't talk that way, sir."

"What's that? Afraid a little German is contagious?" Weston threw back his head and laughed. He laughed a lot. "Language of Mozart, ol' boy."

"Seems a bit . . ." John searched around for the word, "disloyal. Speaking German, like."

"You learned German?" Charlie asked Weston.

"Read languages at Oxford. Good school, Oxford. Better plumbing than Cambridge. Latin and Greek mostly, useful stuff. *Carpe diem, quam minimum credula postero* and all that rot."

Charlie wrinkled his brow. What was he talking about?

"That's right. You're from Africa, or was it Green Land? Barely grasp the English language, say what? I said, *Seize the day, trust as little as possible in tomorrow.* Latin. Words to live by. Get her ready there, John." Weston jutted out his chin.

"Chuck those sandbags out of the front seat."

"Just as you like, sir." John climbed up on the wing and heaved three sandbags down onto the ground while Weston hopped up onto the wing and slipped into the back seat with practiced elegance.

"Get in!" he hollered.

"Right!" Charlie zipped up the cumbersome flight jacket, fastened the straps of his helmet, and, clutching his haversack, he stepped up onto the wing. So this was it. The war, for him anyway, was over. The decision to stay or leave seemed to have been taken away from him, and for that he was grateful. And what a way to go! Boy, if thems at home could see him now.

The seat fit like metal pants. A stick came up between his legs and threatened to do him damage, but, squirming back and forth, he achieved something near to comfort.

"Sir," John yelled over the engine's whine, "try not to bully her."

The old man reached over and strapped Charlie into the seat. "Don't know about this." He shook his head. Weston, his attention diverted by the instrument panel in front of him, waved him off. John jumped down off the plane. "Bloody fool," the old man muttered.

"Contact," hollered Weston. The two men exchanged words and signals but they were lost to Charlie, what with the sound of his heart pounding and the propeller whirling. They were off.

The plane bounced in and out of potholes before rolling onto a rutty grass runway. Weston gunned the engine. Shrieking, the plane lunged forward like a dog to its dinner and picked up speed. Then—it was as if a mighty hand had cupped the plane's underbelly and gently lifted—they were airborne. In less than a minute John and the collection of huts below were reduced to little dots. Up, up, up they sailed. Clouds rolled past like whitecaps on the open sea. He couldn't tell how high they were, only that they were going higher.

Charlie stuck his face out into the airstream. The wind whipped past, taking with it all thoughts, all feelings, leaving him free to fly. He was breathless. He rubbed the mist off his goggles and looked below. He hooted! The plane bobbed below the clouds. He looked back, and for a split second he thought he saw a smile cross Weston's face.

"Look down." Weston mouthed the words, then pointed. There they were, the trenches! Long, black ribbons that might have been strewn and stretched over the ground by a careless child. And over there, the German lines. They seemed to go on forever, snaking their way from the North Sea all the way to Switzerland, cutting a jagged line through northern France. Could each one really be more than four hundred miles long? It was hard to take in. And there, in between, was no-man's-land, that barren, filthy sliver of earth that separated the two enemies. Once it had been fertile land; now it was a thin stream of rolling mud, churned into blackened butter in the summer and frozen into biting-sharp ridges in the winter. But it all looked clean from up there. Tidy. No smells. No rats. No decay. The war in the air was a tidy affair, different from the war on the ground.

Weston seemed to be following the line of trenches. German artillery, dubbed archies, fired, making puffballs of smoke in the distance. They didn't look especially dangerous. The plane continued to soar for a bit longer and then leveled off, and for a long while Charlie settled back, made himself snug, and felt the wind on his face. Time had stopped.

Weston thumped the back of his seat. Charlie ignored him. It had been a long, long time since he had felt such peace— funny to find such a thing in the sky, above a war. He felt he could live up there, and never touch earth again. Except for Weston yelling something incomprehensible, it was oddly familiar. Maybe it was the sky itself, blue like the ocean he'd looked upon every day of his childhood. Just as waves rolled, clouds ebbed. Sailing and flying were one and the same. Again Weston whacked the back of his seat. What was the imperial prig on about?

Charlie turned and looked over his shoulder. There it was. Like a hawk zeroing in on its prey, the black Maltese cross on the wings of a German plane came into view.

CHAPTER 24

CHARLIE CRANED HIS NECK in every direction. Where did it go? The German plane was gone! Then it started.

Tack-tack-tack.

Machine-gun fire. Sparks flew off the wing's struts. The air was dirty with smoke.

Tack-tack-tack.

The canvas skin on one wing ripped, peeled back, fluttered, then whipped and cracked like a loose sail on a ship.

Tack-tack-tack. Ping! Something snapped.

Charlie twisted around and looked at Weston's contorted face. He was screaming something.

Tack-tack-tack.

What should he do? He looked ahead at the gun mount. How did it work? He flicked something. Hit another thing. Where was the lock? Oh, please. There. He released the lock, put his eye to the glass, set to fire, and braced himself for the jolt. Nothing. The gun was jammed. He pulled at it, frantically. Screaming. "It's stuck! It's stuck!" His words were lost on the wind. They were defenceless.

The German plane disappeared again. Their plane

seesawed back and forth, then plunged into the clouds. How long could they hide? Forever wasn't long enough. What was he doing up there? He looked in every direction. Every part of him was frozen with fear.

With a damaged wing, the plane bobbed about like an unmanned ship. The hard thumps of Weston frantically pumping the controls reverberated up Charlie's spine. The plane reared up like a frightened horse, then down it went, a lame duck. Screams he couldn't even hear surged up and seared his throat. The noise of the howling plane spiraling, plunging down to earth blew away any human sounds. Trees were rushing toward them. And, just as suddenly, the plane leveled off. They'd hit an updraft. The plane began to glide.

They didn't so much crash into the ground as the ground reached up and crashed into them. The tip of the undamaged wing hit first. Over they went, cartwheeling, again and again. It sounded like thunder. Then the thunder erupted into a mighty roar. The harness held Charlie fast as his body strained to break free. Something caught. The wheels snapped off as the aeroplane began to slide through an open wheat field. The hull of the plane, wingless, nothing more than an armless, legless torso, came to a grinding, shrieking stop. They were down. Down.

Charlie sat, unable to move. Except for the roar of his heart in his ears, there was silence.

"Grunt?"

He sat.

"Grunt?"

He turned. There was Weston, his face black, his eyes behind his goggles vacant. Charlie removed his own goggles and slumped in his seat. Every bone in his body seemed to have turned to liquid. Smoke drifted up to his nostrils.

"Get out!" Weston cried.

Smoke! Fire! Out, out! He had seen men burnt to a crisp, like overcooked chicken, skin peeling off. No, no. Charlie fumbled with his seatbelt.

"Get out! Get out!"

How? How did the latches work? Charlie tore off his gloves and yanked at the seatbelt straps. The more he pulled, the more tightly the belts bound him to the plane. He took in a breath, had to. Smoke scorched his throat, stung his eyes, and left him parched. And then, flick. One belt fell away. Flick again. The other came off, and, with one mighty heave, he lunged into space and landed on something soft.

"Bloody hell." Weston gave him a sharp shove. "Watch where you're landing. You could do a fellow damage."

Charlie rolled over on the ground and stared at the flier. Damage? Damage? His breath was short; air would not go into his lungs. He looked back at the plane. There was smoke, but no fire. Why?

"Bit of bother, I seem to have twisted my ankle." With one hand pressed to the side of the smoldering hull, Weston struggled up and made an attempt to stand.

Charlie gazed up at the clouds. No sign of the German plane. Air, he had to get air into his lungs. They had landed in a full-grown wheat field. He batted the wheat stalks as he lay flat out on the ground, his chest heaving.

"Bit of luck here." Weston gazed at the plane while testing out his ankle. "Smoke, but no fire. No flamer, say what?

Excellent. Wouldn't take a nap, ol' boy." Weston spoke and hobbled about at the same time. "Not entirely sure we're on the right side, if you catch my meaning."

Slowly, as life returned to him, Charlie took in his meaning. "What?" He spat on the ground and tried to clear his lungs. Complete sentences were beyond him. "Enemy lines?" Charlie sputtered. "We're behind enemy lines?"

"Think we might want to make a dash for those trees." Weston might have been talking about an evening stroll along the promenade. "One can assume that the Boche will be paying a visit shortly. Punctual bunch, the Germans."

Prison camp. That's what would happen to them, if they were lucky. If they weren't shot on the spot. The haversack was at his feet. It must have fallen out the same time he did. Charlie snatched it up, flung it onto his back, scrambled up onto two shaky legs, and began to charge through the field toward the woods.

"Load of bollocks!" Weston grumbled before taking off through the wheat fields as quickly as his bad ankle would allow.

Charlie didn't look back. Run. Run. With flat palms he knocked back wheat stalks, cutting a swath. Wait, he was leaving a trail behind him! He began to dodge and weave, keeping his head low. He wouldn't have lasted long in the trenches if he hadn't learned how to run and duck at the same time.

Sweat cascaded down his face until finally he made it through. He saw another figure—had to be Weston— slumped against a tree and he flung himself down against the roots. If this was shock, then let it last a little longer because, beyond aching lungs, Charlie couldn't feel a thing. Clutching his side he slid down until he was sitting on his haunches.

"Weston." He reached out one hand to rest on the other man's leg. "You okay?"

No answer.

"Weston, I said . . ."

He would have screamed if he could have, if he'd had a voice, if he hadn't immediately pitched himself behind the tree! The leg didn't belong to Weston, it belonged to a German! Breathe. Breathe. He pressed himself so close to the tree that the bark imprinted itself on his chest. He waited. He tried to suck in air. Nothing happened.

Slowly he peeked around the tree. A small handgun lay beside the soldier. If he could just . . . He stretched, quietly, stretched some more, and nabbed it. Right. He pointed the gun at the sleeping soldier. The blasted thing wouldn't stop wobbling in his hand.

"Hey! Wake up." Charlie, still mostly concealed behind the tree, nudged the guy with his foot. "I said, wake up." Nothing. No movement.

His back against the tree, Charlie edged around and peered down at the body. The soldier's head lolled to one side. This time he gave him a sharp jab. The head wobbled and the man, his eyes wide and empty, stared up at him. Jeeze.

Thick, purple blood, like jelly, had congealed above the dead man's ear. It had leaked out of his head and now formed a sticky, dark pool on the ground. He didn't look very old— maybe twenty. At least he wouldn't be any trouble.

Charlie scanned the field. Where was Weston? There! He was staggering through the wheat field and making a beeline for him. Charlie looked up into the sky. Nothing yet. He tucked the gun into his pants, ran out toward Weston, and, with Charlie shouldering his weight, the two hobbled back to the trees.

"What's this? Made a friend?" Weston, clutching his side, fell to his knees and gazed at the body.

"You all right?" For a second Charlie was glad to see him, thrilled even!

"What kind of bloody stupid question is that to ask? We're on the wrong side of the war, my ankle's a bally-hash, and I could murder a cup of tea." Weston spoke in great gasps. The body lay between them. For a moment they said nothing; it was work enough just to breathe.

"See here, grunt." Weston took a deep breath. "I didn't mean to sound so abrupt just then. I must apologize for getting you into this mess. Bloody inconvenient war, wouldn't you say? Always mucking up an afternoon's plans." He grimaced as he felt his ankle. "Of course, it's all your fault." Weston spoke directly to the dead body. "No need to make war, eh? You might have stayed home and had a sausage."

Charlie crept around the body and felt Weston's ankle.

"Yow," he yelped. "Easy on."

Perfect, thought Charlie. He's not only a prig, he's a sissy. Isn't that always the way.

"I don't think it's broken." Charlie ripped Weston's pant leg.

"Easy boy, those trousers cost a bit."

Terrific, he was a prig, a sissy, and a cheapskate.

Weston, his lips pulled tight with the pain, closed his eyes. "It's not like they're army issue. Tailored to fit, don't you know. No, I don't suppose you would know." He glanced down at Charlie. "Look here, I don't want to sound dramatic, but I do think we should expect a visit from our hosts any minute now. As you can see, I'll get nowhere fast. I think, grunt, you should head off on your own. Off you go, boy. Give my regards to the colonies. Shoot a lion or kangaroo in Africa or wherever. Off you go."

"I can't leave you."

"Very sporting. Gallant perhaps, but a rather extravagant emotion under the circumstances, wouldn't you say?" He winced and rubbed his ankle. "All's fair in love and war, say what? Cheerio. Ta-ta. No need to write."

What should he do? Charlie kicked the dead soldier's haversack out of his line of vision and looked him over. The uniform was clean. Not a spot of blood on it. The dead soldier had even taken the time to remove his leather helmet before doing himself in. How thoughtful. Charlie looked back at the plane. Right! He fell over the body and began unbuttoning the soldier's tunic.

"I say, robbing the dead, are we? That's not entirely British."

"I'm not entirely British either. I'm African, remember? Or was it Irish?" The thought that he might well have been killed by this nitwit, and still might die because of him, crossed Charlie's mind. "Help me!"

Weston inched his way over and the two stripped the body in no time.

"I say, our dead friend is a flier." Weston pointed to the wings on the uniform. "I must say, it's rather disappointing to see a flier do himself in. It's not at all the done thing."

"Take off your clothes and put them on him. Hurry!" Charlie flung the German's jacket over to Weston.

"I do see where you are going with this. Our friend here is about to change sides. But I say, ol' boy, how do you plan to explain that rather nasty bullet in his head?"

"We're going to put him in the plane."

"I say, that's a bit much isn't it?"

"Stop saying *I say*." Charlie's nerves were about to snap.

"Do hold on, ol' boy. Courage under fire and all that . . ." Weston put on his new clothes and, for a moment anyway, kept quiet.

"There!" The German, dressed in Weston's uniform, was now a pilot in His Majesty's Service. Weston was a pilot fighting for the Kaiser.

"Rather dashing, wouldn't you say?" Weston modeled his britches. "I'm missing something, though. Ah, the pistol, if you please."

Charlie grudgingly passed him the handgun. Weston buckled his belt, adjusted the knife and holster, and then started an argument with the boots. One was a good fit, and the other might have been too had Weston's ankle not continued to swell. Enough. Charlie picked up the boot, jammed Weston's ballooning leg into it, braced the boot against his own chest, and pushed. Weston squealed like a stuck pig. Jeeze, if he yelled any louder the whole bloody German Empire would hear. But the boot was on the foot.

"Now, how do you propose we get the corpse to the corpse?" Weston, still smarting, looked across the field to the shell of the plane.

"Come on." Charlie stuffed his own haversack, along with the dead soldier's sack, between the tree roots while Weston donned the leather helmet. "Move." Charlie took command.

Shouldering the corpse between them, they staggered back across the wheat field. Sweat trickled down their faces. Weston was in agony, that was plain, but he said nothing about it. No sign of the Germans yet. Surely they must have seen the aeroplane come down?

They came up to the wreck. Charlie climbed up onto the plane and stood with his legs straddling the cockpit. Down below, Weston hoisted the dead flier and heaved him up while Charlie, with his arms under the dead man's armpits and his fingers clasped tight across the dead man's chest, heaved. Grunting in tandem, the two of them lifted him up high enough that his legs dangled into the cockpit. It didn't help that the seat of the plane was bent out of shape. Finally they tumbled the body into the cockpit, right side up.

"Give me your identification. Hurry."

Weston flung up his identification disks. Charlie slipped them over the dead soldier's head.

"That's it. Now run." Charlie jumped down.

"Not yet. Afraid we have to torch the poor fellow." Weston patted his chest pockets in search of a match.

"What do you mean?" Charlie, dumbstruck, looked blankly at Weston.

"There's no way to explain that hole in his head. Besides, let's not give the Huns a gift of a perfectly good engine. Steady on. He's already dead. He really won't mind a bit. Ah, our friend smokes!" He reached into the German's pockets, waved a pack of matches about, then pitched them to Charlie. "Filthy habit, smoking. Just toss a light in that petrol." He pointed to a pool of black sludge that had gathered under the tail. "And you might want to throw in that jacket you're wearing. Give us a tick." Weston picked up a glove that had fallen on the ground, tossed it into the cockpit, then turned and hobbled back toward the trees. "Do hurry, ol' boy," he hollered over his shoulder.

Charlie threw his jacket into the front of the cockpit and struck the match. "Sorry," he whispered.

The fire was instantaneous. Flames leapt up into the air, nasty looking daggers of fire. The heat bent the air around the hull. Something like grief swamped him. No life should end like this. He felt he should say something.

"Our Father, who art in Heaven . . ." There was a rumble in the distance. Trucks. Charlie turned and broke into a run. "Hallowed be Thy name." Faster now. "Give us . . . daily bread. And forgive . . . trespasses, especially mine, But deliver us . . ." He fell to his knees and began to crawl between the wheat stalks. "And forgive me, too." He plunged into the trees just as three armored trucks pulled up in the distance and surrounded the plane.

CHAPTER 25

"SHOULDN'T WE BE MOVING ON?"

Weston was actually *asking* Charlie, and nicely, too. The German trucks had come and gone. They had inspected the downed plane, shrugged, smoked cigarettes, and finally pushed off. Charlie and Weston had retrieved the two haversacks and plunged deeper into the wooded area. It was late afternoon now. Against his better judgment, Charlie had shared his stolen cheese and crackers. They had drained what water was left in the dead soldier's canteen, and now they were waiting for dark.

"See here, Charles, isn't it? I do think I should find out exactly where we are."

So, the pompous imperial knew his name after all. "How do you plan to do that?" Charlie looked up at the sky through tree branches.

"I speak German. I'm in a German uniform." Weston rubbed his ankle.

"What? Are you going to ask some passing soldier where we are?" He leaned on his arm and stared at Weston. "You don't even know *who* you are."

"I'm ahead of you there, ol' sport." He reached into his pocket and pulled out a paybook, a packet of letters, and a crumpled photograph. He held the photo up close and peered hard at it before passing it to Charlie. "I say, look familiar?"

It was the dead soldier as a child, and no mistaking it. The woman in the picture had to be his mother. They had the same round, open faces, the same wary smile. The boy stood grinning in short pants, holding a cone filled with candy. The mother's arm was draped over the boy's shoulder. Proud mama.

"Look at this." Weston, pinching a letter between thumb and finger, waved it about. "Right, you don't read German, either. I'll translate." Again Weston peered closely at the letter, his eyes squinting. "It's from his mother. She says she loves him. That she will always love him and always be proud of him. There's something here about his sister's wedding. Of course it was a quiet wedding, their father having just been killed in some battle somewhere or other. A quick wedding, too, it seems. The groom is being sent off to the front. I say, maybe we'll meet him!"

Charlie folded his arms around his knees and bent his head down. *I expect we'll come to believe that all Germans are monsters. It's easy to kill a monster, now, isn't it? If we thought that they were just like us, with wives and children and such— well, how could we shoot them?*

"Our dead friend's name is, pardon me, *was,* Hans Moser. Good grief. Are all Germans named Hans? These people have no imagination. Now the British know how to name their children. I myself went to school with two Piggys, one Squiggly, and I can't count the Porgys." Weston let out a howl and held up another scrap of paper.

"Be quiet!" Charlie popped his head up and looked around.

"So sorry, but I say, it's Hans's suicide note! Look, it's addressed and stamped. Our fine fellow thinks of everything." Weston looked as pleased as punch and immediately took to reading it. "Ha! Oh my. Tisk-tisk. Seems as though he didn't care for this war experience at all. There's something here about him not wanting to kill strangers. Oh my. He's afraid to fly. Imagine that! Well, can't have Mother knowing that!" Weston was about to rip up Hans's suicide note, then thought better of it and put it back in the envelope and into his pocket. Next to be pillaged was Hans's haversack. "Look, pants!" Weston flung them at Charlie. "Shirt, too. It's bloody Christmas. No schnapps, more's the pity."

Charlie stripped off his clothes and put on the pants and shirt. They made his skin crawl.

"And what have we here?" Weston tossed out a Bible and dangled a medal between his fingers. "I say, an Iron Cross, First Class, too. Much better than the Second Class. A goat could get an Iron Cross Second Class. Tisk-tisk. An impressive military career shot to hell." Weston, with a ceremonial wave of the hand, pinned the cross onto his tunic. "I say, you can't go around carrying that haversack of yours. Use this." Weston flipped over Hans's pack. "Put your old clothes in your own bag and bury the lot."

There was nothing to do now but wait until dark. Charlie closed his eyes and thought of home. Weston retrieved note paper from ol' Hans's haversack and seemed happy to scribble away.

DUSK SEEMED TO LAST FOREVER in Europe. They set off in the twilight. Weston, one arm draped over Charlie's shoulder, tried his best to keep his weight off him. The path underfoot was uneven and they stumbled continually. Twice they pitched themselves into the forest or ditch as trucks carrying water, ammunition, and food made their way to the German front. Their faces were streaked with grease, but it was their parched throats that were crying out. Water. Anything for a sip of water.

"There!" Charlie pointed. As the light ebbed they could just make out a small stream off the path. They stepped, then slipped, then fell, then rolled down a small embankment into the water. Weston yelped a bit. So far, they didn't have much of a plan.

"It's the only way." Charlie splashed water over his face. It was foul stuff and had a whiff of machine oil about it. "We have to cross back over to our side before morning. The front can't be much farther." The right direction was easy enough to tell. All they had to do was follow the sounds of the bombs and artillery. It was an odd thing, hearing the same sounds from the other side. And the look of the place was the same too. Of course, it was all France, just divided like dinner.

"LISTEN!" Charlie stopped so quickly that Weston pitched forward. They were back on the road again, stumbling about in the dark like two old drunks. There was a rumbling coming up from behind. Lorries, lots of them. Charlie was about to make for the forest when Weston grabbed him. Too late.

Trucks rumbled toward them. The two stood to one side to let them pass. A line of fresh troops followed, but none of them so much as acknowledged their presence. Then came a soldier on horseback, an officer. He yelled something, and instantly a beam of light fell on Charlie and Weston.

"*Hallo, Sie da, wohin gehen Sie?*"

"*Zurück zur Einheit, Herr Kapitän,*" Weston answered. "*Vor einigen Kilometer stürzte unser Lastwagen um.*" He stuck his injured leg up in the air and danced around on the other.

"*Gehen Sie in den Esswagen.*" The captain, his eyes focused on his marching soldiers, yanked at the reins and trotted off. Weston gave a German salute, although nobody saw it but Charlie and the horse's ass.

"HEAR THAT?" Weston hissed in Charlie's ear.

It was just after midnight, and the sound wafting through the dark was unmistakable. Charlie could almost hear Weston's heart beating. His own heart seemed to have stopped dead some time ago.

"It's a pub!" If Weston had cried out any louder, the German army would have been on them like flies on a corpse. But then, the music and laughter were loud enough to cover a great deal of noise; even the sounds of war seemed distant and harmless.

"We can't!" He knew it! He knew what Weston was think-ing. The mere idea was horrifying. "We can't go in there! We must cross over tonight." At that particular moment the thought of crawling across no-man's-land was infinitely less scary than walking into a pub filled with enemy soldiers.

"My dear boy, if one's sights are fixed firmly on one's desti-nation, one must ask oneself, is the journey worth taking? Stop and smell the roses."

"What?" Weston was mad, completely mad.

"I'm hungry and I'm parched. Besides, Hans left us enough money to have a very nice meal indeed." Weston plunged into the night toward the bar. Apparently he could hobble at quite a respectable speed if the carrot was food and drink.

"They'll find me out." Charlie was hissing to Weston's back now.

"Right." Weston came to an abrupt stop. He turned, grabbed Charlie by the shirt, and the two crouched behind several barrels and a mound of garbage. He reached into Hans's medic bag and pulled out a length of white gauze.

"Wrap this around your head. Cover your ears. You're deaf, got it?"

Charlie held the gauze aloft. He was kidding, right? This wasn't happening.

"Deaf as a post. Plus you're an idiot besides. A good lie is always more believable than the plain truth. Words to live by. Here, give me that!" Weston snatched back the bandage and tied it around Charlie's head. "Now, your finger if you please!"

Charlie, the innocent, held up his hand. "Oh! Jeeze!" The beggar had cut him!

"Blood, boy. Chin up." Weston replaced his knife, or rather Hans's knife, in his belt, grabbed Charlie's bloody finger, and smeared it down the side of Charlie's face. "There now, pretty as a picture. If one might say a victory is an opportunity for the enemy, then one might also say that in failure there is also opportunity. Let us take up the gauntlet."

"Huh?"

"Come along."

This wasn't happening. This couldn't be happening.

The pub, or rather estaminet, was shrouded in darkness. Even the windows were covered up. If it hadn't been for the noise, no one would ever have known it was there. Staff cars were lined up outside, each with a driver lolling against it. The orange tips of their cigarettes jerked about like fireflies. Weston gave the drivers a regal wave as he swaggered past.

"*Schön' guten Abend!*" He spoke with frightening confidence.

"*Guten Abend.*"

A young driver saluted, leapt forward, and flung the door of the estaminet open with a flourish. It was like opening the gates to a dam. The flood of light and music rushed out and nearly overpowered them. Everything in Charlie said *run*. Run now. But Weston stormed in like he bloody well owned the place. His bandaged head lowered, his chin tucked into his shirt, there was nothing Charlie could do but follow.

CHAPTER 26

"CHAMPAGNE, MADEMOISELLE!"

The way Weston was hollering it was as if he were deliberately trying to attract attention. The place was packed.

Charlie's eyes, smarting from the smoke in the room, flashed from soldier to soldier. There wasn't a glum face in the crowd, just laughing men. Buxom ladies in low-cut, white cotton blouses displaying bountiful bosoms held maybe five or six beer steins in each hand. They flung the steins down on polished tabletops where they were caught, brought to the lips of soldiers, and emptied with gay abandon. Frothy mustaches were everywhere.

The place was split into two levels. Above, toward the back and in full view of the main floor, officers sat up in a gallery. They too seemed to be enjoying themselves tremendously. While the long, narrow tables below were made of rough, shiny wood, the tables upstairs were round, seemed sturdier, and were covered in white linen. All of them sported candles and bottles of wine.

"De la bière pour mon ami, mais pour moi, de la champagne!" Weston shouted in French, pointing to Charlie.

157

A pretty waitress, older than Weston, maybe twenty-five, studied Charlie hard. What was she looking at? If only he could make himself invisible, just fade away. Charlie tucked his chin into his tunic. It wasn't as if she cared about serving a minor. Everyone seemed to drink in France; even children sipped wine mixed with water.

Apparently satisfied, the waitress pulled a bottle out from under the bar and handed it, along with a glass, to Weston. With the bottle of champagne tucked under his arm and the glass poised in his hand, Weston made for a table in the middle of the room. He sat and, with a flourish, waved to Charlie.

"Komm. Komm."

Charlie stumbled forward, inching and squeezing through the throng. Every hair, every nerve, was standing on end.

"Pour vous, monsieur." The waitress plunked a mug of beer as big as a drum directly in front of Charlie. *"Regarde-toi!"* She peered at him. *"Il n'est pas un soldat. C'est un petit gosse!"* She threw her head back and laughed. Her bosoms were huge and white and jiggled as she laughed. Charlie had never seen such breasts. What was she saying? *Petit gosse. Petit* meant small, he knew that much. She'd called him a small *something*. Run. He should run. Now! There were dozens of soldiers between him and the door. They looked tame enough at the moment, but he knew right well they could turn on him in a heartbeat.

"Où est ta maman, mon petit?" She patted Charlie on the head. *"Madeleine, Madeleine,"* the waitress shouted over the heads of the noisy crowd to a woman standing behind a gigantic bar. Why? *"Nous avons un bébé ici. Portez-lui quelque chose à manger."*

A woman behind the bar nodded and waved in their direction. *"Oui, Chantal."*

So, the waitress's name was Chantal. Charlie's eyes darted from Chantal's face to Madeleine's to Weston's. He didn't dare look farther afield.

"Viens, mon petit, t'as besoin d'une caresse." Chantal puckered and unpuckered her lips. She was beside him now, and moving closer.

What was *caresse*? Charlie looked over at Weston. He was laughing so hard there were tears in his eyes. What was so funny? Startled, Charlie looked up. Chantal was coming closer. Closer. Her breasts would arrive before the rest of her. They were huge! Big, white, round things. Closer. She threw her arms around his head. Help! He was being smothered! Air, he needed air. Chantal rocked him back and forth. He was at sea!

"Vas-y, mange." Madeleine came around the bar and placed a bowl of meaty soup in front of him. Chantal let him go with such force his head bobbed back. He took a deep breath. The aroma of percolating vegetables and beef nearly knocked him over. He was rigid with fear but—food! It had been a long while since he'd eaten.

"Mensch, hast du Glück." Soldiers were lifting their beer steins and toasting him. A spoon appeared in his hand. He plunged it into the bowl. It flew from bowl to mouth, bowl to mouth.

"Vas-y, mange, mon petit soldat," said Chantal. She laid her hand over his and applied pressure, as if to say *slow down*. *"T'aime le ragoût, non?"* She was asking him a question. What

should he say? Charlie looked over at Weston.

"*Il est blessé, mademoiselle. Il est quasiment sourd. Et il ne comprende pas français.*"

"*Ah, oui. Je parle un peu l'allemand. Schmeckt dar Essen?*" And to Charlie, Chantal yelled, "*TU AIME LE RAGOÛT?*"

Charlie looked over at Weston. His pinkie moved up and down. Charlie nodded.

"*Comment un tel gosse pourrait-il être un aviateur, monsieur?*" Chantal was saying something to Weston. Still, the spoon, almost by its own self, kept coming and going from his mouth.

"*Il n'y a pas des jeunes en Allemagne, mademoiselle.*" Weston's French was perfect, Charlie could tell. "*Il y a seulement des soldats prêts à donner leur vies pour la patrie et le Kaiser.*"

"*Ah, vous les Allemands. Vous préférez combattre à faire l'amour.*"

"*Ah, mademoiselle, nous les Allemands pouvons faire toutes choses avec finesse.*"

Weston's eyes twinkled as he looked the woman up and down. What was he doing now? Was he flirting? Charlie looked into his bowl of soup. If he could have dived in and hid, he would have.

A man by the bar started a song in German.

Es braust ein Ruf wie Donnerhall,
Wie Schwertgeklirr und Wogenprall:
Zum Rhein, zum Rhein, zum deutschen Rhein,
Wer will des Stromes Hüter sein?

As the song began to ripple through the room like a wave, conversations stopped. Weston picked up his glass, held it high, stood up, and began to sing too. Soldiers lifted their glasses. Was it an anthem? Charlie couldn't understand the words!

Lieb' Vaterland, magst ruhig sein,
Fest steht und treu die Wacht am Rhein!

Charlie scrambled out of his chair and raised his beer stein, like the others. Everyone around him was belting out the song like there was no tomorrow. The words! He didn't know the words!

It was just then that Chantal's elbow came up and knocked his arm. The beer splashed against Charlie's pants like a blooming great wave! It soaked him through. Pants, under-wear—the lot!

Weston's voice grew louder, stronger. He now had one hand poised in the air like a bloody opera star!

Solang' ein Tropfen Blut noch glüht,
Noch eine Faust den Degen zieht . . .

Chantal grabbed Charlie by the hand and pulled. Almost instinctively Charlie reached down and picked up the haver-sack. More voices joined in. The officers up in the gallery, who until now had looked down upon the rabble with benevolent contempt, had jumped to their feet too. One man, a general by the look of him, was especially loud.

Und noch ein Arm die Büchse spannt,
Betritt kein Feind hier deinen Strand!

As the voices rose, Chantal yanked Charlie through the crowd. Where was she taking him? What was going on? He couldn't have escaped even if he'd had a place to go. She had a hand the size of a snow shovel.

Lieb' Vaterland, magst ruhig sein,
Fest steht und treu die Wacht am Rhein!

There wasn't a dry eye in the house.

Chantal stopped at a pair of swinging doors, the kind suited to a cowboy saloon, and Charlie turned back. What was he to do? He spotted Weston through the crowd. Weston held his glass aloft and winked at him. Then Charlie saw Madeleine whispering something into Weston's ear. She was gesturing to a table above. Charlie followed Weston's gaze. The same singing general, apparently none too stable, was waving. Weston, laughing, picked up his bottle and was making his way upstairs.

Chantal pulled Charlie's hand again. The swinging doors hit Charlie in the chest as he went in and belted him in the butt as he passed through.

"*Viens. Viens.*" Chantal gave his arm yet another mighty yank and Charlie was dragged through a bustling kitchen. Cooks were yelling at each other, great mounds of food sizzled in frying pans, heaps of potatoes, onions, and cabbages spilled out of wooden crates. Still Chantal kept marching onward, laughing off comments from the cooks and giving one young man a sharp jab in the ribs.

They stormed through the kitchen, across an old stone walkway, then through a low, small cove that might have been burrowed through rock. She came to an abrupt stop at a wooden door, banged it open, and there they were, the two of them, in a small cupboard stocked from top to bottom with bottles of all sorts—olive oils, jams, pickles. Hardly enough room to swing a cat.

Chantal struck a match and lit a lantern that dangled from above. She slammed the door shut, then turned her great breasts toward him. Her brown eyes narrowed.

"What are you doing here, English? Are you trying to get yourself killed?"

CHAPTER 27

CHANTAL TOOK A SMALL PAIR OF SCISSORS from her apron and snipped the gauze that was wrapped around Charlie's head, tidying the bandages and then tucking the ends in underneath. "It is better, no?" She stood back and examined his bandaged head and her handiwork. "So you, how you say, crack your plane, and now you think to walk home to England. *Mon Dieu*." She wrapped another bandage around his cut finger.

Charlie nodded. Telling her the truth seemed the only sensible thing to do. "How did you know?"

"Know? *Quoi?*"

"Me—English—how?"

"You could not fool a baby. Look at you. That shirt—it is the shirt of someone twice your size. And those pants! And your boots! No German soldier wears boots like that . . . You are, how you say, *lucky* that it is late and they are all drunk. Germans are not stupid. The beer, it has made you wet all through, no?"

"No. I mean, yes." He felt the blood creep up his neck. No wonder babies cried when their nappies were wet.

The door suddenly swung open and there stood Madeleine. She was younger than Chantal, but a little older than himself, maybe seventeen, thin, and her hair was light brown, like her eyes.

"Qu'est-ce qui se passe?" She looked first at Chantal and then at Charlie. *"Mon Dieu."*

"Ferme la porte."

Madeleine didn't need to be told twice. She shut the door and then looked Charlie up and down. "English," she announced.

For the first time in his life Charlie felt no need to give a short course on what it was to be a Newfoundlander.

"Où est son ami?" Chantal spoke in forced whispers.

"Ah, l'aviateur. Il est Anglais aussi?"

Whatever it was that Chantal told her, Madeleine seemed genuinely surprised. "He is," she turned to Charlie and spoke in broken English, "how you say, with the General."

"Vas-y," said Chantal, *"Écoute ce qu'ils disent."*

There were shouts from the kitchen. The waitresses had been missed. Madeleine turned on her heel and ran down the passage.

"What is your name?" Chantal, for the first time, spoke kindly.

"Charlie."

Chantal smiled. She had nut-brown hair, the kind that turns sparkly red when the sun is on it, and brown eyes. *"Mon garçon, Charlie,* you must stay *ici.* I will to find you clothes. They are much around here. A young *garçon,* like you, he died . . ."* Chantal's voice trailed off for a moment and then, just as quickly, she caught herself. "Give me the boots. I must hide them. And the clothes too. Hurry."

Did she want him to strip naked?

"Dépêchez-toi!"

Charlie gave up his boots and his shirt and then shimmied out of his pants. They slid down to his ankles. He handed them to her and stood in soggy Newfoundland Regiment gray underwear. He crossed his arms over his chest.

Chantal pointed to his underwear. "Wet, no?"

"Yes. *Oui*."

"Give to me, hurry."

He wasn't embarrassed. He'd passed that long ago. He was abashed, humiliated, mortified even. Charlie turned his back, pulled down his underwear, and passed them to her. Chantal snuffed out the lantern and left. There he was, in utter darkness, on the wrong side of the war, naked, in a cupboard. If them in Brigus could have seen him now.

CHARLIE PRESSED HIS EAR TO THE DOOR and listened to the sounds of the kitchen as he polished off a jar of something red that had been steeped in pickle juice. At least he thought it was red. Who could tell in the dark? He heard soft steps on the stone path. His body was so tense he thought he might snap in half. What if it wasn't her? How would he explain?

Chantal opened the door. She carried a potato sack. Madeleine was behind her. Charlie's hands flew down. They weren't big enough to cover all the parts he wanted to cover.

"Quick, *habille-toi*." Chantal lit the lantern and tossed him a pair of German britches, a shirt, stockings, belt, soft shoes (worse for wear), and—what were these? They looked like . . . no, it couldn't be! He couldn't wear these! They were bloody bloomers! Women's bloomers! Was there no end to this humiliation?

"Hurry," Chantal urged him.

"Le Général et l'autre Anglais, de quoi parlent-ils?" Chantal asked Madeleine.

"Avions."

"Quoi?"

What were they saying? Jeeze, if he got out of this war in one piece he'd learn to speak French, and German too. Charlie slipped the bloomers on. They were surprisingly soft, comfy in fact.

"What's going on?" Charlie hissed in Chantal's direction.

"She says that the General and your friend are, how you say, speaking aeroplanes. The General, he wants to give him one."

Give him one! A German general wanted to *give* Weston an aeroplane! "Why?"

"Deux minutes."

Chantal and Madeleine left him alone in the cupboard, presumably to give him room to put on the shoes. He didn't need room to change, he needed room to think. Charlie pulled on one boot, then the other. Just before they'd left the British aerodrome, Weston had said, "I plan to make a little detour, nothing much." Was this the detour? Had all of this been planned?

Just like that, he knew! Of course! Weston spoke perfect German, not the kind taught in school. *Perfect German*—he could tell by the way everyone reacted to him. And he spoke perfect French, too. Then there was that song. Not only had he known all the words, he'd sung it *like a German*. And he'd been in a great hurry to leave the British aerodrome while the other fliers were otherwise occupied. He'd even taken a plane with a dodgy gun. Why? And why had Weston chosen to fly over enemy territory? What had he said to that German officer back on the road? And what kind of a German general would turn over a plane to a complete stranger?

It was obvious.

Weston was a German spy.

CHAPTER 28

"*Viens*. Follow me." Chantal pressed her finger to her lips and motioned to a door on the far side of the kitchen. Charlie flipped Hans's haversack onto his back. Good ol' Hans.

The kitchen was empty when they slipped out the back. The night was still as black as pitch. Chantal and Charlie crouched behind a stack of crates.

"See, there." She pointed to an automobile that was parked a few feet away. The trunk was slightly ajar. "Get in, but no to shut. Your friend, he come out soon and they go to airfield. It is near Lomme, only thirty kilometers to Ypres. If you make it to the aeroplane, you will not be, how you say, be long for the air."

Charlie nodded. Chantal was closer to the truth than she knew.

"When the auto, she stop, you get out."

"Why are you helping me?"

Even in the dark he could see the look of surprise on her face. "The Germans must go, leave France. But, after they go, so must you British, too. France for the French."

Should he tell her that he thought Weston was a spy? What if he was wrong?

The driver was leaning against the hood of the car.

"The driver . . ."

"Driver is drunk also. No worry," whispered Chantal.

Why was that not comforting?

"Go!" She gave him a push.

"But . . ."

"Go! *Bonne chance, mon petit.*" With those words Chantal seemed to evaporate into the night. He hadn't said thank you. He hadn't said anything at all.

"Dieter! Feuer bitte," a voice called out.

Charlie, bent like a "Z," scurried over to the car. He lifted the trunk lid, rolled inside, and ever so gently lowered it again. There was nothing but a dangling bit of string to hold on to to keep the trunk from closing.

The rear car doors banged shut. The driver must have climbed in too because a third door slammed. Charlie thought he heard Weston's voice. It was hard to tell, given that the voice was speaking German, there was a bandage wrapped around his own head, and he was in the trunk of a car!

Off they went. The auto wove down the road. The red pickle stuff he had eaten in the cupboard was churning around in his stomach. He was about to lose it. And then a curve. Charlie was pitched around. Something sharp stabbed him in the back. He stifled a groan as the spy glass nearly took out a rib. The trunk lid snapped shut. He was trapped.

"Halt!" Voices. The driver of the car slammed on his brakes. There was yelling, then a jolt, and they were off again. Were they at a checkpoint?

The auto inched along for a while and then came to a standstill. Now what? He could hardly breathe. Silence from the front of the auto. There was shelling in the distance. Were they at the airfield or someplace else all together? He waited. Still nothing. A door opened, then shut.

A voice from outside. "Grunt, you in there?"

"Yes."

The trunk lock clicked open. Weston kneeled down as if he were tying his shoe. He hissed more than whispered, "Listen old bean, don't talk. We're at an airfield. The General wants me to fetch a bottle of his favorite brandy from Strasbourg. Thing is, he thinks I went to summer camp with his son. Thing is—I did."

What the hell was he talking about now? Summer camp? Strasbourg? Wait, Strasbourg was in Germany! They were going to Germany!

"The General and the driver seem to be sleeping. There's an aeroplane just off to the right. Lovely thing, a C.11 I should think. Can you hear me?"

"Yes." Get on with it, Charlie muttered to himself. What does it matter what kind of bloody plane it is?

"We've cleared two checkpoints, but this place will pop once they hear the engine turn over. When you hear it, run like hell. Got that? Just run for the plane."

"Yes."

Charlie pulled off the bandage that wrapped his head. Was Weston a spy or not? Was the General dead or had he just passed out? Were they going to Germany or not? If Weston was a spy, then Charlie had to cross back over to the British side as fast as he could. But, come to think of it, he was going to have to cross over whether he was a spy or not. Weston could have killed him by now. Why was he taking him along? If he was a spy, then what use would Charlie be to him? Maybe he needed Charlie as a cover? And there was still that thing about the detour . . .

"Weston?" Charlie whispered. He lifted the trunk lid just an inch. A sliver of light was showing in the east. He could see Weston loping toward the dawn. He stopped and stood still as if taking the lay of the land. Finally he limped toward a far building and, it was hard to see, disappeared inside!

Charlie scrambled out of the trunk and crouched down low. He should make a run for it, but in which direction? The land in front of him was as big as a playing field. He tried to peep into the car. The General was laid out on the back seat. The driver was slumped against the steering wheel.

Weston emerged from the building. He was carrying something, packages maybe? Oh no, there was another man with him. Weston lifted his hand and pointed toward the car. He was turning him in!

Charlie, crouched low, rolled away from the car and then lay flat out on the ground. The only cover available was darkness. The man turned and started to walk toward the automobile, Weston following behind him. Then suddenly Weston dropped the bundles and the man fell to the ground. Weston spun around, picked up the packages and, never mind his limp, he raced toward a plane.

The General, the driver, that fellow over there—there were bodies all over the place!

No matter what, Charlie had to get in that plane. The whirl of a propeller. The aeroplane's engine turned over. The engine roared.

It was as if a starting gun had gone off. Charlie began to run. The ground was pitted. If he fell in a pothole that would be the end of it. The shoes Chantal had given him were soft and gave a spring to his steps. The engine whined. Charlie's arms were pumping like pistons, his legs whirring like wheels. He ran faster than he had ever run in his life. Go. Go. Go. He wasn't running away from the enemy, he was running to his home. Mother, Father, Claire.

"Halt! Halt!"

The aeroplane began to pick up speed. Run. Spy or not, better to take his chances in the air than die on the spot. Run. The haversack was dragging him down but he'd have to slow down to get it off. The aeroplane pulled alongside. They were parallel now. It was about to pass him. He could see the Maltese Cross on the wings. It bounced in and out of the ruts. Slow down. He wanted to yell but there was no extra wind for words. He wouldn't make it! Slow down! There were shouts behind him. And then a rifle shot.

"Jump!" Weston screamed.

Jump onto what? How was he supposed to get on? His lungs were going to burst. The wings. If he could . . . if he could just get hold of the struts. More rifle fire.

"Jump!"

He leapt into the air and grabbed hold of the thin strut wires that bound the lower wing to the upper wing. Instantly he felt the cold metal strands slice into his hands. They were airborne, and there he was, his legs blowing in the wind like laundry on the line. Dangling, wafting in the breeze, hanging on for dear life.

Weston yelled a "Yahoo!" like a cowboy, then tipped the plane so that the wing Charlie was on was pointing up into the sky. Charlie threw one leg up, then the other. He lay flat out on the wing.

Weston leveled off and struggled with the controls. The plane tipped back and forth. Weston was trying desperately to compensate for Charlie's weight.

"Company . . . the way . . . dearie," shouted Weston. His words were mostly lost to the wind, but their welcoming meaning was clear enough.

Charlie looked down and behind. The German fliers below were racing to their planes like ants to a picnic.

"Might . . . buckle . . . in," Weston hollered.

Inching his way forward, clinging to the struts, Charlie crawled to the lip of the forward seat. The plane tipped. He went into the cockpit head first. Charlie's head was jammed between the floor and the metal seat, his legs kicked the air madly. There was a package on his seat that was taking up space.

The grunts, the groans, the sheer effort of will to turn right side up took up time that might have been spent figuring out how to use the gun mount. Finally he popped up like a groundhog on the first day of spring. Weston was yelling. Charlie couldn't understand a word of it. He heaved up the package and made ready to toss it overboard.

"Noooooo!" Weston screamed.

What? Were there bombs in the bag? Potato mashers?

"... on ... para ... now."

"What?"

"Put ... shoot ..."

Charlie shook his head. What could he shoot? It didn't matter what was in the package. It wouldn't fit inside the cockpit. It had to go.

Tack-tack-tack. The Germans were coming up from behind.

"Parachute!" Weston screamed.

Parachute? Charlie looked down at the sack with horror. Those things didn't work. If they did, surely the Brits would have had them!

"Trenches ... ahead ... Ypres ..."

Charlie looked down. Archies were going off. The air sizzled and a great bloody shell burst right in front of them, making the plane bob in all directions at once. Whose was it? Germans or Allies?

"Strap ... now!"

Charlie looked at the package in his hands. He looked down to the ground below.

Tack-tack-tack. Three aeroplanes were coming toward them.

"It's ours!" Charlie screamed, and he threw his hands up in the air. "Hey, British! British! We're British!"

Tack-tack-tack.

They were being fired on! Fired on by their own people! Charlie's head swiveled back to Weston. He wasn't there! Where had he gone? Had he jumped? Charlie looked down. Nothing. Nothing but puffballs of smoke. The unmanned plane bobbed like a skiff in a storm.

Tack-tack-tack. The Germans were on their tail and the Allies were directly in front.

"Put your bloody chute on!" Charlie looked up. Weston, prancing about on the wing, reached down and grabbed Charlie by the jacket. "Put it on." The wind unbalanced him. Weston rocked back and forth.

How? Charlie couldn't get his haversack off. "I can't . . ." His hands wrapped around the struts.

"Stand!" Weston was screaming.

Charlie scrambled up on the seat. Weston shoved the package over Charlie's arms, over the haversack, and hammered the buckle shut with his fist.

"JUMP."

"I can't!"

"JUMP!" Weston motioned to a cord. "PULL." And that was all.

Weston stepped off the wing. The plane went into a dive.

Charlie couldn't move! Nothing moved! His entire body was utterly frozen. Jump? He couldn't jump. Turned out he didn't have to. Charlie slipped and fell out of the plane.

He spun out of control. He couldn't breathe, he was suffocating. He flipped. His belly was pointing toward the ground now. The wind forced his legs and arms back. The roar of the wind in his ears turned him deaf. He was blinded with tears. Pull. Pull what? Panic. A cord lay pinned by the wind against his chest. He pulled it. The force of the chute opening jerked him back, then up. He began to swing, back and forth, side to side.

Charlie looked over and saw Weston's parachute. His face was contorted. He was screaming. And pointing. To what?

What was he pointing at? The tears rolled out of his eyes. The ground was coming at him. Closer, closer.

Charlie landed like a rock hurled onto a beach. He fell forward. Something hard rammed up against his teeth. The acid taste of blood filled his mouth. A white, billowing cloud wafted from above and nearly swamped him. There was no time, no time to catch his breath.

Charlie unhitched the parachute and rolled away from it. Then he heard the ear-piercing shrill of the shell, like a thin whistle. He flung his arms around his head. Four seconds— that's how long it took from the moment an incoming shell was heard to the moment it landed. And if it landed and you could still hear the explosion, you were alive. That was the rule. Wait for it. Then, the explosion. The earth leapt into the air and for a split second it hovered before crashing back down. Wait. If the earth didn't knock you senseless, it could still bury you alive.

Where was the shelling coming from? Behind or in front? What did it matter? Where was Weston? There was nothing to see but smoke. Charlie, his face mostly in the mud, looked around. A flare went up. Early dawn became midday. A bloody great instant sun hovered overhead, lighting everything up for a mile, revealing and exposing.

Charlie lay stone still, his face pushed down into the mud. Still, be very, very still. His body, half buried, quivered. The very blood in his veins quaked. He waited. Shots were fired wildly. The light died.

Slowly, like an animal rising from a deep sleep, Charlie peered around. He listened. He clambered forward, his belly scraping the ground. It was a cool morning but sweat dribbled down his forehead and trickled into his eyes.

He saw the parachute first. Weston lay just down from it, face up in a small, soggy shell crater. His feet dangled in a pool of water. More shots. They'd be using the chute as a marker.

Charlie lunged toward him. "Weston?" He rolled into the hole and ducked as yet another shower of earth poured down. A dead German soldier was slumped against the incline of the crater directly across from them.

"Weston, wake up."

Weston's eyes fluttered. Charlie unhitched Weston's parachute and felt for a pulse. "Weston!" Panicked, Charlie gave him a good shake.

"Get away from me." Weston pushed Charlie back. He was alive. But probably not for long. They had landed in no-man's-land.

CHAPTER 29

CHARLIE ROLLED OVER and looked up at the early-morning sky. If only he could tell how far they were from their own front lines.

"Do you know where we are?" Charlie hissed in Weston's direction.

"Ypres, I think. No telling who is on the other side. Like to think it's the British, but it may well be the Australians. Bloody awful manners, the Australians. Where are your boys?"

"Who?"

"The Newfoundlanders. Aren't they near Ypres?"

So Weston had known all along that he was a Newfoundlander.

"Yeah, they're here somewhere."

"I didn't know . . ." His voice caught in his throat. "I didn't know it was like this." Weston struggled up on one elbow and peered about him. Everything around them was dead, everything but the army of rats. Dead men, dead dogs and horses, dead land.

"From the sky it looks . . . not like this." He fell back and, for a bit, fell silent. He didn't need to say that his leg was much worse; the tightness around his mouth and the furrow of his brow said it loudly enough.

"The letter!" Weston hissed.

"What letter?"

"To Hans's mother."

"Who?"

"Surely you haven't forgotten dear departed Hans." Weston fumbled inside his uniform and pulled out the note. "Here, tuck it into that one." He passed Charlie the envelope they'd found Hans's suicide letter in and motioned to the dead German who lay a few feet away. "He's the mailbag."

Charlie held the note. "What is this?"

"I rewrote Hans's farewell note. Dickens of a time with his signature. Ripped up the original, naturally. And here," Weston yanked off Hans's medal, which still dangled from his uniform, "put this with it. Jolly nice for the mantel."

Baffled, Charlie stared down at the note. Mailbag? What did he mean?

"Are you thick? Tuck this letter into that German corpse. Go!" Weston roared, then slumped forward.

Charlie nodded. Yes, of course. It might take days or weeks, maybe months, but sooner or later this dead German soldier would be dragged back to his own lines. They'd search him. The letter would be found and sent home. Hans's mother would think that her beloved son had been shot down. Maybe she would think he'd crashed his plane and died on the battlefield. Maybe she would believe that he'd died a hero.

With his head below the crater wall, Charlie fishtailed on his belly over to a dead German, rammed the letter into his top tunic pocket, then crawled back to Weston.

"I thought that you were a spy."

Weston's laughter dissolved into a coughing fit. Another shell landed nearby.

"Why were we on the wrong side of the lines?"

"Oh, that. Spot of bother with my eyes, you see. I'm fearfully nearsighted, bit of a reach to see a foot in front of me. Thing is, I have a photographic memory, ol' bean. Very useful. Memorize everything, maps and such. Always manage to pass those infernal eye tests."

Charlie's jaw dropped. "You are a pilot and YOU CAN'T SEE?" That was it! He'd thought he'd seen and heard it all in this war, but a pilot who couldn't see? Well, why bloody not?

"What about your German? You speak perfectly."

"My mother is German. Spent every summer of my life on the Rhine. I say, in my class at Oxford alone half the fellows speak fluent German and Austrian. A few speak Italian, of course. After all, a really top-drawer education includes summer hols on the Continent! The *Grand Tour* and all that."

"The detour. You said that we were going to make a detour. Where to?"

"I say, ol' boy, is this really the place for the Grand Inquisition?" Shells were peeling off all around them.

"WHY DID WE MAKE A DETOUR?" Charlie could feel his nostrils flare, his eyes pop, and his face redden. "TELL ME WHY."

"To see my mother."

"Your . . ." He could barely say it. He could barely think it.

"Oh, do get a grip. Mama lives just to the east of Dover, in England. It's just across from Calais. There's a bit of a sticky wicket with the neighbors at the moment. Father kicked the bucket, you see, a dicky heart. So she's on her own, ol' boy. Thing is, she's a German. It's not her fault, of course, but the Brits are rather hard on Germans these days. Heard a Brit kicked a schnauzer to death in London. Imagine that! Do you think the dog knew he was a German?" His breathing was labored and his words were punctuated with winces and groans.

Charlie rested his head against the incline of the crater. He was tired, very tired.

"Might you have a mother, ol' boy?" Weston continued.

"Yeah."

"She's worried about you, I should think."

"Yeah."

"I do believe mothers worry because they think that if they don't, something bad will happen."

This time they didn't even hear it. A shell landed. They were tossed into the air like dust. Charlie went one way, Weston the other.

Charlie's back was broken. It *had* to be. Nothing could hurt that badly without being broken. The pain caused his eyes to tear up. He moved. No, not broken.

Weston was a good few yards off. Hand over hand Charlie crawled back to him. Mud clogged his nostrils and nearly blinded him. When Charlie reached him, he saw that his arm lay at a peculiar angle from his body and blood was dribbling out of his mouth. His eyes were big and blank.

"Weston!" Charlie felt his neck for a pulse. Nothing, he could feel nothing. He rested his head against Weston's chest.

"I'm sorry. I'm sorry. You had every right to see your mother. We all do. And you're right, I do have a mother. I miss her too. There's nothing wrong in that. Every man here would do anything just to see his mother's face again. Oh God."

Weston blinked. He lifted his head and spat out a wad of blood. His two front teeth went with it. "Sorry about that, ol' bean. Gave you a scare, did I?"

"You . . ."

Weston smiled.

"That's it. That's bloody it! You son of a . . ."

Charlie stopped. He listened. English voices, off in the distance.

Weston heard them too. "Get undressed." He grunted, then tried to move his arm.

"What?"

"You think we're going to get a warm welcome wearing German uniforms?" Weston groaned. His arm dangled in his sleeve.

Charlie squirmed out of his own jacket and ignored Weston entirely. If he wanted help he could bloody well go ask a Hun.

"You can't keep that haversack. It's German." Weston gritted his teeth.

Charlie looked at the battered haversack. It was stupid, really, superstitious rot, but after all this . . . if he lost the spy glass, he knew he'd lose his life. Charlie reached into the haversack, pulled out the glass, and tucked it under his arm.

Weston tried to unbutton his jacket.

"Oh, let me help."

Weston moaned as Charlie eased the arm out of the sleeve and unbuttoned the top buttons of Weston's pants. "You can take off your own damn pants," hissed Charlie as he pulled off his own.

"Hang on. What's this?" Weston peered down at Charlie's bottom half and, in spite of his pain, began to laugh. Charlie followed his glance. The bloomers. Damn.

With the white bloomers flapping madly about his legs, Charlie climbed out of the crater. Weston's broken arm and damaged foot were on the same side, so Charlie slung Weston's good arm over his shoulder and pulled Weston along with him. Charlie winced once, twice, and then cried out. The pain in his back rocketed about his body. They took refuge behind dead soldiers and rotting horse carcasses. Fear now seemed to numb the pain in his back.

More shells. With a heave, Charlie rolled into another water-filled crater, with Weston right behind him. It was already occupied by three British corpses. Rats were making quick work of them. A shell went off just above them. Charlie grabbed one helmet and pitched a second to Weston. He picked up a Lee Enfield. Wearing bloomers and a helmet and carrying a rifle, Charlie once again crawled out of a crater and began calling out as he approached the friendly barbed wire— if any barbed wire could be said to be friendly.

There were empty saps all over the place, ditches used for observation and grenade-throwing. They weren't far now. *Moaning Minnies* were pummeling away. Dawn had arrived, but the light was splintered by the smoke. They were mere yards away from their own barbed wire.

Shots.

"Newfoundland!" Charlie cried out. More shots. A shell landed and a hunk of rock smashed into the back of Charlie's head. He fell forward.

"Get down," Weston screamed. The two rolled into yet another sap. "This isn't going to work," he hissed in Charlie's ear. "I'm done. You'll have to do the last bit on your own, ol' boy. Take off your bloomers."

"What?"

"We need a white flag. Take off those bloomers."

"No." Jeeze, no. He'd die bare-assed naked!

"Give me those bloody bloomers! That's an order!"

Charlie, his head pulsating with pain, peeled off what was left of his dignity and flung them over. Weston stabbed the bloomers with the bayonet and waved them in the air.

"British! We're British."

"Speak for your bloody self," Charlie muttered.

"Go!" Again he waved the bloomers in the air.

Hand over hand, crawling on his belly, his eyes and mouth caked with dirt, Charlie approached the line. Soldiers making their way through a hole in the barbed wire trained their rifles on him. Their bayonets glittered in the morning light. Somebody yelled. Behind him Weston waved the white flag frantically. Charlie, one hand clutching the spy glass, the other pulling him along, threw himself through the opening. The wire cut into him like a thousand shards of glass.

"Newfoundland!" he sobbed as he pushed the spy glass ahead of him.

"What's the password?" called a voice.

Password? He didn't know any bloody password, but that was a Newfoundland voice, he was sure of it.

"Newfoundland . . . independent forever!" Charlie yelled as loudly as he could.

"Stop! Stop!"

Charlie heard screaming. The soldier, with a caribou blazing on the collar of his tunic, threw himself over Charlie. "Stop!" Who was yelling that? Weston? Someone else?

Charlie felt himself being lifted, then flung into the trench. A voice whispered. "Take it easy, boy."

Charlie looked up.

"Charlie-boy, that you? Don't ya ever wear clothes?" Phil grinned.

CHAPTER 30

CHARLIE LOOKED OVER AT CLAIRE, who was gazing into the clouds, as though trying to picture him up there.

"Do you want me to stop? Are you cold?" He spoke softly, as if the tone of his voice could cushion the horror of it all.

Claire seemed visibly shaken by the interruption of the story, as if jolted out of a deep sleep too quickly.

"What? No, no. Keep going," she whispered, without taking her eyes off the white, billowing clouds above. Yet part of her did want him to stop because, as she well knew, the worst was yet to come.

He studied her profile, then took a deep breath.

"I remember waking up in a dugout."

CHARLIE ROLLED OVER IN HIS COT. He couldn't sleep. At best, he closed his eyes and lost consciousness for a while. And then, *boom*. Just like that. A shell landed, rattling a tin of cake that rested on a shelf above Charlie's cot. Now that would be something—killed by a tin of flying cake!

He turned over again, and groaned—his back! Charlie stared up at the roof of fluted tin and tried to piece together the last few hours . . . not that he could remember much. The cuts on his skin itched and there was more than one bump on his head. He'd been patched up by a field medic, that he was sure of. And there had been a bunch of questions from a Canadian officer: "Who is he?" "Why wasn't he in uniform?" "The Boche have been known to give themselves up, to come scurrying across no-man's-land to surrender. Is he German?" "Where are his clothes?"

Phil was there, speaking up for him. But he was a private, not a commissioned officer and gentleman. Nothing he said mattered. They sent Private Jackson packing.

Charlie repeated his own name over and over. Why wouldn't they listen? He was exhausted. Could he have something to drink? A glass of water? A cup of tea? He was a Newfoundlander. What did he care who the prime minister of Canada was? It was Robert Borden. Didn't they know their own prime minister's name? Who is the prime minister of Newfoundland, then? There is no prime minister. There is a *governor,* and his name is Sir Walter Davidson.

No one knew if Charlie was right or not. Someone sent a soldier out to find a Newfoundland officer. Idiots. He had to sleep. His back. His head. The cuts.

He repeated, "Talk to Dr. Robert Daniels. He'll vouch for me." He said it again and again, over and over and over. Dr. Daniels would set things right.

A Newfoundland officer entered. "What's the name of the governor of Newfoundland?" "I already answered that question. It's Sir Walter Davidson." "How do you make brewis?" "Put hard tack in to soak. Cook the cod. Mix the cod and hard tack." "When is fishing season?" "Sealing—March and April. May—setting the potatoes and putting in the gardens. June— herring. July and August for the cod."

"Dr. Daniels." He was pleading now. "Talk to him. Ask him if he knows me." Charlie's legs were quivering with fatigue.

Someone said something. He felt pain, like a sharp blow to his stomach. Had he been hit? That was all he could recall before passing out.

CHARLIE REACHED FOR A CANTEEN and splashed water on his face. He looked around the dugout. The walls were covered with rolls of dimpled tin decorated with pinups of girls from some French magazines. A German spiked Pickelhaube helmet was hung up beside a more modern German coal-scuttle helmet—trophies collected from no-man's-land. And there was his spy glass. Old friend. He reached over and ran his hand over the dented and tarnished surface.

In the middle of the dugout, flanked by three other cots, stood a scarred wooden desk with a lantern on top. A small coke brazier squatted in another corner. The place stank of paraffin, tobacco, and damp mud. It was hard to think. His body ached and his head throbbed. He was missing some-thing. Something was wrong.

"Charlie, you in here?" Phil stuck his head through the canvas door and cast a quick scun about the place. Dugouts were for officers. He'd had his fill of them for the minute. Didn't the brass make him feel like a barnacle—sending him away like that when ol' Charlie needed him most.

"Yeah, come in." Charlie struggled to sit up. For reasons Charlie couldn't explain, he felt discouraged seeing Phil. He reached up to grab hold of a rickety table beside the cot. Jeeze, that stung some. Gauze was wrapped around both hands. It made it a mite hard to scratch himself, and them cuts sure were scratchy.

Phil flipped back the canvas door. "Good to see you, ah, dressed!" He grinned. He propped his rifle against the wall and flung himself onto a cot. "Lap of luxury! The rat's ass, I'd say." As if on cue a startled rat darted out from under the cot, turned, and gave Phil a nasty look. "Cheeky beggar." He gave it a boot. Missed. "It's freezing in here. Why don't you turn that on?" He motioned to the stove.

"Rather die of the cold than be suffocated by that stench," muttered Charlie as he swung his legs over the side of the cot. The wire that held the cot together jabbed him in the back of his leg. Charlie grimaced. He was done up in an old greatcoat. Two bony white legs dangled out from the bottom and two mittened hands hung out of his sleeves. Jeeze, what a sight, and well he knew it!

"Your British friend, what's his name?"

"Weston."

"Right. It's Blighty for him by the look of that arm and foot."

"I want to see him." Charlie did his level best to stand. He hoisted himself up, wobbled for a bit, then thumped back down on the cot.

"Too late for that. I saw him being carried off."

Gone, just like that.

Phil lit a cigarette. "Say, it was a hell of an adventure you were on. Going down the line like a keg of rum."

Charlie shrugged. Naked boy comes in out of no-man's-land, that was sure to get around. Jeeze.

"It was you, then, who pulled me in?"

"Didn't recognize you 'til the last. It was that spy glass of yours that did it. Saw it shining out like a blinkin' lighthouse beacon. Not too many of them things about the place. You were pushing it ahead of yourself. I saw it afore I saw you. Don't you remember?"

Charlie shook his head. But there was something he did remember, come to think on it. At that moment, it had felt as though his father had been right there with him. Reaching out, protecting him somehow. "Look here, Charlie-boy, seems this pal of yours called you a hero. The brass knows you're here. There's likely going to be a dustup. They'll pack you off home is my guess."

Home. Mother holding the front door open, smiling. A warm bath. Clean socks and hankies in his top drawer. Father sitting in the parlor with a book in hand. Claire telling him off about something. And Jim, even now he could picture his best friend's face curled up in laughter. Then there was the feel of soft sand under bare feet. The look of the waves as they lapped up on Bishop Beach's rocky shore. Charlie sat back. Ouch. The cuts on his backside burned something fierce. Wouldn't it make Robert Daniels happy! After all this he'd be sent home by the army! Charlie chuckled. Maybe it was time to go home after all.

"Last I saw of you, you were on your way to Blighty," Charlie said to Phil as he scratched every place his gauze-covered hands could reach.

"They fixed me up and sent me back. Been up the line for a couple of weeks now. But I don't have much time, and I have something to tell you—about Helena." Phil leaned forward, his elbows on his knees. He had a sheepish look about him. "We're engaged, Charlie." The smile on his face went from ear to ear.

Charlie's mouth dropped open.

"And it's all thanks to you. I know that you didn't think me good enough for her. I knew all along that she didn't have a fella. And then, when you gave me her letter way back when I was in the hospital, I figured you'd changed your mind some. I thank you for that.

"Helena fixed it so that she was my nurse in London. That took some doing, I can tell you. And there was lots of dodging around after that. They should make those head nurses generals. We'd all be out of here a lot quicker." Phil snubbed out the butt. "We were together all these months, every day I was in England. She's an angel, Charlie, I can tell you straight. Then, toward the end, just before I was reassigned, I got a few days' leave and we went up to Scotland to see her old auntie. A hard woman, that one. Can't think what it must have been like to be a young one with only that sour old trout about the place. We weren't there half an hour before she had Helena working like a Trojan. Do this, do that, says the ol' bat. I took my Helena right out of there. Spent a packet, but it was the grandest few days of my life."

Phil was babbling like a fool, or maybe, thought Charlie, like a man in love.

"Thing is, I wants you to know that I'll take good care of her, Charlie. I wills that. I promise you. I know you two are great friends. Can you think of a prettier girl than my Helena? Them eyes, like . . . like . . ."

Like chocolate, Charlie thought, but he said nothing.

"The minute I saw her I knew she was the only girl for me. I love her and she loves me. I've put in what they call a *request to marry*. I'm going home to Brigus and I'm taking my wife with me. You'll stand up for me, won't you? Be my best man? It would mean a lot to Helena. Me too, of course." Phil pinked up a bit. "We just got to get home, the three of us I mean. I'll get myself a fishing boat. She's a girl born to the sea, just like us. It's what she wants, and it's little enough." Phil laughed. "I'd do anything for her, anything."

"Congratulations, Phil." Oddly enough, Charlie meant it. Helena was a grand girl, and she'd suit Brigus, too. But he was tired. He was more tired than he'd ever been in his life. Charlie yawned, couldn't help himself. Phil hadn't mentioned Clint. There would be some heck to pay there, but it was a lifetime away.

"I'll leave ya, then. The Regiment is moving up the line." Phil lifted the dugout flap, then turned back and spoke over his shoulder. "And Charlie, I'm that sorry about the Doc. I know you were close. Helena told me all about him. She was a friend of his too, you know, and a great pal of his wife's. Lily, ain't it?"

The air went out of Charlie's lungs. He was suspended in that moment between hearing and understanding. "What do you mean?" He found himself upright. He heard a voice yelling. It was his voice.

"Ah, Charlie-boy." Phil's face dropped along with his eyes. "They told me that you knew. I asked one of them and he said that you was told. I'm that sorry." Phil looked in pain himself. Charlie wasn't aware of any feeling. Nothing. "I didn't want to be the one ta tells you. I thought, when I saw you lying here like this, that you was taking it pretty well."

Charlie, his face frozen, only stared ahead.

"Your Dr. Daniels, he was hit, Charlie. It was a bomb from an aeroplane raid. The whole operating room went up. Everyone inside was killed."

Charlie slumped forward. "No . . ."

"Ah, Charlie-boy, I'm sorry." Phil moved toward him and rested a hand on the shoulder of the boy who was too shocked to cry and too hurt to move.

CHAPTER 31

IT WAS 1918. The war was four years old and the end was nowhere in sight. Some said—even the prime minister of Canada—that it would go on into the twenties. Most agreed that the end would come when neither side had any more young men. They had a name for it—they called it a war of attrition.

The Newfoundland Regiment had been at rest for a few weeks near Boulogne, on the coast across from England. Then, on October 13, with the band playing "Will Ye No Come Back Again" and a motley collection of locals cheering, Charlie and the Regiment boarded a train. The next eight hours were spent on the train, followed by a few hours' marching before clambering back on a train, only to get off again and arrive on foot in the driving rain at Hellfire Corner—past Westhoek. It was past Polygon Wood and a stone's throw from Ypres.

"Not long now, Charlie." Captain Mark Daw, a good man and a teacher once, flipped back the oily canvas flap of the aid post and ducked his head as he entered. As usual, the post was a dugout in the reserve trench. And as usual it was little more than a hole scraped into the earth and supported by beams of wood. Rough shelves ran up the sides and a makeshift hospital examining table stood in the middle.

"You all set?" Captain Daw eyed the stocked shelves, the neatly rolled bandages, the kits loaded and ready. Young Charlie ran a tight ship. Daw knew right enough that Charlie was a volunteer, that he ought not to have been there, but the lads trusted and spoke up for him, especially Tom Alcock, best stretcher-bearer in the army. Tom had spent his share of time holding a gun, but he was no good at it. Captain Daw saw Tom's other talent. Tom could sniff out the wounded like a Newfoundland dog. And he was short. Short soldiers lived longer in the trenches. Daw had made Tom a permanent stretcher-bearer, which, despite the added danger, was to Tom's liking.

Charlie nodded. "We're low on morphine. I sent Tom for more."

Captain Daw looked Charlie up and down. He was a tall lad. Still, there wasn't much to him, not enough meat on him to feed himself, is what his wife would have said. But the boy was as strong as a horse and no shirker.

"Good man. I'll leave you to it." The Captain left Charlie to his work.

"Hey, Charlie-boy." Phil poked his head into the post and grinned. "Got a minute?"

"No." Charlie grinned back.

Phil propped his rifle up against a wall and flung his helmet onto the makeshift operating table. "I got a letter from my mother. Go on, read it. There's a bit about your family in there too." Phil passed it over.

My dearest Philip,

The winter is coming on quick and the boats are putting in. Brigus is not the place it once was. Not with so many lost to war and the loss of the Southern Cross still so much in our minds.

I pray for you every hour, my son, for you are all I have left in this world. Lucy Wilcox and I read your last letter over and over. Lucy is always on the lookout for word from Charlie. She tells me that his last letter said he is doing a little work in a hospital. She says that he cannot be specific about which hospital he is in because of the censors, but it is good to know that he is out of harm's way. We all miss our sons, but I do believe losing her boy so young, and so unexpectedly, to the war has been especially hard on her.

I have news of that friend of Charlie's, the one who was married to Dr. Robert Daniels. Wasn't it a terrible thing, him dying like that. This war has a great deal to answer for. Lucy told me that his young widow, Lily I think they call her, is to attend McGill University in Montreal, Canada. I don't really know what to think. Woman in university—it doesn't sound quite proper. Her mother-in-law, who was dead set against it, is quite changed after the death of her son. Now the three of them (there is a young child called Charlotte I do believe) are all living near the University. The war is changing our world in so many unexpected ways.

Charlie thumped down on a three-legged stool and smiled. Good for Lily.

"Read this bit." Phil pointed to the back of the page.

I'm sorry to say that your cousin Bryan has got a girl in the family way. The shame of it, Philip, to bring a child into this world on the wrong side of the blanket. What that poor child must bear for the sins of its parents. It's never right to have a child out of wedlock.

Charlie looked up and stared blankly at Phil.

"My mother is right and proper. Thing is . . ." Phil dithered. "We met, Helena and me, when the Regiment was on rest. She got posted on one of the ferries carrying the wounded across the Channel. It's a story, I can tell ya. But the long and the short of it is," Phil looked pained, "Helena's going to have a baby. Ach, Charlie, I've got to put it right. It's not that I'm sorry, I'm not. I love Helena and I love this baby, even if it's not born yet. And I'm going to make a good father. The best, I tell you."

Phil's face angered up. He meant every word, Charlie could see that right enough. War changed men, most for the worse, but Phil had changed for the better.

"I have to get back to England, Charlie. Tout sweet!"

"What do you mean? You're not talking . . ." Charlie couldn't even say the word *desertion*. Soldiers of all stripes were shot for desertion.

"No, nothing like that. There's a raid on tonight. Anyone who brings back a Boche gets a week's pass to Blighty."

"Phil, no. What's the sense in taking a chance?"

"Sure you haven't been listening there, Charlie-boy. The bullets meant for me missed. They won't get me. Besides, you know what happens to babies of unmarried mothers? They end up in orphanages. There's thousands of them, right now, babies of soldiers, abandoned. You mind the story Miss Rabbitt read to us in school? *Oliver Twist* it was called, by that fellow Dickens. No child of mine is going to end up like Oliver Twist."

"Helena wouldn't abandon her baby." Charlie was sure of that.

"Maybe not, but I saw where she comes from. That ol' aunt of hers has a witch's heart, I tell you. Black as a prune. She'll make Helena's life a misery, and that baby's, too. No, I got to get back there, Charlie. I got to set things right. See here," Phil reached into his pocket and pulled out a crumpled envelope, "this just came. It's our permission to get married." He opened a smaller envelope, poured a gold band onto his palm, and looked at it fondly. "Bought it from a tinker. It's real gold, though. I want you to keep them safe for me."

A cold shiver went up Charlie's spine. He backed up until the operating table would let him go no farther.

"No, you said yourself that you'll be fine."

"Come on, Charlie-boy. Take 'em." Phil thrust them into Charlie's hand. "I'll be back tomorrow morning with a German in tow and a ticket to Blighty. This time next week, I'll be a married man." The pleading look on Phil's face vanished, and in its place was the happy-go-lucky smirk.

Charlie looked down at the two envelopes. He walked over to his haversack and pulled out his spy glass. The broken glass inside rattled as he struggled to twist off the eyepiece. There was a sucking sound, then a pop as the eyepiece came off in his hand. He emptied the broken glass into a bucket, twisted the envelopes into cones, and slipped them into the spy glass.

"They'll be safe in here until you come for them, Phil."

"No fear, Charlie-boy. It will all work out for the best. Just you wait and see. It will all work out."

CHAPTER 32

"ATTENTION!"

Charlie froze. The command came from outside the dugout. Bloody hell.

"At ease, men." A British Commanding Officer, fresh from the cricket field by the look of him, parted the canvas door to Charlie's aid post with his silver-topped ash swagger stick. Captain Daw was hot on the CO's heels.

"Is everything in order?" The CO tapped his stick against his thigh. Seldom did a CO visit the trenches. If it was an honor, no one looked thrilled.

"Just putting in for a few more medical supplies, sir," said Captain Daw. He looked uncomfortable, and with good reason.

Charlie tried to make himself as inconspicuous as possible, not an easy job in a small space, particularly since the CO's stomach was taking up most of it.

"Very good." The CO took a step out of the dugout then abruptly reeled around and peered at Charlie.

"Who are you, and what kind of uniform is that?"

Charlie's tattered wool Newfoundland tunic instantly began to itch. Aside from the caribou badge, his only insignia was a Red Cross band over his right arm.

"I . . ." Charlie could feel the blood drain from his face.

"Sir!" The Captain came to full attention. "This is Charlie Wilcox—a, a volunteer," he stammered.

"A bloody what?"

"He's the best medic we have, sir. Trained by Dr. Robert Daniels himself. Sir."

"I have no idea who Dr. Robert Daniels is." The CO looked Charlie up and down.

"Dr. Daniels was a field doctor we had, sir. He was killed a year ago at—"

The CO waved his stick. "A volunteer, you say? Since when do we have volunteers manning aid posts? How old are you?"

"Seventeen, sir." Charlie too stood at attention.

"Are you telling me, Captain, that on the eve of a major battle we have a seventeen-year-old *volunteer* manning a Regimental Aid Post?"

"Yes, sir." The Captain went the color of cement while the CO took on the look of a boiled fish. He huffed, he coughed, and when he took a breath, his cheeks flared like gills.

A shell landed close enough to send boulders of all sizes hurling through the air and down into the trench. The dugout quivered, then imploded, sending the CO careening into a wall. He slid, then thumped, down onto the dugout floor. Sludge oozed up through the duckboards and seeped into his pants. He cursed a storm.

"Sir!" Captain Daw offered his hand to the CO.

Again a shell landed, and another after that. The roll of tin that was used to shore up the mud wall curled and fell like away like old wallpaper.

The CO struggled to his feet. Pushing away Captain Daw's extended hand, he steadied himself against the dugout wall. A strip of barbed wire sticking through a gap in the tin wall tore into his kid leather glove and bit into his palm. Nasty stuff. Bits of wire were always popping out of the mud, shredding uniforms and skin as well as gloves.

"Bloody hell," he muttered.

"I'll look at that, sir." Charlie reached for the wounded hand. He cleaned and bandaged it, all to a chorus of the CO's profanity.

"Here's the morphine, Charlie." Good old Tom, with a cigarette dangling out of his mouth like a wet noodle, came bursting into the aid post carrying a small box. He rammed right into the CO's stomach.

"Oh, sorry, sir." Tom leapt back and spouted out his lit cigarette. Behind him was Johnny, a townie from St. John's. The CO looked from the medic, to the Captain, to Charlie, ignoring Johnny entirely.

"That's enough!" The CO took back his wounded hand. "So you can bandage a hand. So can my wife, but I wouldn't want her running an aid post. Willox, or whatever your name is, you are hereby relieved of aid post duties. Although that presumes that you were officially assigned to them in the first place. Captain, I'll see you in my office tomorrow at 800 hours."

"B-b-but, sir!" The Captain stuttered and went pale. In less than ten hours he would be leading men over the top. "We are in need—"

"You, the one with the pants on fire." The CO pointed to Tom.

Oh, oh, his cigarette! It had landed in a crease of his trousers! Oh Jeeze, oh Jeeze! Tom thumped his thigh.

"Take over the aid post."

"Me, sir? I'm a stretcher-bearer. I don't know nearly anything as much about running an aid post as Charlie here."

"What about you?" He pointed to Johnny, a big, slow-witted fellow, too stupid even to know that he was stupid.

"Yes, sir. I can manage, sir." Johnny saluted, then tried to hide his smirk. Finally, his chance! He'd been in the trenches for months, and the whole point of coming to this filthy war in the first place had been to prove to his father that he was smart enough to take over the shop on Waters Street. (His father owned a haberdashery, the best in St. John's.)

"And you . . ." The CO turned back to Charlie. "This isn't a game for you to play-act in. Either you are a soldier or you're not. Our backs are against the wall—all the more reason to keep up standards!"

The CO stalked away. The back of his pants, which hung down to his knees, was plastered with black goo. In fact he bore a startling resemblance to a portly baby with a loaded nappie.

Captain Daw sighed. "Well, Charlie-boy, time to clear out." Maybe it was for the best. Daw had two teenage sons of his own at home, both itching to join up. He couldn't count the letters he had sent his wife telling her to keep the boys home, tie them down if she had to. Please God, may his own sons never see a day of this war.

"I don't think so, sir," said Charlie.

"What do you mean?" Captain Daw, lost in thought, came back to himself in a hurry. "You don't expect me to go against the CO's orders, do you? I haven't lived this long just to get court-martialed."

"No, sir. The CO told me that I was relieved of aid post duties. Tom and I, we're a team. We used to—"

"Sir. Fire trench is collapsing. Corporal wants you to come up." A soldier, flustered and holding the receiver of a field telephone, ducked into the aid post.

"Sir—" Charlie tried to get the Captain's attention.

"Don't split hairs, Charlie. Make yourself scarce. We'll talk about this later." And with that, the Captain left.

While dim Johnny surveyed his new kingdom, perusing the morphine and fondling the bandages, pretending that they were men's hats, shirts, and button covers, Charlie pulled the straps of a medic kit over his head and hoisted his haversack onto his shoulders.

"Come on," he said to Tom.

They fell back into step as if no time had passed, Tom in the lead, Charlie holding up the back of the stretcher. It was like old times. But one thing had changed, Charlie had grown a good deal in the last year. He had to remember to keep his head down when he was moving through the trenches.

Four stretcher-bearers would die that night, but Charlie and Tom emerged unscathed. They worked through the night, scuttling like rats in a maze of trenches. They scrambled over a parapet, out into no-man's-land, quick as cats, darting, listening, noses up, heads down, ears tuned to a particular sound—calls for help, like wind's whispers on the open sea. It took a trained ear to hear the muted cries amid the thunder of the battle. Charlie and Tom knew whom to save, which of the wounded would make it, whom to make as comfortable as possible. Little time was lost.

"Down!" Tom had heard the sizzle of a flare going up. He and Charlie dove into a shallow sap. Tom twisted in the air and managed to land face up. All around them shapes, hardly men at all, hit the ground and lay dead still, waiting for the flare to die.

"It's a magnificent thing, is it not?" Tom laughed as he looked up into the sky. "God mocks in mysterious ways, eh Charlie?"

"Over there." Charlie pointed to something moving in the mud. Heads down, noses up, they moved forward.

"Have the raiders come back yet?" Charlie yelled to a gunner as he heaved himself over a parapet and slid into the fire trench.

The mostly deaf gunner cupped his hand over his ear. "Ah?"

"I'm looking for Phil Jackson. Red-headed guy."

"Ah?

"Bunch went out on a raid. Are they back?" Charlie yelled again. "RAID—BACK?"

The gunner shook his head.

The night wore on. Twice Tom and Charlie made it down the lines as far as the aid post. Johnny was having a terrible time.

"Just tell me what to do?" he pleaded with Charlie. He was a sight, all bulgy-eyed and panting like a cornered dog.

"Sort them. Make room. Send them on." Charlie knelt down and felt a soldier's pulse. "This one is dead. Get him out of here."

It took twenty minutes to clear out the aid post, and then Tom and Charlie were back up the line. In the forward trench they shared a can of bully beef. In the communication trench they swallowed something foul that passed for tea.

"It's a shite box I'm after, Charlie-boy," said Tom as he made his way down the reserve trench. "Better not be full. I'm not dumping it. That fella Burns got himself killed emptying it. Helluva thing, to die holding a shite box."

Charlie did his business against a wall. The sky was lightening up. The collection of the wounded was almost over for the night. Charlie, exhausted, sank down on his haunches and fell into a dreamless sleep.

"CHARLIE, WAKE UP." Tom nudged him.

"What?"

"Wake up."

"What time is it?"

"Coming on to six I should think."

Charlie looked up to a sliver of sky. Living in a trench was like living in a Cracker Jack box, narrow, deep, and dark. A wall in front, a wall in back, a gunmetal sky above. Charlie eased himself up and rubbed his hands together, then examined them for cuts.

"Where you been?"

"I just talked to Captain Daw."

Charlie tensed. His eyes grew wide.

"No, I didn't tell him I was with you, and he had the good sense not to ask. You wanted to know about the raiders. Only one came back. It wasn't your friend. I hear that they are all dead, no wounded, no prisoners. Sorry."

Charlie nodded. He'd known all along that Phil was dead. Maybe he'd known from the moment he'd accepted the two envelopes.

Charlie collected his haversack. "I'm leaving."

"What?"

"I'm leaving," he repeated.

"Good lad. Save yourself. Get out with your skin."

CHAPTER 33

"I WANT TO ENLIST." Charlie stood at attention in front of the CO's desk.

The CO's fishy face hung down over his chest like a bib. It had been a long night and a longer day awaited. "And how do you plan to go about that?" The CO didn't seem surprised; he didn't seem much of anything.

"I hear that there is an enlistment office in Calais, sir."

"What age are you?"

"Seventeen, sir."

"Enlistment age is nineteen."

Of course Charlie knew that. But he also knew that there were plenty of soldiers who had lied about their age and signed up. Recruiters were turning a blind eye to all sorts of things.

"I've asked around about you. Wilcox, isn't it? You have quite the reputation. Seems you run around on a whim doing whatever the hell you like."

"No, sir . . . I—"

"Heard you were in a plane crash."

"Yes, sir."

"Landed in enemy territory."

"Yes, sir."

"Flew across no-man's-land to get back."

"Yes, sir, but—"

"Had one of those parachute-things on. Floated home, did ya?"

"No. Yes . . . I mean—"

"They wanted to send you home but you disappeared. Just ran off. Hiding out, were you?"

"Yes, sir, I—"

"Seems you like to play doctor."

"No, sir."

"How long have you been skulking about in the trenches like a rat?"

Charlie sputtered. What did it matter? He wanted to join up, and they were desperately short of men. Besides, what had this old man been doing all these years? Sitting back and waving his blooming ash stick like a baton, directing young men to their deaths? Charlie held his tongue.

"What do you have to say for yourself? Speak up. There's no future in modesty, boy. Other than arresting you, which would seem like a waste of my time, what is it you want from me?"

"Travel papers, sir." Charlie took a deep breath. Here came the hard part. "And, I'd like a note from you requesting that I be assigned to an aid post."

The CO stood, clasped his hands behind his back, and rocked on his heels. He gazed up at a portrait of George V that hung on the wall behind his desk, while Charlie, not knowing what else to do, looked at a framed photograph of a young man, in uniform, on the CO's desk. The boy in the photograph had dark hair, a face like one of those angels in those paintings—all chubby, pink cheeks, and a shy smile. He looked like a schoolboy and wore the same insignia as the Commander. A black ribbon was wound around the top of the picture—the boy was dead.

"Tell me, Wilcox, do you think that you will make a good soldier?" The CO spoke to the portrait of George V.

"Yes, sir."

"What was that?"

"Yes, sir." Louder.

"Are you courageous?"

"Yes, sir." If courage was struggling to keep others alive, if courage was putting the lives of others before his own, if courage was loyalty—then yes, he was courageous. Once he had doubted himself, but not anymore.

"A courageous man lives up to his responsibilities, follows orders. Tell me, Wilcox," the CO circled the desk and looked at Charlie with sad, swollen eyes, "will you always follow orders?"

"Yes, sir."

"Even if the orders are wrong?"

"Sir?" Charlie looked at the picture of the boy, then up at the CO. Could it be that the boy had been under his own father's command?

"You see, Wilcox, good soldiers follow orders, *especially* if the orders are wrong."

CHARLIE LEFT THE CO'S OFFICE, hoisted his haversack onto his shoulders, and headed toward Calais. His travel papers and a recommendation from the CO burned a hole in his pocket.

CHAPTER 34

THE GUNS WERE BOOMING, the shelling was constant but a ways off. It was a fair, fall day in early November 1918.

Charlie boarded a train at Poperinge. It moved with the speed and grace of a mop. He slept in fields, wolfed down cans of bully beef and sardines, bathed in a bone-chillingly cold river, and carried on. He passed through small, mostly deserted villages. Vacant lots, where homes used to be, stood out like gaps in teeth. Homeless people shuffled about, unsure of where to go. With kits bouncing off their arses, fresh troops clomped past.

It was here, on a road heading to Calais, that Charlie spotted him in a company of soldiers. They were taking a break by the side of the road. He was lying with his face turned up to the sun like a boy on a beach without a care in the world.

"Hank! Hank Boil!"

Hank looked up, startled at first. Then his whole face cracked into a broad grin.

"It's you! Charlie Wilcox, the idiot from Brigus." Hank leapt to his feet and whacked Charlie on the back. Hugged him, too.

Charlie hugged him back. It was good to see him. "What are you doing *here*? You're a medic!"

"No, I'm a regular now, Charlie-boy." Hank grinned again.

"Oh Jeeze, Hank, what did you do to him?"

"Ol' Pisspot! Got him good. I had a friend at Headquarters get me some of that letterhead, paper like, from the head office of the Regiment. Real official stuff! Got hold of one of those typewriter things and made us up a letter saying he was going to get court-martialed. Busted him to private, too. Should have seen his face when he got it." Hank hooted and slapped his knee. "'Course it all came out in the end, the truth I mean. But I tell ya, it was worth it!" Hank laughed heartily.

"Stand to." The Sergeant rallied the men. The soldiers groaned as they scrambled up and collected their kits.

"Off to fight the Boche. Charlie-boy, you take care of yourself." Hank laughed again. Everything about him was full of fun, hopeful. Charlie would remember that grin forever.

THE NEXT DAY, coming on to afternoon, Charlie arrived in the port town of Calais.

"Cup of tea, please, and two buns." He spoke to a cheery young woman who stood behind a portable YMCA canteen. She smiled, revealing large buck teeth, and handed him the sweet buns and a cup of tea. He peered into the cup. Everything was khaki-colored, even the tea.

Calais was awash in khaki. Soldiers, hundreds of them, hung about the streets. The great buildings were ornate and stately, but still the town had the seedy air of a port. A bunch of soldiers on leave staggered out of a bar. They were laughing and punching each other like boys at play.

On the next street, heads bobbed behind a curtain that ran a good many yards down the cobblestone road. Behind it soldiers showered. They were assisted by stout, dour old women who might just as easily have been dipping filthy sheep as washing young men. There was an extra charge to have your clothes laundered, pounded against washboards with a bar of soap. Young girls, bony and gaunt for lack of food, hung the men's skivvies and drawers up to dry. They ignored the naked boys. There was nothing these young soldiers had that their brothers hadn't, and seen one naked backside, seen 'em all.

Against a far wall, soldiers sat on folding wooden chairs, their bare toes extended. A medic jogged down the line sprinkling powder over their feet while the soldiers joked about, read week-old newspapers, and puffed on stubby cigarettes. Charlie, taking it all in, took a seat on a stone wall and munched on his bun.

A small dog, a poodle perhaps, its matted fur hanging in hanks off its wasted body, barked and danced for scraps.

"Hey fella." Charlie looked down at its big, pleading eyes then gave it a pat. "Good dog," he said as he flung the animal a bit of his bun.

"Hello! I say, hello!"

Charlie looked around at nothing in particular.

"Are you rude, stupid, blind, or all three?"

A woman in a VAD uniform jumped out from behind the wheel of an ambulance and strode across the brick-paved square in long, purposeful strides. She had the look of a modern woman about her, confident and cheerful. Her smile revealed uneven teeth.

"I know you. I never forget a face. You are Helena's friend, the one she took care of instead of coming on leave to Paris. I'm still mad about that. I shouldn't be talking to you at all." She feigned a pout.

"Pardon?" Charlie jumped off the wall. What on earth was she talking about?

"Hmm, good manners, too. No wonder Helena thought you were tops."

Charlie felt as though he had picked up a storybook halfway through. "I don't . . ."

"You don't remember me, do you? I guess I don't make a lasting impression. My name is Grace Fester. You can call me Gracie. Helena introduced us. Don't just stand there, say something."

"Hello. I'm Charlie Wilcox."

"Aren't you the clever one. You know your name and everything. What are you doing here? Not signing up, are you?" The idea sent Gracie into peals of laughter. She really was rather pretty.

"Yes," said Charlie. What should he do with his sticky bun? Should he just set it down? He couldn't continue eating it, not in front of a lady.

Gracie stopped laughing so abruptly that her mouth stayed curled up in a laugh as her eyes grew into astonished circles. "You are joking? You are not serious?"

"Yes." Should he put the bun in his pocket? No, that would make a mess.

Gracie paused, looked Charlie up and down, and then, in a low, slow drawl, said, "This calls for a celebration. How would you like to buy a girl a drink?"

"A drink?" She might as well have suggested a leap off the Eiffel Tower. "I don't drink."

"Dear Charlie, a man signing up to go to war should have a drink or two. Come along."

She plucked his bun and cup out of his hands, tossed them aside, and looped her arm in his. In a half-drag, half-push, she marched him down the road. They passed shops with notices written in English that read "Beer, Chips, Eggs." Other signs said "Washing Done Here for Soldiers."

The estaminet Gracie chose was on the street level of a stone building in the middle of the busy square. Tables and spindly black metal chairs spilled out of its open doors onto the street.

"Come on." Her elbow jabbed him in the back and propelled him forward.

The bar smelled of sour wine and grease, and the farther back they went, the dimmer it got. At the very back of the bar a potted soldier was spewing tall tales to an equally drunk collection of soldiers.

"Bloody biggest shell hole you ever saw. Filled with mud." His arms sliced the air like windmills. "Lost a tank in it, the whole bloomin' tank!"

There were other soldiers too, some eating great mounds of eggs and mashed potatoes, others poised in front of bottles, quiet-like, deep in thought. One soldier, slumped over the table, clutched a bottle for dear life. He looked asleep.

"Madame, un cognac," Gracie called out to a woman behind the bar. The woman nodded.

The soldier's voice rose. "It was this big, I tell you!"

"What's it matter how big it is?" yelled another. "Trouble with this war is there are too many dead men. Clog up everything. And ever see dead men run? They're slow! Where's the wine? *Madame! Madame!* More wine."

"Shut up. I can't hear myself drink." The groggy soldier lifted his head for a moment, then let it thump back down.

"Let's sit outside, Charlie." Again, Gracie tugged his arm.

"I really don't drink. I mean, I have never—"

"Now Charlie, here you are about to sign your life away. We have to celebrate!" Gracie chose one of the tables on the sidewalk.

"Voilà!" The owner of the bar banged a large bottle of cognac, plus two dirty glasses, down on the table. *"Cinq francs."*

Gracie busied herself with pouring two generous portions of gold liquid into the two spotty tumblers.

"Cinq francs." The owner glared at Charlie.

"Oh, yes, *oui.*" Charlie reached deep into his pocket and pulled out a few precious coins and bills. He only had twenty francs to his name, plus five precious pound notes sent from his parents. He handed over the coins.

"To your continued good health and long life." Gracie hoisted her glass and grinned. "Come on, can't have a toast unless we're all in. Lift your glass there, Charlie-boy. Chin-chin."

Charlie lifted his glass and took a sip. It was disgusting stuff, something his mother might have forced down his throat when he was sick.

"Bottoms up!" Gracie hooted. Charlie looked at her glass. It was empty. "Got to keep up!" Gracie slammed her glass down on the table.

Charlie squeezed his eye shut and belted back the alcohol. It dribbled down his throat like glue. The town clock bonged on the half hour. He needed to find the registration office before closing time. Best to drink this stuff and be on his way.

"There's a good man." Gracie filled his glass yet again.

"No, no thank you," he stammered.

"The first rule of good soldiering is to know how to hold your drink. Consider this your first lesson. Down the hatch. Now tell me, why do you want to sign up? Some say the war is almost over."

"Some say it will go on for years yet." The gold liquid was settling in his stomach quite nicely. He was feeling rather warm, come to think of it, very warm indeed. "Why did *you* sign up?" he asked politely as Gracie refilled his glass yet again.

"Oh, the adventure of it all I suppose. There's not much for a girl to do in Vancouver except get married. But even that might not be an option much longer, not with all the would-be husbands pushing up poppies. Just shows you the lengths some boys will go to to avoid marriage. Drinkie, drinkie!"

"Did you find adventure?" He sipped his third glass. The world was taking on a golden hue.

"Goodness no. It turns out that I'm really here to mop up. This war is either pathetically sad or a thumb-twiddling, bloom-ing bore! Never mind, have another." She refilled Charlie's glass.

"No, no. I've had enough." He was feeling very, very . . . the world was doing funny things! It was going very, very . . .

"Nonsense. The bottle isn't empty yet."

"Gracie, what on earth are you doing?"

Another voice. Charlie looked up. A woman, dressed in a VAD uniform, stood beside Gracie. She seemed angry. Now why would she be angry on a nice day like this?

"Oh, Armine, meet a friend of mine, actually a friend of Helena's. This is Charlie Wilcox. You remember her telling us about him. *Underage.*"

She said the last bit out the corner of her mouth. Now what was that about?

He knew he should stand when being introduced to a lady. He tried. What was wrong with his legs? They were rubbery. He shook his head as though he were trying to empty it.

"Gracie, he's dead drunk."

Now this lady . . . what was her name? Armine, yes, that was it. Armine sounded annoyed. She shouldn't have been annoyed. She should have been happy. Happy, happy, happy.

"The point is, he is not dead. And he's not drunk enough, either. Not yet anyway. Come on, Charlie. Here's to the King, God bless him."

"The King!" Charlie held his glass aloft.

"Gracie, I don't know what you're playing at but if the Commander sees you, you'll be out this time for sure. You've had two warnings already." Armine's voice had taken on a pleading quality. It was plain that the two women were good friends. It was also plain that where Gracie went, trouble followed.

"Do you know what he wants to do? Sign up! Over my dead body." Gracie sounded fierce. Now why did she sound like that?

"No one would take any notice of an extra dead body about the place. What are you planning to do with him? And . . . ohhh!" Armine lifted her foot and looked at the bottom of her shoe. "There's something sticky on the ground."

"Sorry, that's where I was pouring out my cognac. Dreadful stuff. Don't know how anyone stomachs it. Come on, Charlie, drink!"

Who were they talking about? Charlie could make out their words but not their meaning.

"Look at the soldiers we can't save. Sure, we can shift them about, but for what? So they can die in one place instead of another? This one . . ." Gracie pointed at Charlie and Charlie smiled back at her, "this one is *not* going to war."

"What are you going to do with him?" Armine flopped down on a chair.

"How do you do?" Charlie smiled at Armine. She ignored him, so he turned his attention to the road in front of them. Now this was interesting. Charlie hadn't noticed this before, but if you looked at an ambulance in a certain way, head on, and then if you tilted your head just so, it looked like it was smiling!

Charlie studied the auto, and as he did his eyes drifted to a figure standing across the road. He looked familiar. Not only did the man stand out because he wasn't in uniform, he was noticeable because of the *way* he was standing—stiffly, as though there was something wrong with his legs. A large, black envelope was under his arm, the sort of thing an artist would carry. What was that thing called? Portfolio, that was it. Charlie began to rise out of the chair. Could it be?

"Davy!" Charlie yelled. His foot caught on the leg of the chair and spun out from under him. "Davy!"

The man across the street seemed to turn toward him just as a line of lorries passed between them. Charlie stumbled forward, falling over the chair.

"Easy, boy." Gracie leapt up and reached for him.

"Oh for heaven's sake!" Armine grabbed his arm.

"That man, he's a friend. Davy!" Charlie yelled as he tried to stand. "He has no legs. From St. John's. It's him!" Now Charlie fell face first onto the cobblestoned road. Blood instantly gushed from his nose.

"You have a friend with no legs who can walk! Armine, give us a hand." Gracie picked up Charlie's arm and tossed it over her shoulder.

"Where is he? Davy!" Gone. He was gone. Where did he go?

"Come on, sit back down."

He felt a chair under his butt. Was it him? Had that been Davy? Charlie wallowed in his chair. He didn't seem to notice the blood dripping from his nose.

"Good. Now stay still while we figure out what to do with you," muttered Gracie.

"What do you mean *we*?" snapped Armine.

"*We* are going to wrap him up and ship him out. We have an ambulance." Gracie pointed to the McLaughlin Buick parked on the roadside. "The next hospital ship to London leaves in an hour. He's going to be on it. We'll address him directly to Helena. When he wakes up, he can listen to Big Ben."

"But he's not wounded!"

"We have bandages, don't we? Look at this, we even have fresh blood." Gracie pointed to the river of blood that was now running down his chin. "I think he should have a head wound. Pass me my medic bag."

CHAPTER 35

"My head," Charlie groaned. It was falling off. Surely a head couldn't hurt that much and still be attached to a body. Water, he needed water.

He tried to sit. His head banged against something. "Ohhh." He groaned, and fell back. His stomach was quaking. He was going to be sick. Wait, his whole body was quaking! He was moving. Not just his stomach, but all of him.

"My head," he whispered.

"Not to worry, my son. Someone will look at that head injury after we have crossed the Channel. You'll be in a proper hospital before you know it."

Charlie opened his eyes. Channel, what Channel? What head injury? He reached up and felt the gauze around his head. Had he been shot in the head? He must have been. It ached so.

"Water," he whispered. He looked up at the man and noticed his collar.

The priest held a cup to his lips. "Bless you, my son. You'll be fine now."

"Ohhh." Talking hurt his head. Listening hurt his head.

"I can see you are in great pain, my son. Rest assured, God is watching."

"Where am I?"

"On a ship bound for England, my son."

England? Ship? The priest moved away.

"Wait!" Charlie peered out of his upper bunk. Bunk! He felt the floor before he'd even realized he was falling. He heard his bones break from the inside. His collar bone cracked, his shoulder popped out of its socket, and his arm snapped. A searing pain shot through his body.

Shouts. Someone lifted him. He screamed. The pain. Let him die. Everything faded to black. Then someone far, far away called for morphine. He felt the prick of the needle, a gentle hand on his brow, heard hushed, comforting words and then, nothing.

"CHARLIE."

The voice was familiar. This had happened before. The same voice. The same feeling of being pulled back from the beyond, of nightmares evaporating before memory had stored them, of deep oceans and bottomless wells. He awoke and looked into chocolate-brown eyes.

"Ohh!" The pain hit with all the grace of a hurtling rock. "Helena," he whispered.

"Charlie, listen to me. Don't move," she whispered in an urgent, pleading voice. "You are safe, but you've broken your arm and shoulder. It seems that you fell out of a bunk. They gave you quite a lot of morphine on the boat because they had no way of setting the bones. Charlie, bonny boy, can you hear me?"

"How?" He opened his eyes—oh, even his eyelids hurt—and spied his arm strung up to a web of bars.

Helena fussed about his bed. "Quiet now. You're in London—in a ward for soldiers. I didn't know what else to do with you. Hush now, pretend that you've lost your memory. Here comes the head nurse."

"I see our new patient has returned to the land of the living." She squinted at Charlie. "Who are you?" She had a pinched, beaky bird look about her.

Charlie tried to catch Helena's eye. What was going on? How had he arrived here? He'd been in France having a drink with—what was her name? Grace. And then what?

"Did you break your tongue, too? Come on, boy, your ID disks are missing, and where is your uniform?"

When in doubt, say nothing.

"He arrived in army-issue pajamas, Matron. I think he's still disoriented." Helena offered up the explanation in a plaintive voice.

Army-issue pajamas! Why were people always stripping him naked when he wasn't looking?

Matron snorted. "I don't care what he's broken, we can't have patients about the place who have no names. This is an army hospital. If he doesn't remember who he is in a few hours, call Headquarters and see if he's a deserter. If not, he's a freeloader." Matron stopped suddenly and peered at Helena. "Should you not be off duty, sister?"

"Yes, ma'am. I just thought I'd tend to this patient."

"Very well. But either he remembers who he is and where he is from, or out he goes." Matron went trundling down the ward, full of purpose.

Charlie touched his head. The bandage was gone.

"I removed your headgear," giggled Helena. "It was a very professional bandaging job, but you were lucky that no one checked you."

Lucky? What was she talking about? He didn't feel the least bit lucky. He didn't want to be there! He didn't even know where he was! What had she said, London? He looked around. Soldiers on both sides of the room lay in single metal beds, each one covered in a gray blanket. Long windows anchored the ward at one end. The walls were painted stale red on the bottom and white on the top. Why was it that the decor of hospital wards seemed to conspire to keep people sad and sick?

"How did I get here?" Charlie whispered.

"Gracie put you on the boat. She wired me and I went down to the harbor and claimed you like the post."

"Gracie?" The memory came rolling back. Cognac. As God was his witness he wouldn't touch liquor ever again.

Helena's brow knitted and her voice grew serious.

"Gracie's wire seemed coded. It said, 'Not to sign up.' What did she mean?"

"I was planning on joining up."

"Why, Charlie?" Helena was near breathless. "You're underage."

"Because . . ." He stopped. She didn't know yet about Phil's death. How could she know? How could he tell her? "Helena," his voice was raspy, "my haversack, is it here?"

"Charlie Wilcox, the war may be won or lost but I swear you will always be toting around a sack." Helena laughed as she dragged it out from under a small table beside his bed. "Here. It was propped on top of you down on the wharf. I must say, the two of you looked rather silly."

"Give me my spy glass."

Helena reached in the bag and pulled out the long, tarnished, and dented brass glass. It hardly looked like a spy glass anymore, just a long, spotty tube.

"It's badly damaged."

"It broke a long time ago. Help me get the eyepiece off of it."

Charlie tucked it tight under his good arm while Helena pulled. The eyepiece popped off in her hand. He tipped it upside down and out fell the small envelope. Getting the second envelope out, the one that contained the marriage permission form, took a little longer.

Helena reached for the small envelope, opened it, and let the ring roll out into her open palm. She didn't cry, she didn't even blink.

"When?"

"A few nights ago. He didn't come back from a raid." Charlie reached out for her. "Phil loved you, and he loved the baby, too."

Helena grabbed hold of Charlie's iron bed frame to steady herself.

"Sister, are you all right?" Matron made another appearance. Why was it that head nurses always popped up when you least wanted them to?

"Yes, ma'am." Helena, her head high, slipped the envelope into her pocket while Charlie tucked the second one under his blanket.

"What's wrong with you? You look quite pale."

"Nothing . . . Sorry, ma'am. I mean to say . . . this young man has recovered his memory." Helena took a deep breath, squared her shoulders, and spoke plainly and directly.

"His name is Private Philip Jackson of the Royal Newfoundland Regiment."

Charlie gasped but held his tongue.

"Well, Private Jackson, your memory has come back just in time. I was about to oust you."

She was pleased by the revelation. There was enough paperwork to do without having to deal with a patient who had no name. Besides, this young man looked a little suspicious, and he seemed quite young. But they all looked young. The less she knew about them personally the better. This war had become exceedingly tiresome.

"Helena," Charlie whispered while keeping his eyes on the head nurse's back as she walked away. "I won't leave you. I'll stay and help any way I can."

"Yes, I believe that you would. Come now, Private Jackson, let's get you well and home where you belong." Helena plumped his pillow.

"Here." He passed her the second envelope, the one that contained the marriage permission form, and Helena slipped it into her pocket. "What are you going to do?"

"Me? I'll have to pick up sticks, won't I? It's back to Scotland for me, eventually."

"But your aunt, will she . . . ?" He could hardly ask.

"Will she accept a wee one? My auntie's a hard case, but she doesn't care a fig for what others think. She'll give me a roof over my head, and the baby's, too. No more than that, mind. We'll earn our keep, you can be sure."

"But what about Phil's mother? I could tell her—"

"No!" The word near exploded out of Helena's mouth. Even the mummy in the next bed jumped.

Helena's hand trembled. She couldn't break down, not here. She had taught herself not to cry many, many years ago. She had lost her parents, her brother, the man she loved, and now her future was bleak. She'd be the mother of an illegitimate child. She'd be shunned by neighbors and friends alike. She dared not start crying now, she might never stop.

"Charlie, what would it be to tarnish a son's name in his mother's eyes? She has lost her only son, her only child! She has no husband. How could I bring shame to her? No one wants a fallen woman, and a grandchild born out of wedlock, about the house. So, what good would it do? Promise me, Charlie. Promise me that you won't tell her?" She clenched her hands tightly as if trying to hold herself together.

This was wrong. He knew it. He felt it.

Helena's brown eyes filled with tears, but they didn't fall. She was fighting, fighting as hard as she could, to hold them back.

"Oh, Helena." Charlie ran his hand through his hair.

"Promise."

"I promise." What else could he say?

"Right then. I'll be back tomorrow, Charlie." And with measured strides, Helena walked down the aisle and out of the ward.

CHAPTER 36

Noise, noise, noise. The mummy in the bed beside Charlie's had been replaced by a man who spoke in riddles and continually flicked his fingers. He was blind and he hadn't much of a face left—no nose at all.

"Clack, clack, clack," he cried as he took in deep breaths like gulps of water. As he inhaled, his chest rattled like broken teacups; when he exhaled, he whizzed like a steam engine. "Clack, clack, clack," he cried. "Clack, clack, clack." Over and over, day and night. No one got much sleep, and the patience of the patients was in short supply.

"What's wrong with him?" Charlie had to ask.

"He's not for this ward, but there's no room upstairs just yet." Helena tucked a blanket around Charlie's feet. She was referring to the mental ward.

"He's a Canadian from Winnipeg, gassed at Bourlon Wood.

"Clack, clack, clack," he cried again.

"They used clackers in the trenches, children's toys, to warn for gas," said Helena. "That's what he's doing, I think. Warning us about the gas. He's trying to keep us all safe. Now, how about a sponge bath for my favorite patient?"

"Oh, Jeeze . . ."

A young nurse came racing down the aisle. "It's over! The war is over! Listen!"

She flung open the glass doors at the end of the room. Nurses appeared out of thin air. They came flying down the ward with veils flapping and skirts swaying, twittering and screeching like birds on a wharf.

"Come and see. The whole of London has taken to the streets!"

Patients who might otherwise have been moved with great caution were flung, or flung themselves, into wheelchairs. The rest hurled their arms around each other. Charlie looked down the ward. A dozen or so wounded men, most propped up on crutches or canes, had now gathered around the great, long windows. The nurses beside them laughed and smiled, hugged, kissed. A few soldiers cried. Church bells rang and cannons went off.

"Clack, clack, clack." The nineteen-year-old soldier in the next bed carried on, warning others about the gas that was coming toward them. "Clack, clack, clack." He pulled his imaginary gas mask down over his imaginary nose.

"What's the date?" asked Charlie.

"November 11, 1918," someone replied.

It was over. And no one was asking "Why?" in case someone dared say, "It was all for nothing."

HIS CAST CAME OFF, and the naked limb was shockingly white and puny.

"Very nice," sniffed the doctor. "It will take time to get your strength back, and it will be a little tender, but you'll have full use of your arm and shoulder as time goes on. I must say, they were bad breaks." And with that he shuffled on to the next patient.

Helena helped Charlie on with his shirt. "I have a surprise for you." She was starting to look heavy now; it would not be long before everyone knew.

"I spoke to the Harbormaster again. He'll take you on, room and board and all, until you can get a passage home. It won't be easy—there's many a soldier left stranded in this country. But you'll have a roof over your head and you'll be getting paid work on the docks. There is a ship captained by a man named Tripp expected in the early spring. The ship is bound for St. John's. He knows your father, Charlie!" A smile a mile wide broke out over her face. For a moment Helena was all teeth and eyes. "Won't ya be pleased?"

"Yes, sure, it's just a surprise, that's all."

"You'll find that all surprises are a little tart in the middle. I'm off to Scotland today." She gave his hand a squeeze.

"It's all over then, just like that?"

"Aye, just like that."

CHAPTER 37

NEWFOUNDLAND, 1919

A SHIP WAS PUTTING INTO HARBOR. Charlie and Claire could see it right enough, snug as they were in a dip in the hillside.

"It looks like Bartlett's *Morrissey*," said Claire as she turned to look at him. "Charlie, are you all right?" She touched his arm.

"Just like that," he whispered. "All those men dead, and then it was over and we were all to come home and pick up where we'd left off. Except there's a great hole in the middle where an entire generation used to be." Charlie's eyes followed a ship skimming across the water. "I used to ask soldiers, 'Why'd ya sign up? Why'd ya come?' They'd tell me it was for God, or King, or country, or to get away from home, or for the adventure of it all. That may be why they came but that's not why they kept on fighting. They fought for each other, for the man beside, in front, behind. And that's why I stayed too, for the fellows around me. It's hard to explain and it's harder to understand, but that's the truth of it."

Charlie leaned back against the hill and it seemed natural enough for Claire to rest her head against his shoulder.

"What happened to them?"

"Who?"

"Martin, to begin with, the one you helped get into an ambulance. Tom Alcock, the stretcher-bearer, and Hank Boil, the medic in the hospital. And Weston. I liked him in the end."

"Martin was sent back to England, then home. I heard that he's up Corner Brook way. Married now, baby and all. Hank was killed that November, just a few days before the end of the war. Don't know what became of Tom. It happens like that. One day you'd give up your life for a fellow and then next day it's over and that's that.

"As for Weston, he mentioned a town where his mother lived, near Dover in England, so he wasn't hard to find. Helena sent him a letter for me. He wrote back and told us that the brass found out he was as blind as a bat. He couldn't figure out how it happened. 'Course, it might have had something to do with the letter Helena and I sent to Headquarters telling them so." Charlie threw his head back and laughed. "The brass might not have cared much about their pilots, but they sure did care about their aeroplanes. They gave him a medal. The locals in his village likely had nothing more to say about his mother being German. He tried to join the army after that but they didn't want him either on account of his bad arm and leg.

"He sent me an atlas. It must have arrived some time back because it was in my bedroom when I got home. He wrote in the inside, *'To my African friend. Carpe diem, quam minimum credula postero.'* Not sure if that's how it's pronounced, mind."

"What does that mean?" asked Claire.

"It's Latin. It means, 'Seize the day, trust as little as possible in tomorrow,' or something like that."

"Something changed, didn't it, about how you feel about Germans? You don't seem to hate them anymore." Claire spoke gently.

Charlie shrugged. "It was the war I hated, not the enemy. Besides, my mother once said that hate is a heavy burden to carry."

"Clint hates, and it's got him all twisted up inside."

"One person picks on another. Then the other gathers together a few pals and they fight back. Then before you know it, there's a war. Once I thought that when people saw how destructive war was, they would stop. But that's not true. You know what I think? I think that now we know how destructive war can be, we'll just do it again, and again. Nothing will change."

"There are some things we can change." Claire bolted up. "What about Helena and the baby?"

"I expect she's up in Scotland now. She'll be fine."

"But she won't be happy."

"No."

"And Philip's baby—it won't be happy either."

"No."

"And Mrs. Jackson is all alone."

"Yes."

"And *she's* not happy."

"No."

"Charlie!"

"What?" He turned and looked at her.

"Crap demon."

"You mean *carpe diem*?"

"Seize the day, that's what I mean. Remember what Dr. Daniels said? He said that any good we can find in this war, any at all, is a small victory. If you can't change the past, change the future. Go and tell Mrs. Jackson that she's not alone. That she has a daughter-in-law, that she'll soon have a grandchild. Tell her, Charlie."

"But Phil and Helena were never married. And I read the letter that Mrs. Jackson sent Phil, about a baby being born out of wedlock. She's dead set against it."

"Oh cripes. People change. Phil changed, didn't he? Who cares, and who's to know if they were married or not?"

"But I promised."

"Were you born thick or did it just happen to ya? You were wrong to promise, and Helena was wrong to make you. People need the chance to change. And if Mrs. Jackson won't accept Helena because she and Phil weren't properly married, then so be it. You tried. That's got to count for something, doesn't it? Tell her, Charlie. Make one thing come out right."

Claire stood up and reached down for him. "Come on!"

What if he made Mrs. Jackson feel worse? But she was already miserable. Phil had wanted him to stand up for him at his wedding. Maybe he could still be his best man.

Charlie took hold of Claire's outstretched hands, leapt to his feet, and, without a thought, he kissed her, quick-like. Right on the mouth.

Claire touched her lips. "Charlie?" But he was off.

Claire, who had no breath to spare, could hardly take in what had just happened. He had kissed her, and he hardly seemed to notice!

"Wait for me!"

"Not in those shoes," Charlie laughed over his shoulder.

"Oh bother."

CHAPTER 38

CHARLIE SCRAMBLED DOWN the hill then set off at a run. In the distance he could hear the *ping* of Mr. Pinkstone's hammer, shoeing a horse most likely. And there were sounds coming from the dock. Shouts from ship to shore, waves slapping against rocks, snipes and gulls screaming. Home, he was home. He turned his head every which-way, trying to take it all in. And then, bam!

"There ya be, Charlie, my son. Not looking where yer going I can see." Mr. Lambe, the butcher, stood solid as a post in the middle of the road. He was round, fat, kind, and older than Moses.

Jeeze, the wind was near knocked out of Charlie entirely. He mumbled an apology while trying to catch his breath.

"Oh never you mind, my boy. Oh my, oh my, it was a fine feed your mother put on, a fine feed. Tasted some sweet. It was a grand adventure you was on, then, Charlie-boy. What's after happening? Tells me all about it. Not that ya missed much here, I be telling you. Not a'tall. Fishing down on the Labrador, good swoiling last year, but them old boats, then, Charlie. Worn out. Good to see our old steel ships come home

239

from the war. And what was you up to? Mucking about in those nasty trenches I'll wonder. Mind, you didn't miss all that much. Good fishing down the Labrador."

"Yes, Mr. Lambe. Maybe I could . . . later?"

"Now, I minds the time my dear father came back from the war. It was the Crimea War, minds, my father being English and all. 'Course, my mother's a born Newfoundlander, no fear on that score I be tellin' ya. What's this I hears about mud, Charlie? Nasty stuff. Can't be a gentleman and have mud on your britches."

Charlie edged forward. If he could just get around him.

"I minds my dear father saying—"

"Mr. Lambe, I would love to hear about your father. Perhaps I could come by tomorrow?"

"Would you now? Would you really? Well, that would be fine, Charlie. I'll have the missus cook us up some brewis. I bets ya missed that! Bets ya can't get enough of it."

Charlie nodded. "Goodbye then." He set out again. He made a turn to head down North Road.

"Alone, are you? Aren't you afraid to be out by yourself?"

Clint. Jeeze, the road might as well have been mined! All that was missing were a few shells popping off.

"I'm in a hurry, Clint." Charlie attempted to sidestep him.

"And what would you be hurrying off to, soldier-boy?" He gave Charlie a sharp jab to the shoulder, and Charlie cringed.

"So, the soldier-boy got wounded? How did you hurts your arm? What great story do you have for us all, then, Charlie-boy? Did you fight off the Huns with your bare hands? Maybe you took on a whole regiment, huh? *Bang, bang.*" Clint threw a few sucker punches.

"If you must know, I fell out of bed. Now get out of my way."

The information left Clint speechless. "You what?"

"You heard me. Now hear this, too." Charlie planted his feet hard on the dirt road and faced Clint square. "It's over, Clint. Over. You're too old for this and so am I. I am sorry you had a rough go of it but it's not my fault."

"What do you know about me and mine?" Clint's eyes grew narrow and dark. His lips and fists curled.

"I know that your father beat you. No one should beat a kid. But I didn't do it. You can carry the past with you and let it burden you down, or you can get on with it. It's up to you. Let this be the end of it, Clint. It's over."

Charlie stepped around him.

"Yeah? It's over when I says it's over, Wilcox. And it's not over." He reached out and grabbed the back of Charlie's shirt.

That was it. That was enough. Charlie, lean, tough, with at least one good arm, wheeled around, hauled back, closed his eyes, shot out his fist and, and then . . . nothing! His fist didn't hit anything! It went out, and Clint went down. How? There was Clint, on the ground. Flat out. Dead?

"How could you?" Emma stood above them with a rage in her that could have set fire to a stone. Her braid, usually wound into a bun, swung back and forth with such speed that it would take the head off ya. She waved a bit of paper in the air.

"Did you . . . ?" Charlie could hardly put it together. "Did you just knock him out?"

"What? Let him kill ya—when I wants to kill ya myself?"

Emma came closer. Jeeze, she could have spit nails, of that Charlie was dead certain. He scrambled away on all fours.

"Emma, I don't know why you're mad but . . ." He looked down at Clint. He was still out cold. "But don't hit me!"

"Hit you? I'm not going to hit you. I'm going to strangle you. You're bait for the cod! How coulds you not tell me?" Again she rattled the paper. Was it a letter or a telegram? Surely this couldn't have been the telegram telling them that Murphy was missing in action. They would have got that ages ago. What was it?

"Read it." She flung it in his face. "It came on the same boat that brought you!"

My darling Emma,

Who in their right mind would call Emma a darling? Charlie scanned the letter. There, in the second paragraph.

I have spent these last many months in a hospital in Scotland. I've been near drowned in tea and biscuits. The hospital I am in is in a castle called Glamis. I am the only Newfoundlander here, this place being a recovering hospital for the British. There's a few others here like myself, with no identification and no memory. Thing is, I'm coming back to myself.

Murphy was alive! He could hardly take it in. Charlie stared at the page.

A young girl who they call "the Imp" runs messages for us all and will post this for me today. She's a lovely wee thing, all curls and laughs, puts me in mind of you as a youngster.

Farther down the page, his own named leapt out at him.

Have you heard tell about Charlie Wilcox? Did he make it home? I was out by myself, you see, in a place called no-man's-land, only Charlie was there. Can't say how exactly. But I heard him right enough. It was just his voice, calling out to me, what kept me alive.

Emma snatched back the letter and once again waved it over her head. "You knew! All this time you knew he was alive and didn't let on. When I get through with you you'll wish the Germans got ya." She made ready to attack. Oh, Jeeze, he knew the look.

"Now Emma," Charlie backed up, near stumbling over passed-out Clint in the process, "I didn't know! I really didn't. Think about it. Why would I keep this from you?" He could outrun her. "Besides, would Murphy want you to kill me? I wouldn't think so."

Emma lunged forward. Charlie turned on his heels and ran right across the road and behind the houses. He hit Mrs. Tucker's laundry line straight on and near strangled.

He leapt over Mrs. Harvey's back wall and almost tumbled Mrs. Weeks's tilt altogether.

"Charlie Wilcox, that you?" Mrs. Weeks came to the back door of her summer kitchen and waved. Wasn't it nice having him home again? Such a nice boy. She waved harder.

Charlie kept on. Clutching his sides, and breathing so hard it hurt, he rounded the corner and collapsed onto Mrs. Jackson's front gallery. Emma was nowhere in sight. His lungs ached. It was going to be awfully hard to dodge her until Murphy came home, especially since she worked in his own house! "Come home quickly, Murphy," Charlie implored.

"Glory be, Charlie. What's after happening, and who be you talking to?" Mrs. Jackson peered through the screen door and stared down at Charlie.

"I have to tell you something, something about Philip and Helena." Charlie scrambled to his feet.

"Come." Mrs. Jackson held the door open.

CHAPTER 39

Mrs. Jackson flew out of the house. Tears streamed down her face and she didn't care who saw them. Clutched in her hand was Helena's address. She was making for the telegraph office, running with the fleetness of foot of a woman half her age. She had a daughter-in-law, and God help the poor soul who said different. And soon she would have a grandchild. Maybe she was a grandmother right this minute! They would come here, if they were willing. And they'd have a good life, a grand life.

"Please let her come," she whispered as she ran. And, "Thank you, God, for giving them to me."

Charlie sat down on the steps of the gallery and watched Mrs. Jackson charge off in one direction as Claire came hobbling down the road in the other.

"Was it the right thing to do?" She stood awkwardly in the road, looking down at Charlie.

"Yes."

"My heel came off." She held up her shoe.

"I can see that." But he wasn't looking at her shoe.

Dr. Daniels had once said that Lily was the love of his life. Well, if it was true that each was born for the other, then

Claire was the love of *his* life, and there wasn't much he could do about it. He could no more get away from the hold she had on his heart than he could escape the tug his country and this village had on his soul.

"What did you do to Clint? He's staggering all over the place. Says you've got a punch that's inhuman. He says that you must have learned it from the Germans." Claire put one hand on Charlie's shoulder, and, teetering on one leg, she slipped her foot back into her heel-less shoe.

"It wasn't me."

"If you didn't, who did?"

"Emma."

"Emma!"

Charlie stood and looked into Claire's eyes. *Carpe diem.* He put his arms around her waist, enclosing her. One hand went to the small of her back and gently he pulled her forward.

"Charlie?" For a fleeting second she looked startled. When he had left they had been the same height, and now he towered above her. Her breath was short and her heart beat so hard she was sure he would hear it. Slowly, he lowered his lips onto hers, then stopped.

"You're supposed to close your eyes."

"Will you be here when I open them?"

"Close your eyes." He laughed, but softly. Then he kissed her. It was soft, and it took a very long time. It was true, what they said, about cliffs and falling in love. Once you stepped off, there was no going back.

"You're here, to stay?" Claire whispered between kisses. He

kissed her again—her lips, her cheeks, her nose. "Say that you won't leave again."

He didn't answer her.

It came in a flash. The thought rose up and washed over her like a rogue wave. Claire wrenched back her head and stared up into his blue, blue eyes.

"You *are* going away again. I can hear you thinking."

"Yes, but—"

"Oh, oh!" She stepped back and wrapped her arms around her stomach as if she'd been punched. "Where to? The ice? Are you planning to sign on with Captain Bartlett?" Tears, angry and hard, filled her eyes. No, not after all this time. Years and years of waiting for him. Years of worry. They had said that she was too young to know her own mind, too young to know her destiny, but they'd been wrong. She had always known that they were meant for each other, always.

"Just let me explain. I promise—"

"Are you or are you not planning to go away?"

"Yes, but I promised—"

"Promised?" Claire spun around and bit back tears. No! She wouldn't let him break her heart. Don't cry. Don't cry. Then she twirled around, riveted her hands to her hips, pursed her lips together and spouted, "You can . . . you can . . . you can put it where the monkey puts his nuts. *That's* what you can do!"

With her head held high, she turned and tried her damnedest to storm away, although the best she could manage was a furious hobble. Damn those shoes! Damn everything!

"Claire, just give me a minute to explain. Claire!" Monkey? Nuts? What could she have meant by that?

"Having troubles?" Skipper Sam, with a parcel tucked under his arm, stood down the road a bit and tried not to smile.

"Just a few," said Charlie. "Where do you suppose a monkey puts his nuts?"

"His what?"

"Nuts."

"In his cheeks, I expect." Skipper Sam nodded toward Claire, who was hip-hopping down the road. "She puts me in mind of your mother at that age."

"I don't think Mother was ever this much trouble," Charlie grumbled.

Sam threw his head back and laughed. "My son, my son, your mother was all that and then some."

Charlie got in step with his father. Still . . . he looked back over his shoulder. Should he run after her? Maybe she needed time to cool off. What did he know about women?

"What should I do?"

"Give her a bit of time, then go talk to her. Not too much time, mind. Stay away too long and you'll get in trouble for that, too!"

"Anything more I should know . . . about women?"

"If they puts on a new dress and asks you how you like it, say it's grand."

"Even if it's not?"

"Oh yes, my son. I've been a happily married man for many years. There's no trick to it, you just have to keep your wits about you."

"I think I'll be needing your advice."

Sam couldn't answer. He didn't trust himself. What a thing, for a grown man like himself to be seen shedding tears in the middle of the road.

"I never thought coming home would be so . . . confusing."

"Sailors come and go all their lives." Sam struggled to keep his voice from wobbling. "It doesn't get any easier. Ease your way back in. You can't do it all in a day or two."

"Too late," said Charlie. Claire was mad at him, Emma wanted to murder him. He'd nearly done Clint in—wait, Emma had done that. Murphy was dead, but now he was alive, and Mrs. Jackson had a family. And there was still a whole evening ahead!

Skipper Sam and Charlie climbed the steps to their own gallery.

"Wait!" Charlie stopped dead. Where was Emma?

"What's wrong?"

"Nothing." He couldn't rightly tell his father that he was afraid of the maid, now, could he? Some hero.

Charlie stuck his head in the door and listened like a dog at a rabbit hole, except he was the rabbit. No, he couldn't hear Emma clumping around. Mind you, she might not kill him in front of his father. Then again, she might.

"Your mother will be making the dinner soon, but let's have a mug up," said Skipper Sam as he took great strides down the hall.

Charlie scampered after him and stayed right close. It would be just like Emma to lie in wait and leap out when least expected.

Sam laid the package on the table, banked the fire, put the kettle on the hob, and took down a tin of biscuits from the shelf.

Charlie sat with his back to the wall and looked around the room. The setting sun laid a stream of light across the wooden table. Over there, behind the screen, was the bathtub, still squatting on four fat paws, and beside it the old rocking chair and the daybed. This was where his mother once read out loud to him, where friends came to tell stories. Towels still hung in the chimney corner alongside the dog irons and copper utensils, and Mother's old wooden muddle still rested on the lip of the deep kitchen sink. This was the room where neighbors cried over the dead that had gone down on ships, where family and friends celebrated births and marriages, where mummers danced. The spell of the room eased him some.

"Your mother's been on the telephone making appointments. You'll have to have that arm looked after in St. John's Hospital. Then there's the dentist, the tailor, the barber. She's over at Eliza's now making lists."

"I can do all that myself now, Father."

"Don't you go interfering. There's a lot of years of mothering lost to her. I'd go along with it if I were you." Sam set out two mugs. "I thought, since there's just the two of us, you might tell me of any plans that you have. No hurry, mind."

"I need to go away."

Sam stopped short and held his breath. Truth be told, the thought of losing sight of the boy for even a day brought him great discomfort. But he wasn't thinking about himself just then, he was thinking of Lucy.

"I want to go to Montreal and see Lily Daniels," said Charlie. "I need to tell her about Robert. I want her to know that he was the best of doctors and the best of men. I miss him, every day I miss him."

"Aye." Sam nodded. He breathed a little easier. It wasn't the ice Charlie had in mind then, not yet, anyway. Visiting Lily in Montreal was the right and proper thing to do. Sam knew well enough that Dr. Daniels had done his best to keep Charlie safe, that this country had lost a great man. But they had lost many a great man in the war. Whole families wiped out, educated men and men born to work with their hands or on the sea—gone. His Newfoundland, his dear country, would never recover.

"Father?" Charlie laid a hand over his father's hand.

Sam came back to himself. "I was lost in thought, my son. What is it?"

"I tried to tell Claire about going to Montreal but she wouldn't listen! Do you suppose Mrs. Guy would let Claire come with me?"

"Unchaperoned, all the way to Canada? You'd be gone weeks. I shouldn't think so, Charlie."

Charlie nodded. It had only been a thought.

"There might be another way, though." Sam gazed at his son. By God, he was a handsome lad. "We could all go. Claire's mother will approve, your own mother will see to that. She's right fond of the girl." Sam laughed.

It was a wonderful idea.

"Your sisters and their families will be here tomorrow for a few days, and you'll be busy enough with all of your mother's planning. We could leave directly after that."

This was better than he had hoped! The house would be crowded for two days, and then they would be gone for a few weeks. Murphy might well be home by the time they got back, or at the very least Emma would have cooled off. It was working out after all!

"Do you have any other plans? Long-term ones, I mean?" Sam dithered. He hardly trusted himself to look directly at his son. But if Charlie wanted to fulfill his dreams and become a sea captain, he'd not stand in his way. Lucy would have to understand too, although he knew it would hurt her some. Sam poured out the tea.

"Yes." It was now or never. All his life Charlie had wanted to go to the ice, to become a sailor and eventually a captain, like his father. He couldn't remember ever wanting another life, ever wanting to leave his country. "I thought I'd look in at McGill University while we're in Montreal."

There was warm silence before Sam asked, "And might you have a profession in mind?"

"Medicine."

Sam nodded. The tears welled up behind his eyes all over again.

"I have something for you," he said. Sam placed a package on the table. "Although you might not be needing it in quite the same way now."

Charlie unwrapped it. Inside was the spy glass.

"Knowing where you're going is good, but it helps to see the journey, land or sea." Sam looked into his son's eyes, eyes the color of the ocean, and chuckled.

"Thank you." Charlie held the spy glass in his hand and whispered, "Old friend." The shine was back on it, the insides new, the feel of it familiar and sound.

"Your mother will be home anytime. She's cooking up another feed. Now, why don't you go and find Claire. Tell her how you feel before she tells *you* how you feel."

"I will, Father." Charlie picked up the spy glass. "But this belongs here, in this house."

Sam chuckled. "Now, are you telling me this dear old glass was a bit of a burden?"

Charlie dithered, then grinned. "No, but my life hasn't been the same since the day it came into my hands!"

"As you like," his father said warmly. "It's yours for the taking, when you're ready."

Charlie walked down the hall toward the parlor and the glass cabinet where the spy glass had once been kept. The glass on the door rattled as he opened it. Carefully, lifting the spy glass up and over teacups and treasures, Charlie laid it back on two scooped-out cradle holds. He closed the case and stood back. It looked just right.

EPILOGUE

I N THE SUMMER OF 1920, Charlie signed with Captain Robert (Bob) Bartlett and sailed down the eastern seaboard, through the Panama Canal, and up to Seattle. Their ship was nearly sunk by a rogue wave twenty miles offshore of Seattle. Charlie failed to report the incident to Claire on his return. (She knew anyway.)

Charlie and Claire both attended medical school at McGill University in Montreal, Quebec, and were married soon after graduation in 1926. Charlie became a house doctor in the same hospital in St. John's where, many years before, he had had his foot operated on.

Claire, also a medical doctor, administered to those who lived around the bays of Newfoundland. She could often be seen putt-putting about in her small motorboat up and down the coast. Charlie worried himself sick about her, but Claire being Claire, well, there was little he could do about it.

They traveled a great deal, mostly to England, France, and Europe, with occasional forays to Africa, South America, and China. Their adventures and exploits are too numerous to mention here. Their involvement in World War II remains a mystery to this day, as their files are sealed at MI5 Headquarters in London, England.

They had two sons, a daughter, and six grandchildren.

HELENA AND HER BABY SON Philip arrived in Brigus on a fair day in 1920. Charlie, Lucy, Sam, and Claire stood with Mrs. Jackson on the dock with open arms. It was a warm and sweet welcome that Helena, in future years, would call her home-coming.

Mrs. Jackson spent many a happy hour watching her beloved grandson race up and down Bishop's Beach. Not a day, not a minute went by that she wasn't grateful beyond words for the gift of her daughter-in-law and grandson. She died peacefully in Helena's arms in 1927, leaving Helena and young Philip financially well cared for.

LILY MACKENZIE DANIELS RECEIVED A DEGREE in the profession of child development and psychology and became a well-respected expert in her field. She did not remarry. Her daughter Charlotte (Charlie) became a teacher, married, and made Lily a grandmother four times over.

EMMA AND MURPHY MARRIED shortly after Murphy's return. Emma never saw the joy of having saucy children hanging about the place, and when babies did not arrive, she was not the least bit disappointed. Murphy remained fragile and was loved and fussed over until the end of his days. He always referred to Emma as the most beautiful woman in the world. The neighbors put it down to shell shock.

SAD TO SAY, Clint was lost at sea in 1932.

CHARLES ASKWITH WESTON did regain the use of his arm and leg. He and his mother moved to New York City in 1921. Using money from the sale of the family estate in England, Weston launched a manufacturing company that survived the stock market crash of 1929 and went on to become a multinational conglomerate. His mother died in 1939, several days before the onset of World War II.

As an ardent anti-Nazi, Weston turned his attention, and considerable fortune, to fighting the threat of fascism and Nazism during World War II. Once again, Charlie and Weston teamed up in Europe. Another fellow by the name Davy (his last name is unavailable as this book goes to press) appeared to be involved. Again, details are foggy as all the files are sealed at MI5 in London, England. Both the Canadian and American governments refuse to shed any light on the matter.

CHARLIE, CLAIRE, LILY, HELENA, and Weston remained great friends throughout their lives.

Note: Perchance you noticed a reference to "the Imp" in Murphy's letter to Emma. This young girl's name was Elizabeth Bowes-Lyon. She would grow up and marry the future king of England and eventually become known as the Queen Mother (1900–2002). And that, at the very least, is true!

POSTSCRIPT

THE GREAT WAR, now called World War I, ended on November 11 at eleven o'clock (the eleventh hour of the eleventh day of the eleventh month), 1918. Five thousand of the Newfoundland Regiment, call *Royal* after the battle at Cambrai as decreed by King George V, went overseas to fight. A quarter of the Regiment died.

The question comes up: could Charlie actually have lived in the trenches as a fourteen-year-old? Boy soldiers (and, in various parts of Eastern Europe and Russia, sometimes girls disguised as boys) have always played a role in war. They worked as hard as regular soldiers and died alongside them. They were also subjected to the same rigid, often excessive, laws of war.

Herbert Morris, a sixteen-year-old black war volunteer from Jamaica, served well for a year. He appeared to suffer a nervous breakdown at Flanders, ran for two days, was caught, and was shot at dawn for desertion. He was then seventeen.

James Crozier of Belfast, Ireland (now Northern Ireland), was sixteen when he signed up. Having witnessed the carnage at the Battle of the Somme, he too ran away. He was caught and condemned to die. The execution squad missed on purpose; nevertheless, he was shot in the head by the Commanding Officer.

In 1915, John Condon, twelve, left Waterford, Ireland, to join the Royal Irish Regiment. He died during a gas attack at Ypres on May 24. While his gravestone in the Poelkapelle British Cemetery, Belgium, says he was fourteen, in fact he was still thirteen, as his birthday was in June.

John Kipling, the sixteen-year-old only son of the British poet and author Rudyard Kipling *(The Jungle Book)*, twice tried to join the army and was twice refused due to his age and very poor eyesight. His father, an ardent nationalist, took matters into his own hands and pulled strings. John, at seventeen, became a second lieutenant in the Second Battalion of the Irish Guards.

Not long after arriving in France, young John was listed as missing. Countless investigations and trips to France after the war by Kipling and his wife proved futile, leading the broken and distraught father and poet to write:

> *If any ask us why we died*
> *Tell them, because our fathers lied.*

GLOSSARY

NOTE: Many of the words listed below have multiple meanings. Definitions listed here relate specifically to the text. For further explanations of Newfoundland words and their meanings, see the *Dictionary of Newfoundland English,* second edition, published by the University of Toronto Press.

ADS: Advanced Dressing Station, a medical unit where the **walking wounded** were patched up and sent back to the trenches, while the rest of the wounded were sent on.

archies: anti-aircraft guns.

barnacle: Newfoundland expression meaning incorrigible or bad person.

bayman (or **bayboy**): derogatory (not nice) term for a man or boy from the outports of Newfoundland. For example, a man from Brigus might be called a bayman.

Blighty: a slang term for England, used in both world wars.

Blue Puttees: Often called the **First Five Hundred,** these soldiers were the members of the first contingent of the Newfoundland Regiment of 1914 (called the *Royal*

Newfoundland Regiment in December 1917 following the battle of Cambrai). They were nicknamed the Blue Puttees because, when the Regiment ran out of khaki material, blue woolen fabric was used to wrap around the soldiers' legs instead.

Boche: a slang word used to describe German soldiers. Another commonly used term was **Hun**.

braziers: small stoves, fueled with coal, used by soldiers in trenches. Toward the end of the war Primus stoves came into use.

CCS: Casualty Clearing Station, a small hospital near the front lines.

communication trench, *see* **trenches**

coppy down: sit or squat down low.

duckboards: On top of the sludge at the bottom of the trenches were strips of wood called duckboards. Only occasionally did they keep feet out of the water. Mostly the duckboards sank, fell apart, or drifted away.

estaminet: bar, tavern, or public house in France. Serves alcohol and food.

fairy path: A little-used path but one that is nonetheless free of overgrowth. It's assumed that these belong to fairies, who keep the path beaten down.

FDS: Field Dressing Station, medical unit where limbs were splinted, shrapnel removed, and dressings applied.

fire trench, *see* **trenches**

funk holes: coffin-shaped holes dug into the sides of trenches.

gasper: slang for a cigarette.

George V, King (1865–1936): second son of King Edward VII, grandson of Queen Victoria (as was **Kaiser Wilhelm II** of Germany), came to the throne in 1910 and was a popular monarch.

go to the ice: Newfoundland expression, meaning to go sealing.

gone west: World War I slang, meaning killed or dead.

haberdashery: a men's clothing store.

Iron Cross: A German medal first established in March 1813. It lapsed but was brought back into use during the second year of World War I by **Kaiser Wilhelm II**. Over 5 million Second Class and 200,000 First Class awards were handed out.

Kaiser Wilhelm II (1859–1941): born in Berlin of Fredrick II and Victoria (the eldest daughter of Queen Victoria), ruler of Germany from 1888 to 1918. **Kaiser Bill,** as he was eventually nicknamed by the British, was born with a withered arm. Largely a figurehead during the war, he was forced to abdicate in 1918 and died in exile in the Netherlands.

kitting out: outfitting a person.

lorry: British term for a truck.

Maconochie: the brand name of a tinned meat and vegetable stew eaten by soldiers during the war.

muddle: wooden stirring spoon shaped like a miniature shovel.

mug up: cup or mug of tea, plus a small snack, taken between meals.

no-man's-land: strip of land that divided the Germans and the Allied Forces.

parapet: sandbags piled at the top of the trench.

potato masher: the German 1915 stick grenade, which featured a pull-cord and a delay. Manufactured hand grenades didn't come into general use until the end of 1915.

punt: flat-bottomed boat, square at both ends.

RAP: Regimental Aid Post, providing basic medical care in or near the trenches.

rigger: man who outfits the planes, not an officer.

runners: message-carriers in the trenches. Their heads would bob up and over the parapet as they ran. Snipers often shot at them. Tall runners did not last long.

saps: shallow ditches out in **no-man's-land** that served as observation, grenade-launching, and listening posts.

sawbones: slang for a doctor.

scoff: a big feed that ends with a party.

scun: a glance, a look around. Also means to direct a sealing vessel through ice floes.

scunning: repairing a fishing net.

skiff: small boat

Southern Cross: In 1914 a ship by this name sank and 250 sailers were lost. Captain George Clark, and many of the crew, came from Brigus. The loss of men to the sea, and then to the war, dealt a double blow to the residents of Brigus and, indeed, to all Newfoundlanders.

swoiling: to go seal fishing. Also called *swaling* or *swiling*.

tilt: a temporary shelter, often made of bark or driftwood and sometimes covered with canvas.

townies: boys from major towns or cities (also called **Corner boys**).

trenches: Trenches were about 2.5 meters deep (some, however, were much more shallow, especially at the beginning of the war). Piles of sandbags, called **parapets,** were at the back and front. Trenches zigzagged to limit the danger of a shell or bomb to killing only those in the "zig" or the "zag." At the end of the war, on the Allied front alone (not including German lines) there were nearly twenty thousand kilometers of trenches including all twists and turns. **Fire trenches** were front-line trenches. **Support trenches** were directly behind. **Reserve trenches** were at the back. **Communication trenches** ran roughly at a right angle to the front-line fire trenches and served as a line to bring up food, supplies, and fresh troops.

United States: President Woodrow Wilson declared war on Germany on April 6, 1917.

vet: slang for doctor.

walking wounded: wounded soldiers who could be patched up immediately and sent back into battle.

WHAT DID THEY SAY?

Some of the characters in this book speak German. We left these lines untranslated, so that you might feel as confused as Charlie did! But this is what they said:

Chapter 19

The German soldier that Charlie is treating says:

"*Mein Schatz, bitte komm zurück. Komm zurück.*" / "My darling, please come back. Come back."

Chapter 23

Weston tells the rigger working on the plane:

"*Johann, Du machst Dir zu viele Sorgen. Wir haben keine deutschen Flugzeuge in den letzten Tagen gesehen.*" / "Johann, you worry too much. We haven't seen a German plane in days."

Chapter 25

When Weston and Charlie are passed by German troops on the road, Weston and the Captain have a short conversation:

"Hallo, Sie da, wohin gehen Sie?" / "Hello, you there, where are you going?"

"Zurück zur Einheit, Herr Kapitän," / "Back to the unit," Weston answered. *"Vor einigen Kilometer stürzte unser Lastwagen um."* / "A few kilometers back our truck turned over."

"Gehen Sie in den Esswagen." / "Go to the food wagon."

Then, when Charlie and Weston arrive at the estaminet, Weston greets the officers:

"Schön' guten Abend!" / "A very good evening to you."

"Guten Abend." / "Good evening."

When Charlie gets a bowl of soup and a kiss, he's told:

"Mensch, hast du Glück." / "Man, are you ever lucky."

And the waitress asks him:

"Schmeckt dar Essen?" / "Does the food taste good?"

Chapter 26

This is the patriotic song sung by the Germans in the French estaminet:

> *There sounds a call like thunder's roar,*
> *Like the crash of swords, like the surge of waves.*
> *To the Rhine, the Rhine, the German Rhine!*
> *Who will the stream's defenders be?*

Dear Fatherland, rest quietly.
Sure stands and true watch,
The watch on the Rhine.

So long as a drop of blood still glows,
So long as a hand the dagger can draw,
So long an arm the rifle can hold
Never will an enemy touch your shore.

Dear Fatherland, rest quietly.
Sure stands and true watch,
The watch on the Rhine.

Chapter 28

Before he hides in the car trunk, Charlie hears a voice call out:
    "Dieter! Feuer bitte." / "Dieter! Give us a light, please."

RECOMMENDED READING

Young Adults

Linda Granfield. *Where Poppies Grow: A World War I Companion.* Toronto: Fitzhenry & Whiteside, 2002.

Linda Granfield. *In Flanders Fields: The Story of the Poem by John McCrae.* Toronto: Fitzhenry & Whiteside, 2002.

Charles Yale Harrison. *Generals Die in Bed.* Waterdown, Ontario: Potlatch Publications. First published in 1928. (Recently reissued by Annick Press, Toronto.)

Iain Lawrence. *Lord of the Nutcracker Men.* New York: Delacorte Press, 2001.

Kevin Major. *No Man's Land.* Toronto: Doubleday Canada, 1995.

General Audience

Sandra Gwyn. *Tapestry of War: A Private View of Canadians in the Great War.* Toronto: Harper Collins, 1992.

Margaret R. Higonnet, ed. *Nurses at the Front: Writing the Wounds of the Great War*. Boston: Northern University Press, 2001.

John Northway Leamon. *Brigus: Past Glory, Present Splendour*. St. John's, Newfoundland: Harry Cuff Publications, 1998.

Francis T. Lind, ed. *The Letters of Mayo Lind, Newfoundland's Unofficial War Correspondent, 1914–1916*. St. John's, Newfoundland: Creative Books Publishing, 2001.

Kevin Major. *As Near to Heaven by Sea: A History of Newfoundland and Labrador*. Toronto: Penguin Canada, 2001.

Websites

www.worldwar1.com
www.canadahistory.ca
www.vac-acc.gc.ca
Sharon E. McKay www.sharonsbooks.com

The award-winning bestseller, now available in mass market from Penguin Canada

SHARON E. McKAY

CHARLIE WILCOX

Winner of the Violet Downey Book Award, the Geoffrey Bilson Award for Historical Fiction and the Hackmatack Children's Choice Book Award. Nominated for the Governor General's Award for Children's Literature. Selected for the International Board on Books for Young People (IBBY) Honour List.

Newfoundland-born Charlie Wilcox wants only one thing in life: to go to sea, like his father, Captain Sam Wilcox. But never a strong lad to begin with and born with a club foot, Charlie seems destined for other, quieter pursuits—at least, that's what his parents think. Determined to prove them wrong, Charlie stows away on what he thinks is a fishing vessel, emerging days later to find himself far out to sea, bound not for the ice, but for France and the battlefields of World War One.

An exciting adventure story that is both heart-stopping and heart-breaking, *Charlie Wilcox* has quickly become a modern classic.